THE ROAD FROM DEATH
SCHOOL OF REBIRTH AND REINCARNATION

TOBIAS WADE

This is a work of fiction. Names, characters, organizations, businesses, places, events and incidents either are the product of the author's imagination or are used fictitiously. Any resemblance to actual persons, living or dead, or actual events is entirely coincidental.

First Edition: July 2019
The Road From Death
Book 1 of
School of Rebirth and Reincarnation

Illustrations by Qari Olandesca
https://www.instagram.com/dot2375/

Copyright © 2019
Tobias Wade

All rights reserved. This book or any portion thereof may not be reproduced or used in any manner whatsoever without the express written permission of the publisher except for the use of brief quotations in a book review.

FROM THE AUTHOR

Read more from Tobias Wade and download free books and stories.

TobiasWade.Com

Join the Haunted House book club and get free advanced copies every time a new book is published.

QARI OLANDESCA ILLUSTRATIONS

MRS. ROBINSON'S ADVENTURE

Mrs. Robinson wasn't in her room where she usually sat by the window. She wasn't on the sofa lording over the TV, nor in the kitchen supervising the cooking, nor anywhere else in her two-bedroom house. In fact, Mrs. Robinson has been missing for three days, and speculation has already begun on whether she would ever return.

"She could be dead," Samantha considered. The young girl spoke casually as if she was wondering whether it would rain tomorrow. "Dead in a ditch, I figure. Went and got smacked by a car on her way home, with little pieces of her raining down all over the neighborhood."

"Surely we would have seen the pieces?" Claire replied with undisguised horror. Claire was considerably smaller of the two girls, though they were both twelve years old, and she seemed even tinier now with thin arms tightly clutching her loose t-shirt against her body.

"Not necessarily," Samantha replied solemnly. "It could have happened at night. If I were the driver who hit her, I would have jumped out and gathered up all the pieces to hide the evidence of my crime."

"No!" Claire whined, shrinking farther into herself to form a sad little huddle which practically melted into her bed.

"Or maybe he didn't have to gather her up at all, see," Samantha continued, leaning forward to drive the words home. "Maybe birds picked up the little pieces, so that by morning there wasn't a single piece of Mrs. Robinson at all."

"I don't believe it!" Claire squealed.

Samantha shrugged, settling back into her seat, her long black skirt swishing over the blue carpet beneath her chair. She began to pick at her lavender fingernails, peeking at Claire from the corner of her eye as she continued.

"Well, I'm not pretending to know for certain. I'm just trying to cheer you up by giving you the good scenario. It could be much, much worse after-all."

Claire bolted upright from where she lay on her bed. Her wide green eyes quivered with apprehension, her skin so flushed that all her freckles seemed to dissolve.

"What could possibly be worse than being smashed into smithereens and eaten by birds?"

Samantha spent several exquisitely long seconds continuing to pick at her nail before looking up at Claire.

"Are we going to stay indoors all day?" Samantha inquired suddenly. "Aren't we going to play any games?"

"What else could have happened to Mrs. Robinson?" Claire shouted. "Tell me or I'm going to tell your mother that you've been horrible to me!"

A sly grin flirted with the corner of Samantha's mouth. She narrowed her eyes and leaned close to Claire so that the girls' faces were only inches apart.

"Well at least if she was hit by a car on her way home, then she would have still been trying to come home. There's always the chance that she doesn't much care for you and would rather not come home at all."

Claire jerked away from Samantha as though struck by an invisible slap, flinging herself face first against her pillow. Samantha had never heard a sound as pitiful as the sobbing howl which blasted from Claire's direction, the pillow only muffling it enough to provide a haunting echo to the cries. Samantha plugged her fingers into her ears and waited for Claire's outpouring to stop—she must draw breath eventually —but even when Claire paused to inhale, the sound only transformed into two cement trucks making love.

The door flew open and in fluttered Claire's mother, Mrs. Thistle. She was a short, stout woman who appeared to possess a very soft hug, and she immediately demonstrated this upon her daughter. Unfortunately, the gesture only seemed to squeeze the remaining air from Claire, whose howl of anguish reached a truly piercing crescendo.

"Easy easy, there you go, I've got you," Mrs. Thistle said, rocking Claire gently back and forth.

"Mrs. Robinson doesn't love me anymore!" Claire cried, heaving for breath.

"Oh, darling, don't say such a thing. Of course she does!"

Samantha silently shrugged behind Mrs. Thistle's back, making a gesture with her hands that looked convincingly like an explosion, complete with the wiggly fingers which surely represented the pieces flying every which way.

"She's been smashed to bits then!" Claire continued to howl.

Mrs. Thistle glared over her shoulder at Samantha, who was now avoiding her gaze by engrossing herself once more in her lavender nails.

"Anyway, I think my mom is going to pick me up soon..." Samantha started to say. But she never got any further, because she made the mistake of looking up and catching a full dose of Mrs. Thistle's thundering glower.

"Well you can't blame me for being honest—" Samantha began again, having forgotten that she was still a twelve-year old girl, and that children could in fact be blamed for just about anything.

Ten minutes later, Samantha and Claire were both standing outside in the warm August sun. Samantha was holding a stack of "Missing" posters with Mrs. Robinson's picture on it, although from the foul expression on Samantha's face one might guess she was actually holding a heaping pile of someone else's soggy underwear.

"Can't you just buy a new cat?" Samantha whined. "Or adopt one from the shelter. It would think you're a hero for saving it."

Claire's glare was cold enough to make Samantha shiver despite the sun.

"Dogs are nice," Samantha mumbled, not meeting Claire's eyes.

There wasn't any fight left in her though. Samantha meekly followed her companion as they began their journey along Bentley Street where they both lived. Every time they reached a light or telephone pole, *slap* goes the picture of a very fat black cat stuffed into a very small glass bowl. *Squeee* goes the electric tape. *Crinkle crinkle* as it's fastened on. Then they're off again, no words exchanged as there was no need. Samantha was beginning to feel repressed and stodgy from holding so many sarcastic comments in for so long, and she was about to quip on how excellent dogs are at finding their way home when Claire spoke first.

"I found Mrs. Robinson three years ago before mom and I moved here. She was in a plastic grocery bag along with four other kittens who were all black like her, brothers and sisters probably. Someone had left them in the trash by the grocery store, right on top of a greasy old pizza box. The bag was tied at the top, and there wasn't even a way for them to breathe. I don't know how long they were in there, but none of them were moving when I found them, not even Mrs. Robinson."

Samantha didn't know what she was supposed to say about that, so she respected the wisdom of silence.

"We named her Mrs. Robinson after the song. There's a line that goes 'God bless you please, Mrs. Robinson', so I just thought that if there was anyone who needed to be blessed, it had to be her. And I guess God really did, because pretty soon she started moving again even though none of the others did. We gave her some milk, then Mom rushed off to the store to get some real cat food and medical supplies because it looked like Mrs. Robinson hadn't eaten in a really long while. And the whole-time mom was gone, I kept thinking that if Mrs. Robinson stops moving again that it would be my fault, because I was the only one in the world she had left to depend on. And every time she swallowed a mouthful of milk, or turned her head a little to look at me, well that was just a miracle that might be taken back any second. And now it has. Three years later, and I still wasn't ready."

Samantha silently thanked her mother for giving her sunglasses to wear outside, because at that moment she was very glad Claire couldn't see her eyes.

"Nobody looks at posters," Samantha replied. "We should knock on doors instead. We can do the whole block in less than an hour, and then we'll know for sure if anyone saw her."

The girls left their posters and their tape at the end of

Claire's driveway and began to knock on every door instead. There was no answer from the tall gray house with the carved lion head railings. There was an old woman named Warlinksi who lived in the next house with its forest of potted plants, but she hadn't seen Mrs. Robinson, and said she wouldn't tell them even if she did. Warlinski didn't understand why people don't just "mince cats up like any other critter". Claire thanked her anyway, for she was raised to thank people for giving you their time, even if they didn't spend it the way you had hoped.

Samantha was making a real effort to be supportive now, but she still wanted to skip the next house. All the kids in town knew that a murderer lived there, even if the adults didn't want to admit it. The house even looked like the type of place a murderer would stay: perpetually dead trees rising like tombstones in the arid and withered garden, a deck that was rotten and fallen through in places, and a large collection of strange ornaments, wind chimes, and bead necklaces with funny stones which dangled from nails haphazardly hammered into the peeling plank walls.

"Mrs. Robinson wouldn't have come here," Samantha declared. "She had—has—better sense than that."

"Then we won't have to stay long," Claire replied as she picked her way between the brown and stringy bushes. She hopped over the first rotten step to alight on the solid one above.

"It's just that my mom's going to be picking me up soon, and —"

"Not until dinner time. My mom called and said you were going to help me because you're a kind and gentle person. That is true, isn't it, Sam?"

"That's not fair." Samantha grimaced. "Your mother knows full well that I'd rather be a witch and put curses on people. I said as much in my Christmas card last year, and I know she saw it because she kept asking my mom whether I would like to join you all at church after that."

Claire wasn't paying attention. She was facing the house, calling, "Hello, anyone home?" She rapped on the door with her fist which caused it to rattle loosely in its frame. Samantha found sudden interest in peering through a hole in one of the dead trees, which was hollow and turned out to be filled with colorful stones and broken glass.

The muffled sound of a chair sliding against a padded floor came from inside the house. Claire looked over her shoulder and gestured emphatically for Samantha to join her on the old porch. Samantha pretended not to notice.

Standing alone in front of the dilapidated house, the idea that a murderer might really live inside didn't sound hard to believe after-all. And what would a murderer do if they opened the door to find two young girls, defenseless and alone? Claire's mother thought they were still putting up posters on the public street. No one knew where they were, and if they were to not come home again…

The door began to open, and all the worst parts of Claire's imagination came out at once. In her haste to flee, she forgot about the decaying step until her foot landed hard on the splintering wood. A shrill little scream preceded a thumping crash as she tumbled to sprawl on the dirt beyond. Claire scrambled to her feet and was about to launch herself away once more, but the moment she balanced her weight onto the offended ankle she felt it buckle in protest. A sharp, stinging pain devoured her senses.

Claire was on the ground again, staring at her scraped hands which had broken her fall. There were footsteps behind her now, and Claire was absolutely certain that the murderer stood only a foot away. Could she outrun him? Not likely. Fight? As if more capable victims hadn't tried before. His shadow was already looming over her, and Claire's lightning succession of thoughts only led to the inescapable conclusion of her impending demise. The sole reasonable course of action was to begin screaming again.

"Cut that out, won't you?" came the kindly old voice behind her.

Claire snapped her mouth shut for a moment before breathlessly demanding, "What did you say?"

"He means that if you don't stop screaming, he's going to cut your tongue out," Samantha volunteered cheerfully, still standing nonchalantly beside her dead tree.

Claire's eyes widened. She began to draw a great lungful of air to —

"That's not what I meant!" the voice behind Claire implored. "I just want you to stop screaming, if you please. You'll wake the little one, and Mandy just got him to sleep."

Claire didn't suppose a murderer would have cared about waking a baby, and he definitely wouldn't say please. If anything, he sounded like he was the one who was afraid.

Claire wiped her eyes with the back of her hand before shuffling around on her hands and knees.

"Of course a murderer would ask that," Samantha added, sagely stroking her chin. "He wouldn't want anyone to hear and save you."

Claire could now see that the murderer in question was a pale-skinned elderly man with a long droopy nose like a sock half-filled with sand. He was tall and thin, very much like a spider which had learned to stand on its hind legs and dress itself in rather baggy and faded clothing, and his wide deep-set eyes were as grey and calm as the sea before a storm.

Claire felt immensely relieved, realizing that a strong tempered toddler would likely be sufficient to push this frail old thing around.

"I'm not a murderer!" the old man retorted, a faint flush rising on his cheeks. "That's Barnes' fault, my daughter's no-good boyfriend."

"Your daughter married a murderer?" Samantha asked, suddenly eager. "How many people has he killed? If it's at least three, then it counts as being a serial killer, but only if they weren't all done at the same time, otherwise he's a mass murderer instead."

The old man shook his head, "He hasn't killed anybody either. But he started telling stories about me and now everybody thinks..." his voice trailed off into indistinct muttering which might have been an attempt to disguise the type of language twelve-year old girls aren't supposed to hear, even if they secretly say those very same words in their head at every opportunity.

"You must be Noah then," Samantha declared. "I heard that people keep catching you with dead animals. They say that you kill them for fun. That's even worse than killing people you know, because animals never cheat on their taxes or lie to their mothers."

"I don't '*kill*' them, I put them to sleep," Noah replied indignantly, "and only if they're very sick and in pain. I do work at a veterinary clinic, after-all."

"I heard you like to watch them die," Samantha pressed.

"What's the crime in that?"

Claire and Samantha exchanged an unsettled glance.

"You *do* like to watch things die?" Samantha asked incredulously, her usual playful tone drenched in accusation.

Noah looked down at the peeling rubber sole of his sneakers. "It's not cruel or anything. I just... like watching what happens next." His eyes darted back to the girls suspiciously. "What are you doing here? Do your parents know where you are?"

"Did you kill Claire's cat?" Samantha demanded. Then, on a lighter note, she added, "Oh, this is Claire, and I'm Samantha, or Sam, but never Sammy."

"Hi," Claire mumbled, flourishing a half-hearted wave.

"Hello, Claire. Hello, never-Sammy," Noah replied, lighting up with good humor as Sam rolled her eyes. "Is the cat black with a white tuft on its chest like a general wearing a medal?"

"You've seen Mrs. Robinson?! Is she in the animal hospital?" Claire exploded, bouncing onto her feet. She had forgotten about her injured ankle in the excitement, so this action caused her to stagger dangerously. Samantha was there to catch her though, supporting her as they both turned on Noah ferociously.

"She's right there, isn't she?" Noah said, pointing behind Claire. The girls spun on the spot while still holding hands, almost knocking both of them to the ground in the process. They stared at the empty patch of dirt for a moment before rounding once more on the old man.

"Right where?" Claire asked.

"He's teasing you; there's nothing," Samantha said. "Don't you know it's not nice to play tricks on innocent little girls? Especially when they know how to trick you back."

"I'm not talking about her body," Noah said, sighing as though the words were weighing him down. He sat heavily on the creaking wooden steps and his remaining air all flooded out in a puff. "I'm talking about her spirit. She's chasing that butterfly, although she's never going to catch it because the butterfly is alive and well..."

The girls looked again, and sure enough they saw a butterfly dancing on the wind. Claire cast an uneasy glance at her friend, and she wasn't thrilled to see Samantha smiling. She always smiled when she wasn't supposed to, and that made Claire cross.

"This isn't a game, you know," Claire said. "Mrs. Robinson really is lost, and I'm worried about her. So if you aren't going to help us, then you might as well be a murderer because Mrs. Robinson needs us and —"

"I'm sorry," Noah cut her off, his voice gentle but sure. "If you don't see her now, then no amount of looking is going to help. But you should know that she is having a wonderful time, which means she didn't suffer much. When animals have a painful death, they tend to mope around and complain for a good deal afterward."

"Can you really see spirits?" Samantha inquired.

"It runs in the family," Noah replied, a bit defensively. He cast a wary glance around as though worried he would be overheard. "Cats can too, you know. Whenever they're fascinated by something you can't see, you can be pretty sure there's a spirit there. Dogs can't of course—too many distractions in this world, I suppose. Most people can't either, but people can't see their own nose and that's right in front of their face. Would either of you like a cup of hot cocoa?"

Claire seriously considered her nose, judging the merit of this explanation. She didn't seem satisfied.

"Yes, please," Samantha instantly replied. Standing, Noah offered a hand to help her over the rotten step. She chose to hop it on her own instead of accepting his assistance. "What does a spirit look like?" she pestered.

"It looks like how Christmas feels," Noah remarked

instantly. "Would you take a cup as well, Claire? It's the least I can do."

Claire had absolutely no desire to enter the crumbling house of the strange old man whose denial of being a murderer was dubious at best. Her ankle was starting to feel much better, and she could turn around right now and be back on the street to resume her search. To continue a seemingly endless search, ignoring her best clue which was the first person to have accurately described Mrs. Robinson.

"It's only polite," Samantha said, her face refusing to match the gravity of the situation.

"Oh, very well, but only if Mrs. Robinson can come too," Claire relented.

Noah crossed the porch and opened the door, and the two girls followed him, completely oblivious to Mrs. Robinson's spirit which hopped up the stairs behind them. So too were they unaware of the gaunt stony creature sitting on the mailbox at the end of the driveway. They weren't aware of the long, hooked claws on the end of its wings or its yellow lidless eyes which watched them enter. Noah's gaze lingered on the creature for a moment, but he quickly averted his gaze as he smiled down at the girls who were walking past him into the house.

"I just want you to know," Samantha was saying to the old man, "that I will find out if you're trying to play a trick on Claire. Then you really *will be* seeing spirits, because you'll be one of them."

Noah chuckled and bowed low as he held the door open for the children. "I shall take your warning to heart and tread the line of truth with the utmost care."

That was good enough for Samantha, and so it was good enough for Claire as well.

The interior of the house was in no better repair than the run-down front. The carpet was patchy and threadbare, and only occasional tufts of color hinted that it might have been red in a previous life. Splotches on the ceiling marked where water had once dripped through, and the sofa and chairs had stains on them in enough colors that it was difficult to determine which were part of the actual design.

"We have visitors, Mandy," Noah called softly upon entering. He held the door open for considerably longer than necessary, his eyes presumably following an invisible cat which was taking time deciding whether to follow. The children sat carefully on the couch as though expecting it to collapse as soon as they rested.

"Hello, darlings."

The girls jumped, not having realized that Mandy had been sitting in the dark chair beside them this whole time. She looked to be in her thirties, wearing black all the way from her long brass-buttoned coat and her lacy blouse to her high leather boots. Her skin was as pale as a corpse, and the only color about her was the short golden hair which sprayed wildly from her head like a hose blocked by a thumb.

"Claire, Samantha, this is my daughter Mandy," Noah introduced the newcomers, a touch of pride in his voice. "She's such a devoted mother it was like she was born to raise little Lewis. I swear she could be all the way across town and still hear him cry when he falls down."

"Oh please, you'll make me blush," Mandy said, her white skin showing no sign that this biologically was possible. "I suppose you're here about the kitten?" she added, looking at the same empty spot in the doorway.

"Mrs. Robinson is fully grown," Claire replied. "Perhaps you've got the wrong cat after all…"

"Not on that side she isn't," Mandy responded amiably. "They're always young again after they die. Didn't you know?"

"The cat doesn't want to come in," Noah grumbled, still holding the door. "Make up your mind, won't you?"

"Not so loud, he's still asleep," Mandy said. Then to the girls, "I'm so sorry about the mess in here. As soon as Lewis' father gets home we're going to move into a nicer place, so we haven't been worrying so much about keeping up with things."

"*When his father gets home,*" Noah mimicked. "Never mind that we haven't seen him since the baby was born, surely tomorrow is the day!"

"What's Mrs. Robinson doing?" Claire interrupted, trying to refocus the topic.

"She's walking away now," Noah sighed. "Just as well really. There's the spirit of a raccoon living upstairs, and they might not get along. He's been there ever since before the place was built, and he's never quite forgiven us for it."

"We have to follow her then!" Claire leapt to her feet, grateful for an excuse to leave.

"There's really no point," Noah replied. "Are you sure you wouldn't rather have some cocoa? We already have milk on the stove for Lewis."

"There's every point!" Claire insisted, hurrying back onto the front porch. "Where is she? Over here? Am I close? How about now?" Claire stretched her hands, feeling blindly through the air.

"Lower," Noah said. "Over there, rubbing against the railing."

Dusk was already gathering outside, and Claire had trouble following Noah's finger. She moved to where she thought he was pointing and reached out again. "How about now?"

"She's heading through the yard, toward the sidewalk."

"At least she doesn't have to worry about cars anymore," Samantha interjected. She'd just emerged from the house with a steaming cup in her hands. Mandy's pale face loomed behind her in the shadows.

"What are you waiting for then?" Claire asked, bounding down the steps, careful to skip the rotten one this time.

"I don't think that's a good idea," Noah cautioned. "Spirits can go places that people can't follow. What will you even do if you catch her?"

"She followed me here though, so she still sees me," Claire announced stubbornly. "I bet she's trying to send me a message or lead me somewhere."

"You have to come," Samantha said firmly to Noah. "We can't follow her without you."

"I've tried following spirits before," Noah despondently replied. "They always walk through a building or a highway or something. You can't keep up."

"The dead aren't nearly as stubborn as Claire," Samantha said, dragging the old man down the steps by one of his bony, wrinkled hands with their veins that could be felt through the skin. "Just point the way and we'll figure out how to get there."

"Oh go ahead, dad," Mandy bade them off from the door. "Lewis will have a chance to sleep, and then he'll be able to stay up late and watch your old movies with you by the time you get back."

"Dr. Strangelove is not an old movie!" Noah retorted. "I may be getting older, but movies aren't. Unlike me, they look exactly the same as the day they were made. Oh bother, this must be how dust-bunnies feel being swept away against their will from home."

Despite his protests, the old man allowed Samantha to lead him to the sidewalk. Claire and Samantha didn't have any definite target to follow as they couldn't see Mrs. Robinson, so they kept their attention fixed on Noah as he loped in front of them. Noah would often pause to wait for Mrs. Robinson to finish smelling a plant or roll in the dirt, and he commented on this for the girls' benefit. Other times he would declare that the cat had walked directly into a house, forcing all of them to race around to the other side. Noah was worried that the cat would then retrace its path, or exit the house from a side, or even stay in there, but so far Mrs. Robinson showed no inclination to deceive them.

Off they went between the houses, over the low brick wall, along the sidewalk and up to the intersection. The sun had now completely set, and the street was aglow with racing blur. They were approaching midtown where the buildings soared imposingly and the lights glittered like a million unblinking eyes.

"Why doesn't Mrs. Robinson just come home?" Claire dreamily inquired, her unfocused gaze tracing the steel and concrete heights. Samantha grabbed her friend by the hand to prevent her from stepping off the sidewalk while their traffic light was still red.

"Keep walking during the red light and you'll find out," Samantha said. "Hey, Noah, did she cross here?"

Noah nodded and pointed toward the left side of a large apartment building ahead. The light turned green, but Noah hesitated to cross as the other people streamed past.

"Hurry up then!" Samantha insisted. She grabbed Noah's

limp hand in the one not holding Claire and pulled them both forward. "She's getting away, isn't she? Come on!"

"It's not just her," Noah said, his sunken eyes blinking slowly. He followed Samantha's lead while panning his head to the left and right. "I've never seen so many in one place before."

"Why would so many animals want to hang around where it's so busy?" Claire puzzled.

"Not animals. People. Or... what's left of them anyway," Noah said. "There are three teenagers over there, sitting on the steps of the bank. Then a little girl sitting on the bus stop, and a bunch of old men gathered around the apartment. It's mostly children though—dozens of the recently dead all moving in the same direction as us. I think they know we're following Mrs. Robinson; they keep looking our way and whispering to each other."

Noah and the children stepped off the sidewalk on the far side of the street. Samantha dropped Noah's hand right away, but her grip tightened on Claire.

Claire was looking at the places Noah referred to, though in each case she couldn't see anyone there. She could tell out of the corner of her eye that Samantha was trying to get her attention, but she stubbornly avoided looking at her friend. Samantha would know that Claire was only pretending to be brave, and Claire refused to give her the satisfaction.

"Mrs. Robinson is inside that apartment complex now," Noah said. "I don't think we can go any farther."

"We've come this far," Claire said, trying to keep her voice casual. "Let's just see if it's locked."

Still clutching each other's hands, the girls walked briskly to the glass door leading into the apartment lobby. For a moment Claire thought she could smell an ancient musty leathery smell, but it was gone a second later. Had she just walked through the old men?

"They're still watching you, in case you were wondering," Noah said from where he'd remained on the sidewalk. "One of them has followed you to the door."

"So what do you want me to do about it?" Claire turned in exasperation.

"Nothing. Just thought you'd want to know," Noah added.

"Well I don't!" Claire shot back. "They can't do anything to me, can they?"

"The people? No, I've never seen one of them interact with the living world. If I were you, I'd be more concerned about that stony creature with the claws on the end of its wings though. It's been following us since we left the house, and it's got the nastiest upside-down smile I've ever seen."

"You must think you're pretty funny," Claire replied with dignity. She tried the door in vain. She peered through the glass, but she couldn't see anyone but potted plants in the lobby on the other side. She then began to study her reflection, searching for any sign of the stony thing or the dozens of invisible children or the stinking old men. She would have laughed at herself for being foolish enough to believe if she hadn't just taken another big lungful of that old musty smell.

"What's that supposed to mean?" Noah asked after a long silence.

"I didn't say anything!" Claire responded, still studying the glass. Samantha at her side was only looking at her own reflection. She settled the age-long debate whether sarcasm was limited to words by striking several sarcastic poses.

"I wasn't talking to you?" Noah huffed. "There's a fellow next to you who looks straight out an old-timey movie. He's got one of those striped hats, and a waistcoat with big gold buttons, and —"

Samantha fully turned around to face Noah, wriggling free of Claire's hand. "We don't care what he looks like. What did he say?"

"He said today is an excellent day to be dead, and asked if we wouldn't care to join him?" Noah coughed. "Now he's sniffing your hair. Seems to be rather enjoying himself at that."

"And that's how the party ended," Samantha declared emphatically. She swatted around her head as though pursuing a relentless fly. "Claire? Are you ready to go home?"

"Not without Mrs. Robinson!" Claire cried. "We've just got to wait until someone who lives here opens the door."

"Then what?" Samantha asked. "Search every floor for her? Maybe knock on all the doors too, asking if anyone's seen your dead cat?"

"She's not dead!" Claire grew increasingly red in the face. "If she was dead then she wouldn't be walking around. She's just somewhere else, and I need to find her."

Samantha was still swatting around her head, dodging in anxious zigzagging lines as though that would lose her invisible pursuer. "Even if you do, you can't pet her. You can't pick her up or hold her or feel her next to you when you sleep. She's gone, Claire. And nothing this weirdo says is going to bring her back, so let's just go home."

Claire kept staring into the glass, watching her reflection as the tears started to swell in her eyes. Samantha made an exaggerated motion to block her ears, but Claire didn't scream this time. She only glared at her friend's reflection in silence with dark angry eyes, and that was a hundred times worse than the screaming.

"Let's go home, Claire," Samantha repeated more softly. "Our parents will be wondering where we are. You can still have your hot chocolate at your house, then you'll feel a lot better than if you were—"

"I don't want to feel better. I want Mrs. Robinson back."

The kids remained silent for a moment. Noah stared at his feet with his hands in his pockets. Claire and Samantha glared back and forth as though the other was personally responsible for everything that was wrong with the world.

"The old timer says he'd like to keep the cat then, if it's all the same to you," Noah's voice cracked slightly like a Captain telling everyone the boat is sinking while trying not to cause too much of a fuss about it. "I think we should all be getting home."

Claire's lip began to shake, but she said nothing.

"You absolutely cannot," Samantha stepped up to argue into thin air where she assumed the spirit to be. "Mrs. Robinson isn't a possession to be traded about. Either she's coming with us or she's going where she decides."

Samantha searched for the invisible man around her with mounting frustration before turning on Noah to demand, "Well, what did he say?"

"He said 'Cats are the only thing more stubborn than the dead. You'd have better luck ordering the sun to set at noontime than telling a dead cat what to do.'"

"Obviously you've never met Claire then," Samantha replied, trying to focus on the same patch of empty air that Noah was. "She's twice as stubborn as the dead, and she doesn't rot and stink like old leather either!"

"He says 'I'm not the one you smell'. Samantha, stop looking there. It thinks you're staring at it."

"Tell him to look away first," Samantha retorted. "I'm not backing down."

"Samantha, look out!"

This would have been better advice if she could actually see the thing she was supposed to be looking out for. Samantha only managed to turn her face halfway toward Noah before her vision was replaced a line of searing agony. She felt like a bucketful of water that had been suddenly filled with hot steel. Her insides all wanted to be on the outside to cool off, and her outsides wanted to be safe inside for a change. It was the worst feeling she'd ever experienced in her life.

"Sam? What happened? Noah, did something hit her?"

Samantha was on her knees, although she couldn't remember how she got there. Her vision was starting to return in her left eye, but her right might as well be staring into the sun. The musty smell came back in an overpowering wave, and it was all she could do to keep breathing and not vomit from the shock.

"Get away from her!" she heard Noah shout. His voice sounded like it was coming through a hundred miles of tin cans. The musk lifted for a moment only to be replaced by a towering shadow.

"We've got to get her out of here," Noah urged.

"What happened to her? Why'd she fall?" Claire asked.

Samantha felt a hand under one arm, then two more hands on her other side. She lurched to her feet, staggering to keep up with Noah and Claire who dragged her along. They were almost at the sidewalk of the intersection, and again the light was red.

"We have to go back for Mrs. Robinson!" Claire cried.

"Not safe," Noah grunted, invisible on Samantha's blinded right side.

"That's why we can't leave her!" Claire insisted. "If that old man attacked Samantha, then we can't let him have Mrs. Robinson!"

"He's not the one who attacked her. It was the clawed thing. And I don't think you have to worry about Mrs. Robinson, because the thing is still following us."

The red streetlight glared malevolently overhead, as comforting as an umbrella full of holes in a storm.

"Where is it?" Samantha hissed.

"Behind us. No—don't turn around. They don't usually bother people unless they think they've been noticed. It must have thought Samantha could see it because she kept looking through it without noticing. Keep staring ahead. It will lose interest if we don't acknowledge it."

"So we're supposed to just stand here and pretend the thing that attacked me isn't standing behind us right now?" Samantha questioned in disbelief.

"Uh huh," Noah mumbled, meeting her eyes. "How are you feeling? Your right eye is all…"

"Cloudy," Claire replied from the other side. "It's going to be fine, really." She did not sound very confident.

The musty scent engulfed them once more like a heavy blanket, weighing them down. The streetlight seemed to burn redder out of pure spite. "Seriously," Noah warned. "Don't look back."

"Well, screw waiting here then," Samantha said defiantly. She looked both ways down the intersection before darting across the street toward the patch of grass and trees which separated the traffic lanes.

"Wait for us!" Claire called, breaking after her. Noah was

close behind, muttering curses to himself as he hurried beneath the halo of red light. They caught up with Samantha where she crouched beside a bush, ready to sprint again. In the near-distance another traffic light turned green and headlights began to rush past. The party was tense and ready to run as soon when a space opened between the cars.

"Is it still there?" Samantha asked. She already knew the answer because the smell was as strong as ever, but any words were more reassuring than the oppressive silence.

"Don't look," Noah repeated softly. He seemed to be listening to something only he could hear.

"Is my eye going to be okay?" she continued.

"The old man is talking about it, but—"

"Tell me!"

Noah sighed sharply, looking hopelessly from side to side at the impenetrable wall of rush-hour traffic.

"He says your eye 'might shrivel up to a prune and drop out, or spring a leak that drains all the liquid out and leaves only a sad empty pouch.' I said don't look!"

Samantha's head was beginning to turn, but she quickly snapped it back.

"Will I go blind?" Samantha murmured.

"No. Samantha this really isn't the time—"

"Tell me exactly what he's saying!"

"He says 'If the eye stays in, it'll start to see again. But it won't be seeing what's in your world.' He says 'The things you'll see will take your *breath away*.'"

Just as Noah said '*breath away*', the words were accompanied by a hot, dry breath on the back of Samantha's neck. Something inside her became unhinged after feeling such a thing. It wasn't a physical pain; it was more of an intrusive thought which wormed its way into her head. It told her that she was a scared, helpless little girl in a great, big world that had no possible need for her. That no one would notice much less care whether she lived or died. It didn't feel like a passing opinion either, but rather a law of the universe that she had just stumbled upon, such as the law of gravity, that once noticed could not be overturned. Since she couldn't escape a thought, she did the best she could using her legs instead.

Samantha was halfway into the oncoming traffic before anyone could stop her. A yellow jeep appeared suddenly, roaring across the asphalt directly toward her. The events of the next few moments couldn't agree on which would happen first, so they all crammed through the proverbial doorway and happened at exactly the same time.

Noah followed Samantha into the street. He didn't think of it as risking his life to save her. He only felt an instinctual responsibility for her, and he had to quiet that voice in his head that said it was his fault for leading the children here at all.

Claire jumped up and waved her arms to get the driver's attention. It must have worked too, because the jeep slammed its breaks.

If he hadn't hit his breaks, then Noah wouldn't have had enough time to catch Samantha by the flying end of her long skirt and swing her back toward the island of grass.

The vehicle slammed to a stop exactly 1.2 seconds after the front bumper connected with Noah's right shoulder. The jarring impact buckled his neck and body, allowing the vehicle to make a second point of contact on his temple. His thin frame was lifted by the force and thrown carelessly into the air like a rag-doll.

Noah was aware of his flight, though he wasn't in any pain. He felt the massive wall of pressure from the collision, but this caused more numbness than discomfort. His whole body felt like static, all pins and needles, like a foot that had just taken its first step after being asleep. It didn't seem so bad, except for the inner voice which told him in no uncertain terms that he shouldn't be in the air this long and that either he would continue to float away indefinitely, which seemed unlikely, or he was about to make a close acquaintance with the hard, unsympathetic ground.

QARI OLANDESCA ILLUSTRATIONS

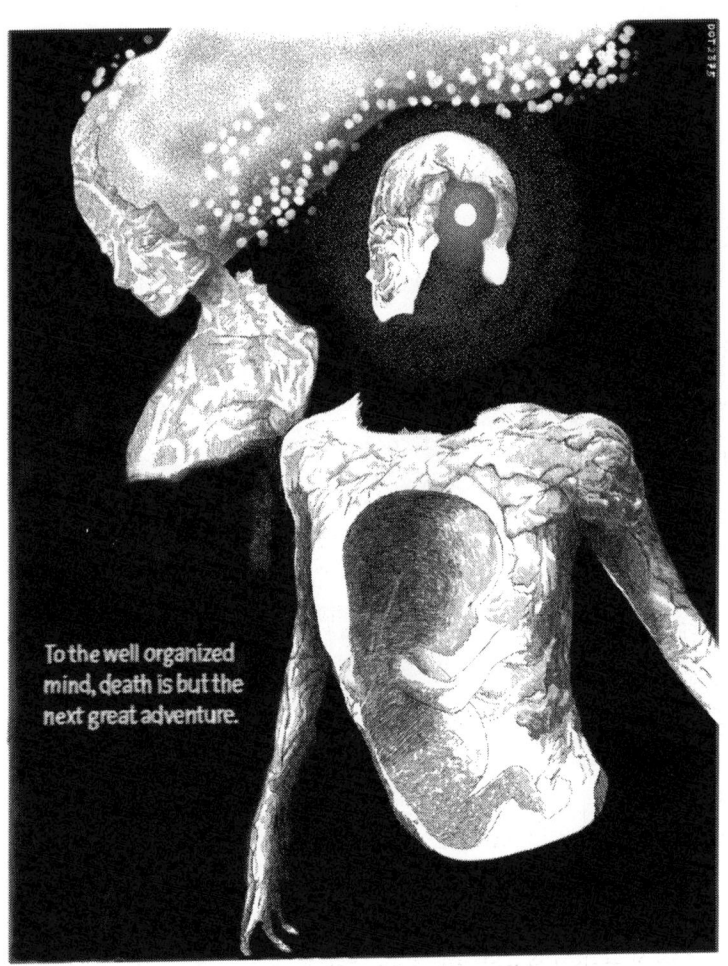

WAKING UP AGAIN

Noah must have landed on the asphalt eventually, but he was quite oblivious to the impact. He only knew he was on the ground because he found himself staring into the pool of blood spreading from his temple along the road. It seemed interesting that people in the reflection were running toward him with open mouths that weren't making any sounds. It was ridiculous that they would make such a fuss when he wasn't hurt at all, and he looked forward to their excited relief when he stood up at any moment.

There was something about the puddle of blood that concerned Noah, although his thoughts weren't clear enough to understand what was wrong with this situation. He could see Claire and Samantha leaning over him: Claire with tears flowing down her face while Samantha looked as though she'd been turned to stone except for her wide quivering eyes, one of which was now pure marble-white.

A bearded man had exited the jeep, yet he hadn't approached. His breathing was ragged as he held a cell phone to his ear, yet still there was no sound coming from him either. A thought floated through Noah's head that perhaps it shouldn't be so quiet if everything really was fine. He kept staring at the puddle of blood, trying to focus his fuzzy thoughts on exactly what was wrong with everyone.

"You noticed, didn't you?" uttered an aged voice, the first sound Noah heard since he'd been hit.

"We're on the wrong side of the reflection," Noah replied, not turning away from the puddle. Had his voice always sounded so thin and high?

"There isn't a wrong-side. No before-side, no after-side, no upside or downside. There's just the other side, the side you're now on."

Noah sat up at last. His body stubbornly refused to rise with him. He looked down to see himself still lying face down in the blood, which by now looked more like a lake than a puddle, complete with little streams that gushed through the cracks in the road to cascade down toward the gutter.

"That's disgusting," Noah remarked, scowling.

The old timer removed his striped hat and held it to his chest, closing his eyes in an apparent gesture of reverence. His head was bald underneath, and his thick wrinkled skin made him appear more turtle than man. "Beats going in your sleep. Dying is a once-in-a-lifetime opportunity that's not to be missed."

Noah began to stand to completely remove himself from his old body. He ceased abruptly when he realized his new body that was emerging was completely naked. Besides that, his skin was smooth and hairless. The scar on his chest from a heart surgery a few years ago was completely gone. He pulled himself entirely free from the carnage to stand over the pool of blood and saw himself as the child he could barely remember ever being, no older than the two girls who were still in shock about the mangled corpse he'd left behind.

Suddenly self-conscious, Noah sank back into the ground, blushing as the old man began to laugh.

"Shut up, will you? This is your fault," Noah huffed.

"If it's anyone's fault, blame the gargoyle. Anyway the girls can't see you, if that's what you're worried about. Here, try this on."

The man began to sketch in the air, and wherever one of his fingers went there remained a bit of soft fire which continued to smolder. The fire seemed to be spilling from a thick white ring Noah hadn't noticed before which traced the outline of a pair of trousers. As he went, the fire began to spread, knitting itself together to populate the space between the lines. The pants proceeded to burn in mid-air as a shirt was conjured beside them. The fires burned out into a bleak gray color before the clothing dropped to a heap on the ground.

Noah hastily scooped them up and self-consciously donned them while facing away from the old man. The clothes had fallen directly into the puddle of blood, but even so are soft and dry against Noah's new skin.

"Don't I get any shoes?" Noah inquired.

"Most spirit bodies don't bother with them. It's hard to find your balance walking up things like stairs when you can't feel them, but going barefoot helps grip the air better, if you know what I mean."

"No," Noah was now feeling flustered and obstinate. "I don't at all."

An ambulance had arrived on the scene. One of the paramedics was dragging Claire away from the body, and she kicked and swung her elbows at them as she was forcibly removed. Samantha walked willingly when she was asked, her face stiff and frozen. The silence of the scene made it even more unsettling.

"Isn't there some way for me to let them know I'm okay?" Noah asked.

"Sure there is. We'll need another jeep though."

Noah, now fully dressed, turned to scowl at him. The old timer grinned and placed his hat back on his head.

"Where's the thing that attacked Samantha?"

"The gargoyle didn't stick around. Took off when you got hit. Cowardly creatures, I'll never understand why the department puts so much faith in them. I've never seen one go after a human like that though, most curious indeed."

Noah watched as his body was covered in a white sheet and carried into the back of the ambulance. Part of him still hoped that it would stand up and shake it off, but that seemed to be growing less likely by the moment. He really was dead. Why did those words sound so strange to him?

"Mandy will still be able to see me though," Noah said. "I should go and tell her what's happened."

The old man shook his head. "Wouldn't recommend it. The T.D.D. is very particular about spirits communicating with unregistered mediums."

"The T.D.D.?" Noah asked, distracted by the progress of his body.

"The Trans Dimensional Department," the old man said. "You'll get that on your permanent record, then fat chance getting into a good school then."

"What would I want to go to school for?" Noah turned to face him. "It's not like I need to earn a living."

"You don't want to spend your next life sweeping graveyards, do you?"

"No, of course not. Why would I—"

"That's what will happen, you know. Or maybe haunting a teddy bear because that's all you'll manage, not having taken your possession work seriously. See all those children passing you by? They're headed for The Mortuary. Brilliant demonology course they've got, real cutting-edge summoning program. Not to mention one of the best necromancy curriculums you'll find this side of the ocean. They've got second year students already raising their own ghouls. Can you believe it?"

"Um, not entirely," Noah replied quite honestly. "Why did you say today was an excellent day to die? Are you the grim reaper or something?"

"George Hampton, a pleasure to meet you," the old man said, shaking Noah by the hand. Noah was surprised to feel how real and solid the other's hand felt. "And no, I'm not going to harvest you, whatever that means. You do have good timing though, because the bus leaves in…" he checked his watch, then the stars, then his watch once more, "about an hour. Little less."

"I don't want to go anywhere. I have to take care of my daughter and her son. Her husband isn't around anymore, and I know she tries her best but she hasn't had a real job since the baby—what are you doing now?"

George Hampton's tongue was out of his mouth and he seemed to be tasting the air like a serpent. He turned suddenly upon being addressed as though he forgot Noah was even there.

"Your daughter and her son are already dead," George said. The words felt like a punch in the stomach.

"What?! How—"

"Well, not exactly, but they are to you," the old man

corrected. "There isn't such a thing as dead really. There's either this side or the other side. When you aren't in one, you're in the other. Now if you do as you're supposed to, you study very hard in all of your classes, then in a few years you'll have graduated and will be ready to go back to the other side. In your words, pass the final test and you'll be back alive again."

That didn't sound quite so bad anymore. Noah reflexively breathed a sigh of relief, surprised to find his lungs still making the motion out of habit despite not feeling any air enter his body. A siren illuminated the scene in flashes of harsh red and blue, and the sound was beginning to trickle back as though someone had turned the TV volume up from mute to low.

Noah watched as a policeman wrote down the statement of the bearded man in the jeep. Claire's mother was there, and Claire had buried against her mother's side. Samantha was sitting on the sidewalk beside them, her arms clutched around her drawn knees.

"They don't seem dead. But I don't feel dead either, so I suppose it doesn't matter either way. How far is the bus?"

"That's the spirit!" the old man chuckled to himself. "Not far at all, we just need to follow all the other children."

George Hampton placed a gentle arm behind Noah's shoulders and steered him away from the bloody street. Away from his body that was already passing him in the ambulance. Away from every mistake he'd ever made, every place he'd ever been, and every person he'd ever loved. He wasn't sure whether to laugh or cry, or perhaps both at the same time.

The volume in the living world never turned all the way back on; all the rush and commotion of the street kept buzzing away barely above a whisper. Likewise, it all had a certain translucence to it in the same way that spirits had once appeared to him when he was alive. And while he had only ever seen the occasional spirit before, now they were everywhere, as real and solid and true as his brand-new body.

Owls—herds of deer—prowling wolves—all right in the middle of the city, in the middle of the street, heedless to the ceaseless traffic. Flights of birds swooped straight through the pellucid towers, and other strange creatures unseen in the living world strut their impossibility brazenly before all to see. One by one they came sparkling into existence before his eyes like the blossoming of a starry night. It immediately became very clear to Noah that all his life he had only seen the faintest edge of the other world which lay hidden over the one he knew.

George Hampton and Noah walked through buildings that couldn't possibly belong to this city. Tucked between a grocery store and a gas station rose a high tower which looked to be entirely built from jagged black glass, more real now than the familiar commercial buildings on either side. There on the other end of the street sat a fat round building whose brown walls rippled like a chocolate waterfall. A few hundred yards ahead, Noah could clearly see where part of the street was abruptly blocked by a marble mountain with a Grecian shrine like a miniature Pantheon carved directly into its mass.

"Some people of faith prefer to pursue resurrection at a temple rather than a school, but they aren't as popular on this side," George Hampton rambled, noticing Noah's fascination in the structure. "It's hard to convince people that you follow the one true God when he never shows his face, and right next door is another faith offering a different variety of resurrections at half the price. Of course none of them can guarantee it—all souls find their way back in their own ways—but The Mortuary will teach you all the essentials and give you your very best shot."

Noah suddenly became aware that humans have been dying for almost exactly as long as they'd been living. That he could run into Napoleon, or Caesar, or a Neanderthal which died before two sticks were rubbed to make fire. As long as their spirit didn't return to the other side, they must have stayed here.

"Why are you old?" Noah inquired.

The old man tapped the side of his nose and his eye twinkled. "Excellent question! Everyone who comes here begins their journey young. There is only one currency on this side: the years of your life. It's the only thing of value on the other side too, though you all hardly seem to notice it being spent. The more someone decides to spend, the older they get, until one day they spend themselves completely and disappear, never to be seen again."

"You must have bought a lot of things," Noah said.

"They sneak up on you," the old man replied. "One day here, a week there—you don't even notice until they're gone, nor how precious they were until it's too late."

"That's rubbish," Noah said. "After you realized that you were getting older you should have stopped right away."

"So you never wasted time again after realizing that it wouldn't come back?" he asked, rather smugly.

"But it does come back though? You can pass the test and come back as many times as you want?"

Noah stopped to watch a pair of horses pulling a carriage directly through oncoming traffic. Maybe it was just getting dark, but he kept counting the wrong number of legs on the beasts. His brain refused to believe half the things that his eyes were extremely confident about.

"As many times as you *can*," George Hampton corrected. "It's not easy to get back. Some never manage it, though they try for a thousand years. Others do it by accident, or maybe it won't happen until a conflict in their previous life was resolved or their soul mate has died and joined them. The way back is so different for everyone that it's quite impossible to have a reliable method."

"What good is trying to teach it then?" Noah asked.

"Schools aren't meant to teach you all the answers. How could they fit the whole world into such a small container? A good school should instead teach you to love the truth so you will search for it on your own."

"How come we could see stuff that was on the other side?" Noah asked. "My daughter Mandy too, and sometimes I thought even the baby was keen on them."

"You're Chainers, that's why." The old man grinned, evidently delighted by this. "Chainers keep repeating the cycle. You've been back and forth, dying and getting reborn again, over and over, until you've done it so much that you started holding onto something about the journey. Some people will come back still holding secrets from the other side. They might even remember spells or powers after learning them so many times. Of course the magic over there isn't nearly as strong as it is here, but every once in a while there goes a psychic with a neat trick or a man with a bit of old predators still in him. Or in your case, a family who can still see glimpses of the other side. Ah, but here we are with time to spare."

The bus stop ahead wasn't like any bus stop Noah had ever seen. It was closer to the size of an airport hanger with a single massive cavity. The building was entirely black, and inside loomed a towering bus, two lanes wide and at least five stories tall. Heavy clouds of purple-tinged steam flooded from somewhere underneath in regular pulses that looked almost like the bus was breathing.

"That's not a bus!" Noah exclaimed, feeling both deceived and delighted by the revelation.

A fresh gout of purple mist billowed from beneath the monstrosity and Noah covered his nose and mouth with his arm. In contrast, the old man spread his arms and inhaled deeply, wafting the mist up toward his face with both hands.

"It's grape flavored this time," George uttered with content. "Hurry up now, you've still got to buy your ticket."

The old man led Noah through the waiting area outside. Dozens of children filled the space, several sitting at each of the stone tables which were scattered beneath bright orange umbrellas. It wasn't just human children though—on one table a golden retriever puppy twirled in happy circles in the center of attention. There were all manner of domestic cats and other animals that were likely to be found in a city, including a very young hippo that must have come from the zoo. Noah paused in surprise to see Mrs. Robinson stalking along the top of the stone wall which surrounded the area.

"You weren't planning to leave me, were you?" Mrs. Robinson snapped, her voice sharp and accusing.

Noah opened his mouth to reply, but in his shock he couldn't find the words. Mrs. Robinson turned up her nose and strutted past, not showing the least concern that Noah had actually died in her pursuit. She cut the line in front of a pair of excitedly chatting girls and hopped directly onto the counter.

"One way ticket to Barbaros please." George Hampton was speaking to an adjacent attendant through the glass.

"Are you sure you've got enough left?" the woman behind the counter answered. She was dressed in a smart business suit with an orange tie and white gloves.

"Maybe so, maybe not," he replied. "It's for the boy, not me.

Noah had picked his way through the tables to reach the counter, and the saleswoman reached out a hand holding a neatly printed ticket. Noah reached out to take it, and white gloves seized his wrist.

"You'll be paying, correct? Can you confirm that your name and date of death is printed correctly on the ticket?"

Noah hadn't told her this information, but he could see that Noah Tellaver, August 22nd, 2018 was correct on all accounts. He nodded and tried to pull his hand away but was unable to break the woman's grip.

"If you'd died one day later then you would have had to wait a whole year," the attendant said, whistling low. "Someone out there is really watching out for you, eh? That will be two weeks."

"Two weeks? How far is this bus going?" Noah demanded.

The ticket woman smiled patiently as she rolled her eyes. "That's not the distance; it's the cost, silly. Two weeks for the fare with your luggage included."

"But I haven't got any luggage," Noah argued, quite confused.

"Your body. You *will* want to take it with you, I assume?"

"Yeah... Of course... I mean—am I supposed to?"

"Yes, dear," the woman replied kindly. "Deep breath now; this won't hurt a bit."

Still grasping his wrist tightly, the woman pressed a brilliant aquamarine stone into the back of Noah's hand. The stone turned on like a Christmas light, the aquatic glow bathing them through its numerous facets. Noah felt intensely groggy for a moment as though he'd just woken from an abrupt nap and was trying to decipher whether the clock read AM or PM. The white gloves released his wrist and allowed him to pull away with the ticket in his hand.

"I don't feel any different," Noah said.

"You won't until around forty," George Hampton responded. "Then it starts to sting a bit. No matter though, you're set to go. Remember not to talk to strangers unless they have something worth saying. and all that sort of thing."

A loud whistle blew from the direction of the bus. There was a stout man with a mustache wearing an identical orange tie and white gloves standing in front. He was checking the tickets of the first children who were beginning to board. At his side was a similarly uniformed opossum standing on its hind legs, checking the tickets from the animals.

"Can you let them know I'm alright? My daughter, I mean. That it didn't hurt, and that they don't have to worry about me."

"I'll tell them you're going to the best place in the world," George Hampton assured him. "Besides, you can always check in on them from the Whispering Room when you arrive."

The whistle blew again, this time a tad more shrill and impatient.

"What about Samantha and Claire?" Noah pressed, not having time to ask all the questions he wanted. "We've only just met me, but I think they'd want to know since it must have been horrible for them to actually see me go. And oh, I can give you more names if we have the time—"

George tapped the side of his nose and smiled. "Find your

way back and tell them yourself. That's how it's supposed to be done."

The third blast of the whistle sounded from directly behind Noah. He flinched and spun to find himself face-to-face with the bus attendant who promptly snatched the ticket from his hand.

"All aboard!" Mustached Man bellowed. "Daymare 7 is departing, one way to The Mortuary on Barbaros Island. Last call!"

"Shut up, will you? If you tried to leave me, I can promise you'll be looking for a new job before sunrise," shouted a portly, red faced boy whose beady eyes were almost invisible in his pudgy face. "What ever happened to resting in peace?"

"Don't mind him, darling," cooed a tall, thin girl racing to catch up. "No-one would ever dream of leaving you behind."

"They'd better not. I'm not staying one more minute in this vile town. You told me Heaven was going to have everything I wanted in it, but nothing here is made of gold and I can't find a thing to eat."

The thin girl caught up and handed two tickets to the Mustached Man who nodded sharply. "Brandon and Teresa Hides, you're just in time. Get inside, three floors up, middle row."

"I don't think so," Teresa remarked curtly. "We'll be sitting on the top with the best view. We'd prefer a row to ourselves, but if we must share we'll be taking those closest to the window."

Mustached Man folded his hands behind his body and swayed back and forth on the balls of his feet. Noah keenly hoped that they wouldn't be allowed on at all, and he looked around for George to tell him so. The old man was gone without a trace though, and in his place sat only Mrs.

Robinson who must have followed Noah from the station. She looked a little bigger than Noah had seen her last, and in her mouth she carried her own ticket.

"Very well, the top it is," the attendant conceded. "You'll have the whole place to yourself, if that's to your liking."

"If that's the best you can do, then we'll take it," Teresa said. "You'll like that, won't you Brandon? Not having to share with any of those dirty animals?"

Brandon screwed up his pudgy face as though trying to work out a particularly unpleasant math problem.

"The top is always the best," Teresa reasoned. "Come on, sugar, let's go check to be sure. If it isn't everything you could have ever dreamed of then I'll make sure they find you an even better spot."

"You'd better," Brandon snarled as he climbed aboard. "It's your fault I'm dead in the first place."

A few more stragglers came rushing from the station while they'd been talking. The attendant turned to take their tickets. Most of the human children were wearing plain white gowns made from a slightly shimmering material. Noah felt slightly out of place in his gray shirt and trousers, but no one seemed to be paying him much attention. Mrs. Robinson spat out her ticket distastefully and trotted at Noah's side as he stepped into the vehicle.

The inside of the Daymare 7 wasn't in the least recognizable as a bus. He used to ride the 247 city line when he'd had to let his car go. How was Mandy ever going to get by without him? Noah had been given his old job back at the veterinary clinic, despite being eight years into his retirement, and the daily commute had been the low part of his day. All the seats on the 247 were always mysteriously damp, and the windows were so filthy he could barely see out.

The city line would have been much more fun if it had a spiral staircase in the center with each step reminiscent of a coffin's lid, as was the case with the Daymare 7. The steps floated unassisted in the air, although they did have a shining brass railing and a fine brass mesh between the steps to prevent anyone from falling through. On each floor was a wooden walkway that extended to a floating platform which was filled with dozens of nervously chattering children and animals. More sets of stairs peeled away from these platforms, with steps going sideways or even upside-down to seat people in such ways as to make a physicist extremely uncomfortable. The people sitting upside-down on the underside of platforms didn't seem to mind, and their hair and clothing didn't hang downward but fell naturally upward as if the people were right-side up.

Noah had never felt further from home than he did staring at the mad scene before him. He'd never felt further from his daughter, Mandy, who must have noticed he was gone by now and was going to pieces trying to find him. He'd never get to watch another movie with Lewis, or hear Mandy singing the songs his wife had once sang to her as a child. But how could he allow himself to stay morose with such a brilliant mystery unraveling itself before his eyes?

"I'm really dead," he told himself aloud, the fact fully sinking in at last, "and that's fine with me."

QARI OLANDESCA ILLUSTRATIONS

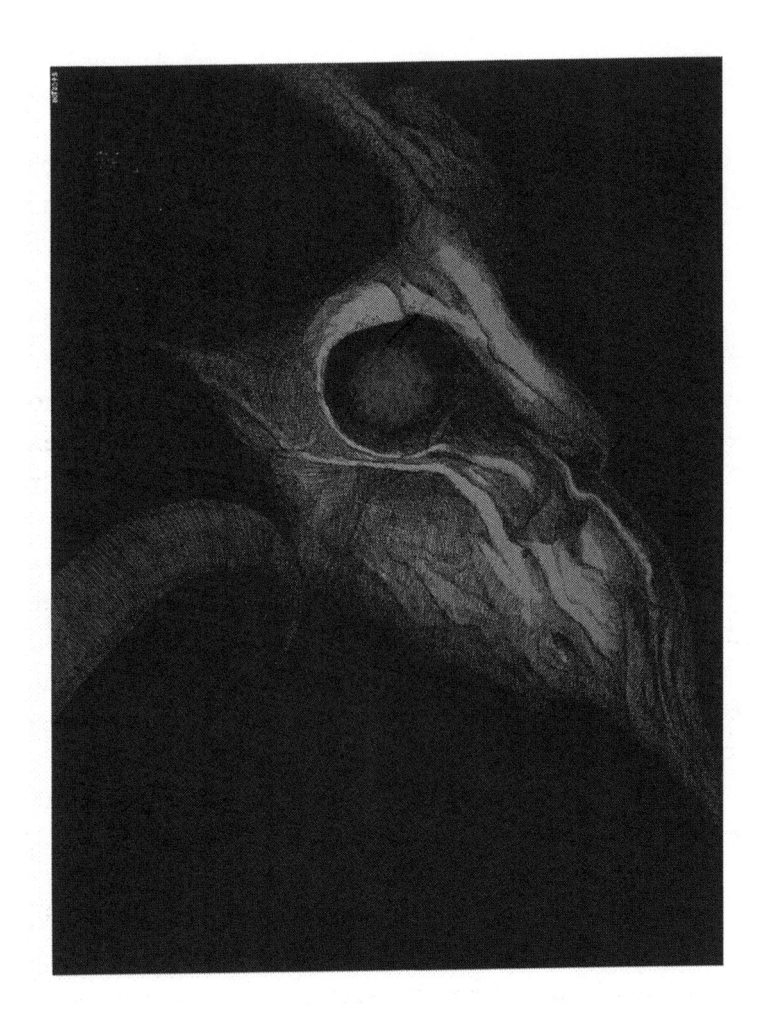

DAYMARE 7

❧

"May I hold your kitty?" a ginger haired girl asked Noah. He blinked in surprise, realizing that he had been blocking the traffic by standing and staring. He quickly stepped aside to allow the other children to pass.

"Go ahead, ask him for permission. Why would you ask me?" Mrs. Robinson lamented. "Why should I have a say when some stranger decides to grab me for her enjoyment?"

"Oh, I'm so sorry," the girl mumbled in embarrassment. She knelt down to speak to the cat directly. "I'm so used to—may I pet you?"

Mrs. Robinson turned to allow the girl scratch her back, which she did with a practiced motion that seemed to hit all the right spots.

"I used to have one just like you named Sebastian," she told Mrs. Robinson. "Or is that rude? I don't mean 'have' like a possession; I mean 'have' like someone has a brother, or a sister."

"I shall choose not to be offended if you don't stop until

you're told," Mrs. Robinson replied, flipping onto her back to expose her tuft of white fur.

"My son got Sebastian for me after my husband passed so I wouldn't be all alone. I hope someone is looking after the poor thing now."

Noah studied the girl's fair, smooth skin and tried to imagine her as a little old lady sitting alone with her cat. There was something wise and patient about her eyes that made the imagining easier, but the contrast still seemed too incredible to picture.

The formerly-old-lady made the bold move of picking Mrs. Robinson up, and after the initial suspicion the kitten settled quite comfortably in her arms. Noah was beginning to feel a little jealous that the cat preferred the newcomer to him after everything he'd gone through for her.

"Maybe Sebastian will find you again when it's his turn," Noah said.

"Do you really think so?" the girl asked hopefully. "My name is Jamie Poffin, by the way. I'd shake your hand, but I don't want to let go of…"

"Mrs. Robinson," Noah said. Then quickly added: "That's the cat's name, not mine. I'm Noah."

"You didn't strike me as a Mrs. Robinson," Jamie smirked. "Could I sit with you, Noah? I don't know anyone else here."

"Let me check my seat number…" Noah replied, but Jamie didn't wait. She was already leaping up the stairs, still cradling Mrs. Robinson.

"It doesn't matter, there are lots of empty seats," Jamie called back. "Oh, hello there. What are you supposed to be?"

Noah had to climb the stairs to see the thing Jamie was addressing. Only about a foot tall, it looked rather like a stuffed animal covered with soft red fur. Along its back was a line of hard ridges that looked like a series of shark fins, and its face was coarse and broad like an ugly little monkey. Mrs. Robinson was beginning to squirm, so Jamie set her down on the ground where she made a low growling sound at the furry red creature.

"Do you think it's a spirit?" Jamie asked. "Maybe an old one, something from an animal that doesn't exist anymore?"

"I don't think it wants you to pet it," Noah warned.

Jamie was already reaching for it though, her palms facing upward in a harmless display. The monkey-faced creature snarled and seized one of Jamie's hands with its stubby black fingers, biting viciously. Jamie howled as she jumped back. Mrs. Robinson hissed and all her fur stood on end, apparently scaring the creature which scampered down the wooden walkway. Mrs. Robinson sprang into action, chasing in hot pursuit.

"Don't touch the imps, please," shouted Mustached Man from below. He'd just closed the door behind the last children.

"Sorry!" Jamie shouted back. Her index finger had two prominent holes in it, but they weren't bleeding.

"Don't shout either!" roared the attendant.

"Sor—" Jamie began to yell, cutting herself off when she thought better of it. She gave the man a thumbs up with her free hand instead.

"No blood," she whispered enthusiastically. "We don't bleed anymore! That's fantastic, I always hated blood!"

The attendant moved toward the front of the bus where he seized a long brass tube, the other end of which connected with the brass railing around the stairs.

"Ladies and Gentlemen," he announced into the tube. The sound was amplified into a magnificent booming echo which radiated throughout the railing all the way to the top of the bus. "My name is Mr. Ludyard of the T.D.D., and welcome to Daymare 7, destination the island of Barbaros. We will be departing in a few minutes as soon as the last luggage has been stored."

"Were we supposed to pack luggage?" Jamie whispered, distraught.

"He means our bodies, I think," Noah whispered back.

"But I was cremated!" Jamie hissed. Noah shrugged.

"The Daymare 7 will depart at 10 PM and take approximately seven hours and twenty five minutes to arrive at its destination. To those of you who recently died in your previous life, congratulations for making it here in one piece. Please save any and all questions relating to the nature of death and the eternal secrets of the cosmos for your professors at school. Make yourself comfortable, and feel free to ask one of the imps for help if you need anything."

Mr. Ludyard dropped the brass tube and saluted to no-one in particular. He turned and made his way farther toward the front of the bus where a dark wooden door concealed the driver's compartment. Shortly after, the whole place began to rumble, and thick clouds of grape-flavored smoke began to flood past the windows outside. They were beginning to move.

Noah and Jamie climbed to the fourth level where there were more open seats. An imp dashed across the aisle in front of them, making odd panicked chittering noises with Mrs. Robinson in hot pursuit. There were more imps up here, grinning, and leering, and sticking out their tongues at the children as though daring them to do something they would regret.

"Do you want to sit in one of the upside-down ones?" Noah asked.

"No thanks," Jamie said. "I already get travel sick without hanging like a bat."

"Do we still get sick? Now that we're dead, I mean," he pondered.

"We're not really dead at all. We're just alive somewhere else. Didn't you read the pamphlets they have at the station?"

"No, I didn't have time," Noah said. "There was a man who helped me find the place though, and he explained some of it to me."

Noah paused; he watched a new boy sit down on his other side. The boy had dark skin and a cleanly shaven head, and he was nervously fidgeting and looking about all over the place.

"Hey, excuse me," the boy said. "Did you see where the imps went?"

Noah shrugged. They'd disappeared from the stairways, though he could still hear the scampering of their claws against the wooden flooring somewhere.

"Hey, imps!" the boy shouted. "Get your furry asses over here. I need something."

"No shouting!" boomed the echo which reverberated from the railing.

Claws immediately appeared to latch onto the platform, and two imps crawled over the edge to glare suspiciously at the boy. He glanced uncertainly at Jamie's wounded hand before clearing his throat.

"Yeah, hi, thanks," he said. "My name's Walter, my girlfriend's name is Natasha. We lived together at 423 E Ventmore Street, and I was hoping you could send her a message."

The imps looked at one another slyly. They started speaking an awful guttural, chirping sound rapidly back and forth. After a moment they faced Walter again with rather wicked grins spreading across their faces.

"So, um, you can do it?" Walter asked.

Both imps nodded enthusiastically, their grin spreading even wider to reveal at least two layers of razor sharp teeth.

"You're wasting your time," yipped a voice from behind. The golden retriever puppy was sitting there with a human girl on either side, both unable to keep their hands off him. "They don't understand a word you're saying."

"Didn't anyone read the pamphlet?" Jamie asked. "Demons are very intelligent and can understand every human language, even if they don't speak it themselves."

"What are you defending them for?" The dog asked. "You were the first one to be bitten."

"It doesn't hurt much, and it was my own fault for not asking first," Jamie huffed.

Walter cleared his throat again, embarrassed. "I just want you to tell her that I love her, and that she should wait for me. A few years at the most, tell her I'll be back as soon as I can."

The dog behind them snickered, and Walter looked even more embarrassed.

"Even if you do make it back, you're going to be a baby again. You won't remember a thing."

"You don't know anything, Bowser," Walter replied stubbornly. "I can possess someone else's body who is fully grown, now can't I? Or I can make myself remember a spell to grow up again real quick."

"Not unless you're a Chainer, and those are super rare." Bowser said. "Did you remember your other times?"

Walter's face soured. He shook his head.

"So what makes you think you'll remember next time?" Bowser asked. Walter turned back around in his chair to face the imps.

"Just tell her I love her then. That I didn't—that I won't ever forget her."

"You will," Bowser gloated. The two girls sitting beside him giggled, although Noah couldn't quite find the joke.

The imps didn't budge and only continued to stand there grinning.

"Go on then, you ugly little twerps," Walter said angrily, waving them away. "And don't let her see you. Just put it in a letter, or burn it in a piece of toast, I don't care. As long as she knows."

The imps darted along the wooden bridge and begun chasing one another in circles, chittering and laughing.

"They aren't going to do it, I can tell," Walter sighed.

"You didn't have to be so rude to them," Jamie said. "Not even a please or thank you…if I were them I'd never do it."

"You don't have to be nice to imps," Walter sounded doubtful. "They've got contracts to obey, they don't have a choice. I know the contract isn't with me, but I figured whoever did own it would have ordered them to serve the students."

The prospective students alternated between nervous chatter and reflective silence for some time before a sudden commotion on the stairs brought the next disruption. Noah and Jamie rushed to lean over the railing to see what was going on above. Brandon was bounding down the stairs after a pair of imps with Teresa chasing after him. The imps were cackling gleefully and seemed to be the only ones having a good time.

"Why are you so slow?" Brandon scolded Teresa. "Catch that little monster!"

"I'm trying!" Teresa whined. She lunged awkwardly at one of the creatures who dodged off the side of the stairs, scampering along the bottom with careless agility.

Brandon knelt to peer beneath the stairs. "I'll have your skin hanging in my room. Or are you too stupid to even understand? Get back here!"

One of the imps popped its head back above the stair to stick its tongue out at Brandon who was peeping over the opposite side. Brandon didn't appear to notice and continued to shout underneath the stairs on the other side.

"I used to have a whole room just for the animals I've killed. I'm going to start a new one on this side just for you and your family. Assuming you even have one and didn't crawl out of a cesspool somewhere."

The imp grew emboldened and crawled right behind Brandon who remained oblivious to it. The little demon was silently dancing now, obscenely thrusting its hips in Brandon's direction much to the delight of the other imps. The distracted creature didn't notice Teresa charging from the side until she launched into a flying tackle which pinned it to the floor.

There was a chittering uproar as the onlooking imps gnashed their teeth in fury, but none of them came to the aid of the pinned creature. It buckled and thrashed on the floor and looked about to wriggle free until Brandon joined Teresa to help secure her hold.

"What's the meaning of this racket?"

The voice came from a tall thin man mounting the stairs who Noah hadn't noticed board the bus. The skin on his face seemed to be pulled much too tight and was discolored in places as though he'd found it and tried it on rather than having grown it himself. This had the side-effect of pulling his eyes into narrow slits, barely wide enough to see the red iris within. He was dressed in a perfectly fitted black suit with a black silk vest and tie which commanded a sense of power despite his sickly appearance. A long, thin dog trotted submissively at his heels, although instead of fur it only had black leathery skin which wrinkled up when it moved.

"They trapped us on the roof!" Brandon raged, his face twisting into the ugliest livid shade Noah had ever seen. "There isn't any top floor at all. As soon as we stepped up there, the beastly things locked the door and wouldn't let us down until..." He grimaced and turned away, too angry to even finish the thought. "They ought to be killed for this, or banished at the least."

"Until what?" the emaciated figure asked, apparently bemused. Nearly a dozen other imps had leapt and bound from the other floors to gather on the stairs behind him. They peered around him or through his legs, leering and giggling to each other in their strange tongue.

Brandon scowled and turned away. Teresa had to answer for him. "We had to do the apology dance," she sniffed indignantly. "Right on top of the bus for everyone below to see. I've never been so humiliated in my life."

The imps began to howl with laughter, even the one that was still pinned to the ground. Brandon's face contorted into a darker shade of purple. Without warning he rose and stomped on the imp that Teresa still held to the ground. There was a loud crack like snapping twigs when his foot impacted against it. The rest of the imps immediately stopped laughing in unnatural unison. The boisterous atmosphere was replaced with a sudden eerie silence.

Most of the children were on their feet now, peering over balconies several floors above and below to watch the drama. The imp on the ground gave a pitiful little moan.

"How could he!" Jamie hissed, outraged. "They're so small!

And so what if they played a harmless trick? It served him right after how he's behaved."

"Apsolvo," the thin man said at once.

The imp on the ground began to dissolve into a thick black smoke. Its moan grew louder, turning into something like a shriek before it stopped abruptly. Brandon and Teresa gagged on the smoke and hurried up the stairs to get away from it. By the time the smoke had cleared, the imp was gone.

"Where did he go?" Brandon demanded of the thin man.

"The first lesson students in my class learn is that the demons we summon are our partners, not our servants," the man replied severely. "When one has been wounded in our service, it is our obligation to release them. To do anything other would be less than human. What is your name, boy?"

"Brandon Hides," he replied mistrustfully. "And I—"

"And you, girl?" the skeleton man interrupted.

"Teresa Hides," she replied, standing protectively in front of Brandon. "His mother."

"They look the same age though," Walter muttered. "I don't think I'll ever get used to that."

"You may call me Professor Salice," the man continued smoothly. "If I have the misfortune of meeting either you in my class, then a humiliating dance will be the least of your concerns. From what I've seen so far, I would not be surprised if you fail the weighing ceremony and are sent home at once though. You will behave yourself on the remainder of this trip."

The dog at his side opened its mouth, and instead of teeth a blossoming of cornflower blue tentacles emerged to spread impressively around its face. Brandon's mouth dropped open in dumb terror.

"How much longer is it, professor?" a brown haired, frightened looking girl on the opposite platform asked.

"We have two stops to make at Genesis General Hospital and the Rainbow Valley Vet," Professor Salice replied. "Make yourselves comfortable, and let us hope the freshly dead are more grateful for their second chance than you lot."

Professor Salice turned indignantly and swept down the stairs, his demonic dog and a small army of imps swirling around him and chattering amongst each other, some casting mistrustful glares back in Brandon's direction. The mood in the bus was more subdued after that, and Brandon and his mother Teresa found isolated seats in the back of a platform and showed no interest in talking to the others. Jamie, Walter, and Noah passed the time reviewing the pamphlet which Jamie had brought with her. Big purple letters at the top read: "The Road From Death."

The pamphlet folded out considerably like a road map with each square devoted to a different topic. "Cassandra's Corpse Comforting" offered counseling for traumatic deaths, and there was a special on "Wallace's Whimsical Windows" which promised such a "realistic view of home that you'd forget you were dead." There were magical stones that possessed various powers, including the "Eternal Spring Aquamarine Line" which allowed the transference of life force such as what the woman selling bus tickets used.

"These are all advertisements!" Walter complained. "I don't want to waste my death on these things."

"That's because you're looking at the wrong part. All the stuff about the school is over here," Jamie pointed out patiently. "Look here's a bit about the professors. It says that Salice is the new demonology teacher this year. He's credited as the inventor of the modern contract which has revolutionized the whole demon industry. They used to be forced to trust the demons at their words, which it says here was about as 'smart as making an omelette with harpy eggs'. I'm not sure what that means, though."

"But look on the other page!" Noah said, flipping back. "They're actually selling Harpy eggs on the first page."

"Yeah, but they say 'for external use only'," Walter said. "Do we still need to eat over here? I haven't felt hungry since I... well, you know."

Noah suddenly regretted not taking a hot chocolate of his own. As it were, the last meal he'd eaten was just a boring ham sandwich at noon. Was that the last thing he'd ever eat? Perhaps the others were reflecting on similar things, because most fell into silent introspection after that. Walter kept bringing up his girlfriend without being prompted, but he didn't seem to be expecting an answer from anyone and seemed more intent on preserving every detail about her to make sure he wouldn't forget.

The Daymare 7 made two more stops as promised, several children or animals boarding each time. Some were laughing, others crying, others wide-eyed with speechless amazement. Ludyard bellowed his short welcome speech verbatim each time, and the empty seats filled up with the freshly dead. The newcomers gave Noah a sense of confidence as he realized that as little as he knew about this new world, at least there were others who knew even less.

The general chatter faded again as the road wound on. The city thinned into suburbs, then to isolated houses dotting the countryside. The bus barreled directly down the streets regardless of whatever traffic might be going in the opposite direction, sliding straight through the other cars more gently than a passing mist. The rest of the world was still going about its business, completely oblivious to the spirits going about their own.

The first shafts of morning light were amplifying into a bright, warm day when Ludyard blared his next announcement through the brass railing.

"Look ahead, and to your right. Behold the only known island entirely within the spirit world, completely imperceptible to the living. Welcome to Barbaros!"

All the children on the left side of the bus hustled toward the right or stood on their chairs to see out the porthole windows. The bus was driving along the beach, rumbling through families and their umbrellas and sunbathers stretched out on blankets. Noah was almost trampled to a second death as several people strained to look past him, and he only got the smallest glimpse out of the bottom of the window.

The bus hissed, releasing great gouts of purple steam which spread across the water before it. Collective gasps resounded as the bus turned from the beach to drive directly onto the water, apparently buoyed by the purple clouds which it continued to dispense.

"It looks like a tombstone," Walter remarked in a somber tone.

"Only because you're thinking about being dead," Jamie replied.

One side of the island was dominated by a sheer stone cliff which produced the effect. Lush grass and thickly wooded areas covered the top however, rolling down in gentle slopes along the other side of the island until it met with a black sand beach which glistened in the sun. Thatch roofed cottages and long wooden houses littered the grassy hills which grew more densely populated as they neared the cliff. There, at the edge, a single prominent stone building which resembled a cathedral loomed over the precipitous drop.

Noah would have liked to watch for longer, but there was too much bustling for the window and he soon grew tired of being pushed and stepped on. He pulled himself through the forest of legs until he emerged near the stairs, face-to-face with Mrs. Robinson again. Noah thought she looked rather forlorn and moved to pet her, but she dashed away again before he had the chance.

"Well don't just sit there counting your toes," Jamie said, pursuing Mrs. Robinson. "We have to make sure she gets off the bus."

"Why?" Noah asked, following her down the stairs. "She can follow the instructions as well as anyone else."

Jamie's expression over her shoulder clearly stated that Noah was speaking nonsense, but she answered anyway. "She's so frightened! She needs someone to look after her. This world must be even more confusing for an animal which hasn't learned to think like humans have."

Noah could have rightly pointed out that none of the other animals seemed to be having trouble adjusting, or that Mrs. Robinson clearly wanted nothing to do with them and would refuse their help even if she needed it. The bus would be arriving at the island soon and they'd need to be downstairs anyway though, so he kept those thoughts to himself and followed Jamie downward.

Mrs. Robinson paused at each landing as though to verify that her pursuers were keeping up before bounding off again whenever Jamie was almost within reach. Others noticed their movement and were quick to follow, so that by the time they reached the bottom of the stairs there was already a crowd of other children pressing for the doors.

Mrs. Robinson was the first out as soon as the doors were opened. She vanished into the final blast of purple steam which flooded around the bus as it reached a complete stop. Before Noah could even think of pursuing her, he collided with a wall of noise blasting from all directions through the open door. A pounding sound—roaring and shouting, then a scream. All his budding fantasies about the other side seemed to evaporate, replaced by the nameless dread of the macabre unknown.

QARI OLANDESCA ILLUSTRATIONS

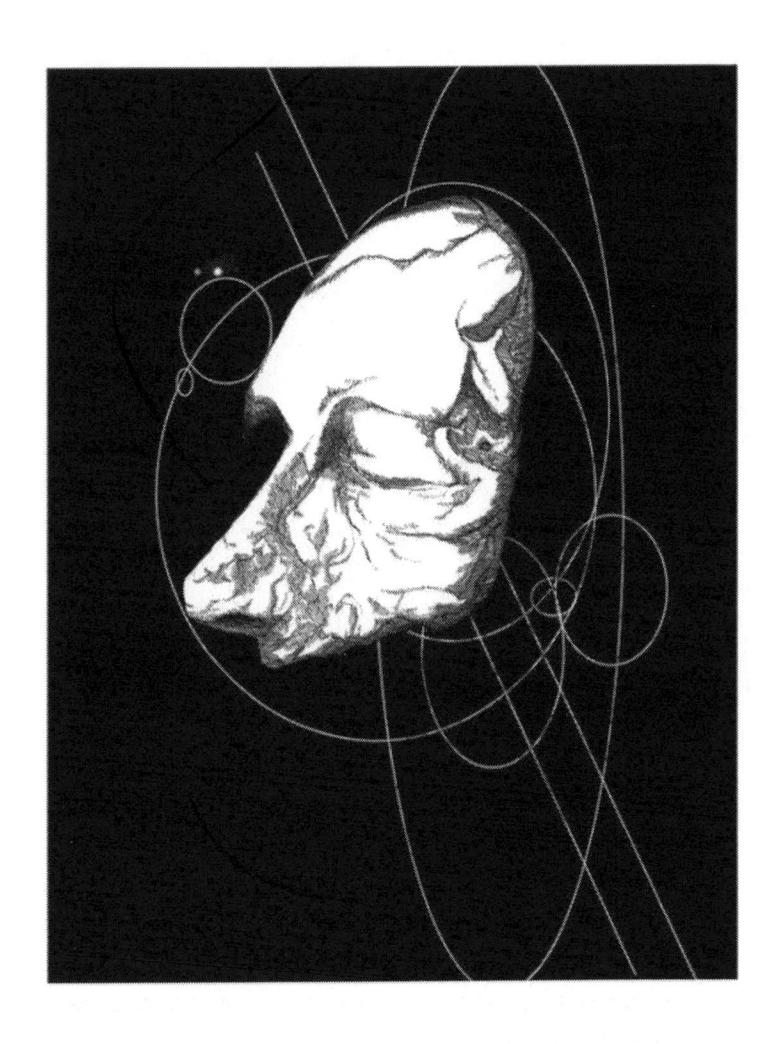

THE WEIGHING CEREMONY

Screaming, stomping, pounding, and... cheering? The scented smoke cleared to reveal a large crowd of howling and clapping people who formed a semi-circle around the bus. It hadn't looked like there were that many houses on the entire island from a distance, so the whole town must have turned out to welcome the new arrivals.

"Happy death day and welcome to The Mortuary!"

An elderly lady with the rigid posture of a drill sergeant stood at the front of the assembly to greet them. She was dressed all in red from her exaggerated high-heels to her black buttoned coat and wide-brimmed red hat which was tied with a black silk ribbon.

"Oh, I know that some of you aren't so fresh," she continued in a warm, velvet voice, "but even if you had to wait a whole year for the bus I promise you'll be glad you came. Don't be shy—and don't block the exit, please and thank you—come on out everyone. Feel the sun on your new skin and the grass between your toes. There's never been a better place to be dead."

The children were hesitant at first, but the lady's gracious smile and the cheering of the people behind her created an infectious, electric atmosphere. The bus quickly emptied onto the grass still heavy with the swirling vapors of grape flavored steam.

"Still in one piece, eh?" shouted a sturdy woman from the crowd. "Death wasn't so bad, now was it?"

"Good for you for making it," called a tall man with a silver buttoned vest. "Jolly worth the wait."

"Any nasty deaths? Remember Cassandra's Kill Counseling!" shouted a woman covered in jangling bracelets and ornaments. "It won't cost an arm and a leg this time!"

"Don't forget to call home with your spiritual operator!" a tall man in a yellow striped suit added, bobbing and nodding as he thoroughly agreed with his own proclamation.

The stately lady in red beamed as she raised her hands, slowly lowering them to still the crowd. It seemed to Noah that she was looking straight at him all the while, and his insides squirmed under her scrutiny. He ducked behind Bowser the golden retriever and his cluster of fawning girls who were now pushing towards the front, only to catch the Lady's eyes still tracking him when he emerged on the other side.

"And special welcome to our returning guests," the lady continued, turning away from Noah at last. "I am called The Matriarch, Headmistress of The Mortuary. Thank you Ludyard, your Daymare must be exhausted. Please relax, the both of you, and don't tarry on my account."

A last purple gust swept the ground, seeming to Noah like the bus was heaving a sigh of relief. Ludyard waved a smart salute with his gloved hand in the door of the bus before vanishing inside once more. The bus purred as it glided across its own steam to completely capsize onto its side on the grass. Noah couldn't help but stare at the thousands of legs like those of a centipede which wriggled and stretched luxuriously along the bottom.

The lean figure of Professor Salice cut through the assembly of children, which wasn't difficult considering how eager everyone was to get out of his way, to join the headmistress. She smiled and inclined her head toward him, allowing him to whisper something in her ear. Again she seemed to look in Noah's direction.

"If you have not already met Professor Salice, allow me to introduce this semester's new demonlogist," The Matriarch announced.

Professor Salice smiled as though the gesture physically hurt him—and considering how tight his skin stretched, maybe it really did. His leathery dog released its spread of tentacles in an arc that almost appeared to be a grin of its own.

"On my right, returning for his two hundred and twelfth year of distinguished service is Gregory Wilst. He will be overseeing your necromancy studies," The Matriarch said, gesturing to a figure that Noah hadn't even noticed a moment before. Perhaps that was because his bleached bones reflected the sunlight so strongly. Apart from a complete absence of skin, his most distinguishing features were the twisted metal staff he leaned upon, and the gold-trimmed, white linen wrapped around his bony waist. The skeleton nodded his head respectfully.

"A privilege, as always," the skeleton said dutifully in a voice like dry sand in the wind.

"On my left is Borris Humstrum. He will be instructing

your transhumanism courses. This naturally includes reincarnation studies, morphology, and animal linguistics."

"An honor Matriarch. And I'm so glad to see so many new furry faces this year."

Borris' clear, high voice was audible before he was visible, which took a moment as he had to climb on top of treestump in order to be seen. It's not that he was small—he might have been as tall as The Matriarch if he stood upright and he surely weighed many times as much—but his characteristic slouch was understandable considering that he was an orangutan. His wild orange hair sprouted out of his forest-green robes, and he leaned upon a thick wooden staff with an antelope head on the top. The antelope head seemed quite happy for the attention and brayed loudly in response to the applause.

"But what are we waiting for?" The Matriarch asked, her voice taking on the hush of sharing a conspiratorial secret. The children were in thrall to her captivating presence and drew closer to hear what she was saying. "Wouldn't you rather skip right ahead to the main event?" Each word was softer than the last, so that the children were drawn inward with the nearest being almost within arm's reach before she stood rigidly upright and shouted, "To the Weighing Ceremony!"

The leading few children scrambled backward and fell into one another when she shouted. The Matriarch laughed and turned with a red swirl, marching toward the looming cathedral on the cliff side. Some of the town's inhabitants peeled off to return to their homes, but a good number continued to follow the children in an enclosed semi-circle as they approached the ledge. Professors Salice, Wilst, and Humstrum took up positions around the perimeter of the children as if herding sheep.

"Did they say anything about the weighing in the pamphlet?" Walter asked Noah. "I didn't see it."

Noah shrugged. "It sounds so arbitrary. All the different animals must weigh completely different"

Jamie began folding through the pamphlet to check as they walked. "Hold on, I'm sure I saw it," she said. "The Daymare 7... The Mortuary... Welcome to Barbaros... It says here that 'Everything you need will be provided for you on the island of Barbaros. There are shops in the town which will provide all of your school supplies, although no student is allowed to spend more than six months per semester to maintain uniform aging.' Here we go, the Weighing Ceremony. 'The Weighing Ceremony will precede your first classes at The Mortuary. Those who do not pass will be sent back on the Daymare, and will not attend during the current school year.'" Jamie's last words shook uncertainly as she read.

"Okay, how do you pass?" Walter asked.

"It doesn't say," Jamie groaned. "It just goes on to talk about the Bestiary, and the Coven, and the Graveyards, and all the other attractions on the island."

"I don't want to go home yet," Walter said in a small voice. "Natasha wouldn't be able to see or hear me, and I wouldn't know how to come back. I'd just be... lost."

Jamie's brow furrowed as she flipped the paper back and forth. "That's not right of them to keep it a secret. Do you think we should ask someone to explain?"

"Shhh," Noah hissed. "It looks like she's about to tell us something."

The Matriarch had turned to face the children and was walking backward up the grassy slope now. Despite her apparent age, she moved with a sort of careless agility that turned the simplest gesture into the next component of a never-ending dance. Her rhythmic motions were soon joined by a sing-song honeyed voice.

My father was a soldier man
Who served his nation proud.
The battle lost, he turned and ran
And was shot down to the ground.

He's good and dead, the doctor said,
Still and dead as he can be.
He's got no head, his pillow red,
He sleeps eternal as the sea.

I'll never watch him growing old,
Or catch him walking down the street.
But I know if my heart is gold,
Then he'll be watching me.

Whether I go now or if I wait,
Until I've passed ninety-three,
I worry not, because it's our fate,
To dream each other in sleep.

The destination for the Weighing Ceremony was readily apparent from a fair distance away. A massive tree ruptured from the edge of the cliff with two ponderous limbs outstretched in either direction along the edge. From each limb hung a cage made of twisted black wires. As Noah drew nearer he noticed that one of the cages was already occupied by a solitary heart which must have belonged to a giant as the organ was several feet high and wide. The size wasn't nearly as troubling as the fact that it was beating on its own, pushing and pulling in wet gasps of air in place of blood.

"Don't be frightened, now," The Matriarch announced as she approached the base, still walking backwards to keep her eyes on the flock. "There's no beating around the bush with this one. The fact is that not all of you will find a path back to the other side. That not all of you *deserve* another life based on how you behaved in the last one. A simple calculation reveals there have been approximately 110 billion humans in the history of the world, whereas only about 7 and a half billion have currently found their way back. As a necessity, some of you will have to be turned away."

An uneasy hush fell over the assembly. The Matriarch's smile was inviting though, and her warm words continued to draw the students inward.

"One at a time—just like that, thank you. You there—with the ponytail, yes—step right up. You'll be the first."

The girl being referred to tried to melt back into the crowd, but the lady caught her by the wrist and dragged her forward. The girl looked at her feet and trembled from head to foot while the lady spoke.

"What's your name, dear?"

"Do-Dolly Miller," she stuttered.

"Well Do-Dolly Miller," The Matriarch mimicked with a reassuring smile, "why don't you tell the class a little about who you used to be?"

Dolly glanced at the cliff edge behind her as though seriously considering whether that might be the preferable route. Instead she swallowed hard and answered, "I was thirty two when I..."

"When you what?" The Matriarch prompted, leaning in with eager anticipation. "How did you die?"

Dolly looked down at her bare feet again and gripped the grass with her toes. "I did it myself," she said, barely above a whisper. Almost as if by magic the words seemed to catch in the wind and blow across the assembly, clearly heard by Noah despite how far back he was.

"Shh… shh… that's all over now," The Matriarch cooed. "Please step into the open cage, Dolly."

She did as she was instructed, glancing at the heart opposite her with unease.

"Don't Dally Dolly," gurgled the air from the beating heart in short, rhythmic bursts. "You are safe." Needless to say this did little to comfort Dolly who was now shaking from head to foot. She clasped the bars of the cage with her hands and watched The Matriarch close the door behind her.

Over the next several seconds the girl's weight slowly lifted the heart off the ground as it began to level out. The heart huffed and puffed faster now, seeming to grow excited by the process.

"How heavy is your soul, Dolly?" The Matriarch asked eagerly, like a starving woman asking about the daily special.

"I d-don't know," Dolly stammered.

"There are many things that can add weight to a soul," The Matriarch said. "Great emotions are important. Happiness, grief, fear—it doesn't matter, so long as you've *really felt* something. Making hard decisions adds weight. Imagining interesting thoughts, telling funny jokes, perhaps a burning passion—anything that will make us look back at the end and say 'I lived because…' That *because* is what the scale is measuring. That *because* is the weight of your soul."

While she'd been talking, the scale had continued to shift in Dolly's favor until it reached a perfect level. Gradually

Dolly continued to sink below that of the heart in the opposite cage.

"Dolly Miller!" the heart wheezed enthusiastically. "She lived to be loved. She is worthy to. Live again."

The townsfolk who had accompanied the children began to clap.

"Congratulations, my dear!" The Matriarch cheered with them and opened Dolly's cage, giving her a hand to help her back onto the grass. "You are most welcome among our company."

"I'm not going to move the scale an inch," Walter grumbled. "I never did a thing worth remembering."

"Don't say that," Jamie said. "Having a girlfriend will give you some points. You must have really loved her."

"I'm the one who hasn't done anything," Noah sighed, shuffling into his place in line. "I did get married, but it didn't last long. Always the same job, ever since I got out of school—seventy-five years of comfortable routines and daily habits and nothing to show for it."

"That's funny, I thought you were much younger," Jamie said. "You must get some credit for keeping a youthful spirit all the way to the end."

"What about you?" Noah asked. "Did you love your cat *passionately*?"

Jamie snorted in a not uncharming way. "Hardly. And I'm sure I miss Sebastian more than I do my husband. My son Erik might have noticed I'm gone by now, but then again he might not notice for a year on his annual visit. I've been to France though, do you think that counts for anything?"

Noah shrugged. "It can't hurt."

They waited in line while the students were weighed one by one—the first four all passing and being cheered by the crowd. Even the heart in the opposite cage seemed pleased, announcing each name with satisfaction. Noah didn't catch all the names, but he noticed Jason Parson was a human who lived to improve himself while Elizabeth Washent, the rabbit, lived to make the people around her happy.

There were a lot of students to weigh however, so whenever the beating heart wasn't making an announcement The Matriarch filled the time speaking about the school.

"The Weighing Tree was here even before The Mortuary was founded in 1647, although of course the living couldn't see it.

"The story begins with a ship named Alexandria which was carrying tobacco from America toward Europe. The ship was attacked by pirates, and every man and woman on board was slaughtered and burned aboard their looted vessel. Their spirits were not lost upon the ocean however, because on the other side they discovered the secret island of Barbaros. The men of Alexandria made an oath to one another that day, to never leave this place until they discovered a road back to life.

"In that pursuit they founded The Mortuary and began their studies. By the time one man had stumbled upon a way back to life, the whole community had become steeped in the knowledge of the spirit world. They decided that rather than let this knowledge disappear with them they would found a school so that each generation might pass on these secrets. Although each of the men has long since found their road from death, there remained one scullery maid who refused to abandon her school. Hundreds of years before women could even vote, yet since that day The Mortuary has been run by a Matriarch. *The Matriarch*, if you will."

At this she bowed low and flourished her red hat, leaving no doubt that she was claiming credit for this staggering act of good will. "Can you imagine?" she went on. "Giving up my own resurrection for the sake of forever leading others to that lofty goal? Of course I've already lived *so many* lives that I hardly need another. We should all be grateful that such a high-minded person as that has gathered you all here today."

Much of the assembled townsfolk moaned and shook their head at her boastfulness, but it was done so in good nature like someone pretending not to enjoy a good pun.

"Nigel Bronheart," the heart interrupted, "never understood. What he was living for."

The jovial atmosphere was replaced with many somber faces. Noah had been watching The Matriarch during her story and hadn't noticed the scale, but it was clear now that the heart sat considerably lower than the doughy boy dangling in the air. Nigel's eyes were wide with fear, and he began to jump up and down as though to force to scale lower. His efforts didn't move the metal cage in the slightest.

"Please step out," The Matriarch commanded, a sharp edge in her melodic voice. "It's time for you to go home, Nigel."

"That's not fair!" he protested, retreating to the opposite end of the cage. "I lived for plenty of things. I had a wife!"

"Did you love her?" The Matriarch asked patiently.

"The third one, sure I loved her," Nigel insisted. "At first anyway. And I had a steady job, and I never caused anyone any problems."

"Maybe you should have. Hush now," The Matriarch said. She opened the cage door and guided him out. "I can forgive mistakes, but I cannot forgive a blank page."

"I'm not blank!" Panic crept into Nigel's voice.

"*You* are not your experiences," The Matriarch explained patiently. "*You* are not your memories. *You* are not even your decisions, which many times are nothing but a spontaneous reaction. *You* are awareness itself, and if you failed to really feel the life you've lived, I don't see what good you'll do with another one. You have one year to revisit your old life and think about the person you used to be. If in that year you have learned what you must do differently next time, then you are welcome to come and try the scale again."

Nigel hid his face in his hands and refused to look at anyone. The Matriarch guided him gently by the shoulders to where Borris Humstrum stood leaning against his wooden staff. The orangutan nodded and wrapped a hairy arm around Nigel to lead him back the way they came. The surrounding townsfolk pushed each other out of the way to make room for them as though they were afraid of catching a disease.

"That must be so embarrassing," Jamie whispered. "If I were him I wouldn't ever come back."

"Bet he's going to go haunt somewhere now," Walter said. "Go haunt his ex-wife, throw some dishes around or something. That's what I'd do."

Noah didn't say anything though. His mouth felt like it was full of cotton, and his fingers wouldn't stop drumming against his thigh. He was next in line, and he could imagine the whole crowd sneering at him when the heart turned him away. How was he supposed to have truly experienced his own life when he'd always been focused on someone else? From his own sick mother whom he'd looked after until her passing, he'd barely had a moment to focus on his schooling before his daughter was born, and then everything he'd done was for her. Why hadn't it ever crossed his mind to spend more effort on himself? A sharp, loud sob broke the air from Nigel as he was led away, replaced by heavy silence.

"And you?" The Matriarch purred, appearing not to hear the crying boy at all. "What is your name, dear?"

"Noah Tellaver," he replied, keeping his voice as steady as he could.

"Go on then, Noah. Show us why you matter."

Noah swallowed hard, then nodded. He opened the wire cage, but hesitated before he stepped on. He glanced over his shoulder to see Jamie and Walter speaking in hushed tones. Jamie looked up and waved encouragingly, but Noah didn't feel the least relieved. At last he closed his eyes and stepped into the cage, jumping nervously as the door clanged shut behind him.

Noah couldn't feel the cage moving. There was no sound from the surrounding crowd to indicate his fate. They would have been cheering if he'd passed though, wouldn't they? There would only be silence if—but he couldn't open his eyes, because he was too afraid of seeing all those people looking down at him in disappointment.

"Noah Tellaver," the gurgling voice announced. "How many lives. Has he lived? Such a complex tapestry. I see a common thread. Runs through them all. From start to finish. With an unparalleled passion. He has lived each life. To kill. He is worthy to. Live again."

Noah opened his eyes to see a hundred eyes studying him with a range of curiosity and disgust. His cage was completely resting on the ground, the heart hoisted high above him. Hardest to bear was The Matriarch's deep brown gaze which felt like a spike impaling him against the wall. The fact that she was smiling did nothing to alleviate the pressure of her stare.

"Who did I kill?" Noah whispered to the heart in a gusty breath.

"Would you like. Their names?" the heart chortled. "It would take a while." Noah found small comfort in the fact that the heart didn't have a face, and therefore couldn't have been smiling as much as the voice suggested.

A murmur rose among the crowd of onlookers—first soft as the wind through reeds, yet steadily rising into a clamoring chorus. The Matriarch turned away from Noah to wave and smile, capturing their attention and urging them toward begrudging stillness.

"An unparalleled passion!" The Matriarch declared with excitement. "That's what I like in my students. Ladies and gentleman, please be at peace. So what if our young friend was a killer?"

"I wasn't, I swear!" Noah chimed, his voice seeming very small in the large open space. The Matriarch continued as though he hadn't spoken.

"There is no more evil in destroying life than there is in creating it. Who can say that it is worse to kill an evil man than to bring one into the world? Did the man being born have any more choice than the man who was killed? Both belong to the eternal cycle, and we do not condemn such expressions here. Welcome, Noah, to The Mortuary."

Noah glided back amongst the rest of the students, but there wasn't anyone to cheer for him as they did with the others. People stepped away from either side to make room, and even Brandon's lip was curled with disgust. Noah made his way toward Walter and Jamie again, but stopped when Walter turned suddenly to begin a conversation with a boy named Sandy behind. Jamie elbowed Walter fiercely in the ribs, prompting him to spin back once more.

"Play nice, will you?" Jamie scolded. "Does he look like a mass murderer to you?"

Walter grimaced and averted Noah's eyes. "It's none of my business," he grunted.

"I never killed anyone!" Noah insisted, hot in the face. "I sometimes had to put a dying animal to sleep at work, but I certainly never enjoyed it."

"It's not just your last life that counts," Sandy said, sweeping his shaggy blond hair out of his eyes. "It could have been your life before that.

"Or every life before that," Walter added ominously.

"I absolutely would not," Noah repeated stubbornly.

"You already did though," Walter said, still not quite meeting Noah's eyes. "You're still the same soul, don't you get it? We might not remember, but the soul we were then is the soul we are now, and it's the soul we're always going to be. You're a killer, man. I don't think that's ever going to go away."

QARI OLANDESCA ILLUSTRATIONS

Bless me father, for I have thinned.

THE MORTUARY

The rest of the ceremony must have completed, but Noah wasn't paying much attention. He sat away from the others on the grass with his eyes closed, wondering whether Mandy was able to look after Lewis, or whether she'd be too stricken by grief to even take care of herself. She'd always relied on him so much...

There was a thunderous round of applause, but Noah kept his eyes pressed tightly shut. Another person with a blessed life, how nice for them. Noah knotted the grass around his fingers and flung the loose blades into the air.

"Why didn't you tell me you'd found Mrs. Robinson?" Jamie asked.

Noah opened his eyes to find Jamie standing in front of him with her arms crossed. He hadn't noticed that Mrs. Robinson was stretched onto her back with curled front paws right beside him. Noah reached out to rub the cat's belly and was rewarded with a bear trap of claws.

"Ow, get it off me!"

"Ungrateful," Mrs. Robinson growled. "I came here to comfort you, and this is how you repay me."

"I was just going to pet you. Let go!"

"Hold on, you big wuss." Jamie unhooked the claws and pried the cat away to nestle it against her like a baby.

"Why are you okay when she does it?" Noah asked, nursing his hand.

"She's not a killer," Mrs. Robinson replied indignantly.

"You're one to talk," Noah grunted. "Bet you killed all sorts of mice and things."

"I even got a squirrel once," Mrs. Robinson boasted. "Took his head clean off and gave it to Claire. I think she liked it, because she ran to show it off to her mother right away."

"See? How's that any different?"

"It's not about what you do, it's about who you are," Mrs. Robinson lectured condescendingly. "When I was on the scale, the heart wouldn't shut up about how much Claire missed me. He said anyone who was loved so much must bring that love into the world again."

"Well you were both let in," Jamie said, "so you must both deserve another shot. Let's stop bickering and hurry up or everyone is going to leave us behind."

Mrs. Robinson allowed herself to be carried off by Jamie. Noah sat up to see everyone moving in the same direction.

"Where are we going?" Noah asked, hustling to catch up.

"The Mortuary! Come on!" Jamie called over her shoulder. "I can't wait to see our new home."

The Mortuary looked less like it was built and more like it was grown straight from the earth, as though it belonged as much as the forests or the cliff or the ocean itself beyond. The climbing ivy which engulfed the grave structure added to the effect, and thick moss upon every visible stone. Noah could only relate it to old gothic cathedrals he had seen in photographs, although it was impossible to compare those perfectly interlocking ancient stones with something as fragile and artificial as the buildings in his world appeared.

The far wall of the building was continuous with the cliff face as though the entire structure had been carved straight from the rock. There was a single round central tower which was composed of hundreds of smaller spires, as well as two smaller flanking towers. Each of the three towers was dominated by huge stained glass windows, and every inch of stone was intricately carved with miniature figurines, each nestled in their own alcove.

"They're gods!" one of the girls exclaimed, pointing at the closest figurines. "I never would have guessed there were so many religions. There must be thousands of them!"

"And look at the glass!" echoed another girl beside her. "What do you think the animals mean?"

From left to right, the three stained glass images were of heroically posed camel looking into the sunrise, a wide-eyed child beneath a blazing sun, and a snarling lion before a crimson sunset. There were words inscribed in the stone above the door in the central tower.

Life and death are each other's shadows,
Cast by the light of eternity.

The last of the curious townsfolk who had straggled along branched off here and returned to the cobblestone road, which in turn wound down through the grassy hills toward the town. The real sun was high overhead now, although Noah felt less tired and more like a deflated balloon. He shielded his face from the light, feeling as though he was fading beneath its relentless fire.

"Ah ah ah, not yet," The Matriarch said, calling back one of the boys who was already approaching the massive iron-studded double doors in the central tower. "It's so bright out, and you must all be so tired. Classes won't begin until tomorrow night. Mr. Wilst, would you be so kind as to show the students their resting place? When you're finished, you can join myself and the other staff in my chambers."

"Certainly, Matriarch," replied the dry, cracking voice. The Skeleton's metal staff clanked threateningly against the stone path as he turned away from the front doors. A few apprehensive glances were exchanged, but no one protested to following the morbid figure along the side of the building. He brought them around the building's flank to a tall black iron fence with severe spikes lining the top. Professor Wilst led them through the gate, and then waited there as the students filed in.

"We're going to sleep in a graveyard?" a blonde girl asked, her nose wrinkled in displeasure.

"There's something very comfortable about being with your own body that never goes away," Wilst replied.

"Ewww, they brought our bodies here?" she whined.

"Shhh Grace. Just let him talk," a taller girl beside her hissed.

Grace raised her hand instead, holding it excessively vertical.

Wilst stared at them expressionlessly for a moment before continuing. "The imps should have already stocked your bodies in the Mausoleums. There will be two names to a structure. Find the one where you belong and lie down.

Professor Salice will retrieve you at sunset to collect your books and school supplies."

"How come we still need to sleep?" Grace asked, unable to contain herself any longer. "We don't need to eat, do we? I don't feel hungry anyway."

"Silly human," Wilst replied in a voice that implied he didn't have the first clue what silliness was, and only a faint recollection of being human. "Spirits don't need to eat or sleep, but even the dead must dream."

With that the Professor swept his white linen about him and exited the graveyard. Several other people were beginning to ask questions, but their voices were cut off by the loud grating sound of metal clanking against metal. Professor Wilst had fastened a chain around the gate and locked it with a heavy padlock.

The Professor turned stiffly on his heel bone and walked away, ignoring the mounting protest from the students locked inside. Within seconds there were students leaping onto the fence and clutching the bars. Others shouted after Wilst or rattled the chain around the gate, but none succeeded in turning the skeletal figure around.

"It's not so bad, look," Walter said, emerging from one of the stone mausoleums. He was holding a stuffed reindeer in his arms. "I don't see any bodies in there. I think he was just being dramatic to scare us."

"Did it work? Are you scared?" an older boy with a face that permanently appeared to be tasting something sour asked. He'd just emerged from another of the mausoleums.

"Oh boy, I love stuffed animals! Where's mine?" Bowser said. Then louder, the dog howled "Anyone see Bowser? Where's Bowser supposed to sleep?"

The hunt for their personal mausoleum quickly distracted

the students who spread out through the graveyard. Walter had already found his place, but Noah didn't mind not sharing a place with his new friend after how he'd reacted at the weighing ceremony. Mrs. Robinson had wriggled free once more and Jamie was chasing her between the structures, so Noah didn't bother them either. He hunted on his own until he found his name, He ducked inside the low stone arch, grateful to finally have a chance to rest. He felt a lot less grateful when he saw who else was already inside.

"Why do I have to share with the murderer?" Brandon sneered. He was sitting cross-legged on the ground with his back against the coffin, holding a stuffed rhino on his lap. The inside of the mausoleum was small but clean with bare stone floors and a cushioned coffin against either wall. A burning lamp rested in the center, although the ball of fire which lit the enclosure floated unsupported in the glass. There was no curtain or barrier or any form of privacy between the two sides. On top of Noah's coffin sat a stuffed tiger waiting for him.

"I won't bother you if you don't bother me," Noah said, sitting down on his side of the room.

"Just looking at you bothers me," Brandon said. Noah was beginning to wonder whether he was really sneering at all, or whether that's simply how his face looked.

"I was expecting to find our real bodies in here," Noah said, trying to divert the subject.

"Look inside, idiot," Brandon said. He held up his rhino to reveal that he'd already ripped it open along the seam on its back. The skeletal remains of a hand clearly protruded from the white fluff, the curved forefinger making up the rhino's spine. Noah looked at the stuffed tiger and shuddered, preferring not to imagine what part of him might be inside.

Brandon waited for Noah to reply, but he didn't. Brandon sighed and climbed inside his coffin to lay down, still holding his stuffed rhino. "It's really not so bad," Brandon said, his voice seeming smaller and less hostile than it had a moment before. "If I close my eyes, it feels almost like I'm home."

"Why, did you sleep in a coffin at home too?" Noah replied sarcastically. He picked up his tiger and immediately understood what Brandon meant though. He felt a presence apart from the soft fur, a sort of harmony like an out of tune note that had just been adjusted to fit again. Noah climbed into the generous padding of his own coffin and held his tiger close. It was a perfect fit.

"Screw off, what would you know," Brandon replied. "Your home could have probably fit in my garage." He swung his lid shut to close himself inside.

Noah double checked to make sure there wasn't a lock on the coffin before carefully lowering his own lid. The darkness grew heavy, and this too felt nourishing somehow. The madness of the day faded into the comfortable buzz of voiceless thoughts, which in turn gave way to the haze of dreams. Violent dreams, bloody dreams, one after another, with Noah himself committing each atrocity he saw.

∽

"Don't hit your head when you wake up!"

Noah jolted upright, trying to escape his dreams more than he was trying to lurch back into wakefulness. He immediately smacked against the lid of his coffin and flopped back onto the cushions.

"The moon won't wait. Come on now, you can rest when

you're alive." It was Professor Salice, but the voice was muffled and moving away.

Noah opened his coffin with his hand this time. Brandon was already gone, and he'd taken his stuffed rhino with him. Noah couldn't imagine what he'd need it for, but the presence was so familiar that he couldn't resist taking his tiger along as well.

Professor Salice was standing near the open gate. He was scratching his demon dog behind the ears, which caused one of its tentacles to flop out of its mouth and twirl in sinuous spirals. A dozen imps had scattered through the graveyard to knock against the mausoleums and rouse those who resisted.

Noah moved to join the mass of students gathering around the gate, but most of them would take one look at him before quickly finding an excuse to stand anywhere else. Noah caught the eye of Walter, but he immediately looked away again without offering any sort of greeting.

"Noah! Over here!" Jamie called, waving and hopping up and down to be seen. "Look at this."

"Please do not touch the imps," Professor Salice drawled, looking in her direction. "I thought you would have learned your lesson on the bus already, Mrs. Poffin."

"He remembers me though," she insisted. "I think he's trying to say sorry for biting me earlier. Look he even let me pet—ow!" The imp bit her once more, and the students howled with laughter. Noah smiled and moved to join her, and, at least for the time being, everyone seemed to be too distracted to take any notice of him.

Professor Salice led the students through the gate and onto the cobblestone road. In the near distance, Noah could see open gates in other sections of the graveyard which allowed the free passage of older students. It appeared that only the youngest ones were locked in during the day.

"The sum of your supplies for the semester should cost no more than two months," the Professor said. "You should have all spent two weeks on your passage here, which leaves three and a half months available for discretionary spending. I strongly encourage you not to spend anything unnecessarily today, however. You are all without exception still very stupid and ignorant about matters of death, and the townsfolk with have no qualms about taking advantage of your unsuspecting wealth. While you may prevent yourself from aging by acquiring other people's life force later, you will never be able to reverse its process and become younger again while you remain a spirit."

The students pressed him with questions about what to expect, but he assured them that they would discover it for themselves soon enough.

"We will meet back here at the crossroads at midnight when I will escort you back to The Mortuary," Professor Salice instructed. He was passing out sheets of paper from a stack in his arms now. Some students were tentative to approach the professor and retreated the moment they received their note. "You will find the required items on the list along with a map of the town. Note the hourglass on the paper—when that is empty, it will be time for us to head back."

The words on the paper burned as though glowing hot, making them clearly visible even in the pale moonlit night. Grains of sands like sparks drifted down from the hourglass to fill the glowing base. Noah scanned the list of required items, which included three textbooks by the names of:

Understanding Undead: The Spirit's Guide to the Other Side
Twelve Signs Your Imp Might Be Plotting To Kill You: And Other Demonological Advice
Don't Be A Cow, Man: Reincarnation The Right Way

"What are we going to use Voodoo Dolls for?" Walter asked, reading the lower half of the sheet.

"Clearly to stick it to the man," Salice replied dryly. "Get going or you'll still be out when the ghouls wake up. Noah, you may stay with me."

Noah hadn't gone five steps before the note was whisked from his hands by two long and dexterous fingers. Salice handed the paper to one of his imps instead and shooed it away.

"See that it's filled," Salice said, dismissing the imp toward the village without taking his eyes off Noah. "We wouldn't want to burden our new Chainer with such trivialities, now would we?"

Noah wasn't sure who the 'we' being referred to was. He was acutely conscious that a disproportionate number of the students were staring at him. It made him immensely uncomfortable.

"I really don't mind getting my own books," Noah said quietly. He tried to surreptitiously retrieve his shopping list from the imp, but it growled as he reached for it and Noah backed off.

"Nonsense. Come. I have something else to show you that will be more worthy of your... lineage. Have you ever heard the story of the blind men and the elephant? Walk with me."

The sallow faced man pivoted sharply and reversed direction, making a direct route back toward The Mortuary. Noah shook his head, allowing himself to be led away. He felt as though he had no choice but to follow, although at that moment he would have rather done anything else even if it meant burying himself on the spot. It was bad enough everyone thinking him a murderer without being singled out again. He could already hear the word *'Chainer'* being whispered up and down the assembled students.

"One blind man stands at the elephant's tail, and he's asked by the others to describe what the elephant is like. The blind man grasps the tail and feels it up and down, confidently telling the others that the elephant is like a rope. Another blind man stands at the legs, and feeling these argues the elephant is a tree trunk. A third feels the tusk, saying the elephant is a sharp spear. Are any of these men wrong?"

"Couldn't they just keep walking around feeling the rest of the elephant?" Noah reasoned.

"Such is the life of a common soul," Salice said, ignoring the reply. "No matter how long they study what is within their grasp, they will only understand life through a single perspective, and thus they will not understand it at all. Only a Chainer may learn the truth of the elephant, and no secret of life may be hidden from one who experiences many lives. In the pursuit of truth and power, there is nothing more important than Chainers. How is it to be back?"

"I don't even remember being here before," Noah replied. "I don't remember any of my previous lives either. What good is it being a Chainer if I can't remember anything?"

Salice's tight skin seemed close to snapping as he grimaced. "Nothing? I wouldn't expect you to remember exactly how you made it back, but at least you must remember the other times you've died. Not every day that you die—very memorable, impossible to forget, I'd imagine."

"All I remember is being chased by something—A

gargoyle, I heard it called—and then I was hit by a car while trying to get away. And that was only in my previous life."

"Mmm," Salice said through pursued lips. He appeared disappointed. "A gargoyle doesn't chase the living. Your mind must have already started to decay before you died. There are some things that can't be erased, even if they are forgotten. Experiences, people, even skills and powers—they become so ingrained in your being that they become inseparable from the soul. I've heard that Mozart was a pianist in every one of his lives, and that he would always master it again regardless of his opportunities to play."

If Professor Salice had been trying to make Noah feel better, then it wasn't working. It was impossible not to wonder for the hundredth time how many people he'd really killed. With an *unparalleled passion*, no less.

"No matter. I have no doubt that you'll find it all coming back to you sooner or later," Salice added languidly. "Perhaps the Whispering Room will jog your memory. It's typically reserved for staff and special guests, but I don't think anyone would protest to a Chainer making use. After-all, you're much older than even I."

The Mortuary doors ahead were open and a steady flow of older students were piling through. They all wore plain gray trousers and t-shirts, just like Noah had received from George Hampton what seemed like a lifetime ago. The Professor's imps were scurrying ahead as they walked to clutch and claw at the legs of students who were standing in the way. The demon dog never left its masters side though, not even by a few feet.

"Do you know how many lives I've lived before? Could you tell from the weighing ceremony?" Noah asked.

"More than ten—perhaps many more," Professor Salice

answered. He disdainfully swatted a boy on the back of the head who was taking too long to move aside. "Enough for there to be power in you, if one knows where to look."

Noah considered asking again whether he could have really murdered people in all of them, but there were so many other students about now and he didn't want to draw more attention than was necessary. Besides, he was entering the main doors and was distracted by his first look inside.

It was a rather imposing structure on the outside, but at least it still looked recognizable enough for him to think of it as a cathedral. Inside the whole central tower contained a single cavernous room which soared at least a dozen stories above his head. He stood upon a circular path which traced the perimeter of the tower with eight doors spaced evenly around.

The tower above him was only the tip of the iceberg though, for the center of the space was dominated by a massive pit which must have been carved directly into the cliff it rested upon. Within that pit a gargantuan tree soared up from unseen depths. Its highest boughs filled the central tower above ground, and its innumerable branches stretched out to the circular pathway to form natural bridges leading to the tree itself where doors were carved directly into the trunk. Noah rushed to the edge of the pathway and looked down over the brass railing to see another circular pathway on a floor below him, and another below that, and more beyond until they were lost in the inscrutable darkness below. The whole scene was illuminated in a red-tinged moonlight which poured through the stained glass window with the child and the blazing sun.

"Unless you plan to jump, I advise following me," Professor Salice said darkly. He was already striding across one of the thick branches which spanned the pit to the main trunk. "Contrary to the fondest wishes of many naive first years, the reckless dead can still die. It isn't easy to destroy a spirit, but once gone you are gone with it. We will be taking the stairs."

Noah hastened across the bridge after Salice who was opening the door within the tree trunk. The brass railings felt woefully inadequate over the abyss, and Noah made the mistake of looking down when he was about halfway across. The tree seemed to go on forever, and deep below two shades of darkness seemed to slide past each other as though some monstrous creature was stirring in the depths. It was fortunate that the space below the railings was too interwoven with branches to allow him to fall, because Noah wobbled dangerously before catching hold of the railing once more.

"Today, Noah," the Professor barked.

Noah tore his eyes away with difficulty and forced his weak knees to stumble along the remainder of the bridge. He was only too grateful to step through the door to enter the tree, which turned out to be filled with a two spiral staircases which wound around each other in a double-helix. These too seemed to wind down indefinitely, although at least it was well lit by an array of small burning orbs which floated randomly throughout the space. No—not orbs—he could clearly see the little winged bodies wreathed in flames. Noah reached a hand toward one, recoiling immediately after feeling its warmth.

"Will-o-wisps are for looking, not touching," Salice said without even glancing over his shoulder. "First floor is the living quarters for the teachers and staff. Do not disturb anyone unless you've been specifically invited." Noah was still transfixed by all the new sights so he did not answer. "Confirm that you understand me, Noah."

"Yes sir," he replied automatically.

"Second floor is dedicated to necromancy studies. You will find rooms for animation, possession, and other occult matters."

"Yes sir," Noah said again, immediately feeling foolish by the condescending look he received. They passed the second floor headed downward.

"Third floor is run by Professor Humstrum," Salice continued. "I wouldn't expect a Chainer to bother with something as lowly as reincarnation though. Why would someone who has already proven their ability to return on their own terms wish to waste their time as a rat or a cockroach? I've never understood it.

"On the fourth floor you will be receiving instruction from me. Do not dismiss demonology as the mere imps you see around you. This branch of science deals with much more profound and practical uses that can both aid your existence here as well as provide new routes back to the living world. There is nothing more powerful in this world or the next than the magic spun from the Nether."

Noah expected them to exit on this floor and even reached toward the door, but Professor Salice continued his descent. There was not a single student to be seen on the stairway below the fourth floor. Salice didn't stop until he reached the fifth floor where he held open the door for Noah. The stairway beyond this point was blocked by a metal gate which was fastened by many sets of heavy chains.

High overhead, Noah could see the students going to and fro across the bridges, but the circular floor on this level was completely deserted. The light from the stained-glass couldn't penetrate this far down, and everything was obscured in a thick layer of shadow.

"The fifth floor contains the Whispering Room, as well as the seven unspeakable words. Students are not permitted here without invitation. Come."

Noah couldn't help but look down once more while crossing the bridge, and this time he was sure he saw two great eyes blinking deep below in the darkness.

"Below this begins the Road From Death. A student may choose to walk it upon graduation, or more commonly, they continue their studies independently while finding work in the town below. Others will return to the living world as a spirit where they will watch over those they have left behind, although the T.D.D. has strict rules about permitted interactions. Don't be so slow—my students will be expecting me shortly."

Noah hurried across the remainder of the bridge to join Professor Salice on the circular floor. He was already unlocking and opening the first door to disappear inside. Noah hesitated before entering, noticing a wave of cool steel-blue mist pouring out of the room to stream about his feet and legs.

"Why do they call it the Whispering Room, Professor? What's it for?" Noah asked.

"In the Whispering Room, one might hear everything the living are still thinking and speaking of them. It is a valuable chance to connect with your previous lives, even more so for a Chainer who might possess an enduring legacy. Aren't you curious what they have to say?"

QARI OLANDESCA ILLUSTRATIONS

THE WHISPERING ROOM

The Whispering Room was small and round, looking to be designed for no more than one or two occupants. Most of the space was filled by an elevated marble dais on which a large mystical circle was carved into the stone. Its outline was filled with occult writing and strangely interlocking geometrical shapes. The pale blue mist was bleeding from the carved lines.

"I don't think I want to hear," Noah said, reluctant to enter. "Mandy will be in pain, and there won't be anything I can do for her. Can we try again another time when it isn't all so… fresh?"

Professor Salice watched Noah in silence, the colored mist casting odd shadows across his angular face.

"Do you know what I hear when I stand in circle?" Professor Salice asked.

Noah shook his head. Salice pursed his lips, for the first time appearing vulnerable.

"When I first died," Salice continued, "it used to be almost deafening in here. I had a big family—three sons, two daughters, brothers and sisters. I owned my own business and a hundred people owed their jobs to me. I had two homes, and four cars, and a boat that I would take out on the lake during the summer. And that's what everybody was talking about. All I ever heard in here was people trying to figure out which of my things they would get to keep. And now..." the Professor cleared his throat. "I haven't heard so much as a peep for a long time now. Listening to the Whispering Room is rarely easy, even for the purest souls. But the earlier you listen the truer it will be, and such insight will aid you in preparing for the next time round."

Noah nodded as he cautiously mounted the marble dais. The Professor slid along the wall behind him to shut the door. The mist began to pool on the ground and fill the room now that it wasn't leaking out, and in that mist Noah could hear a soft murmuring. Noah stepped inside the circle and the sound immediately became clear.

"I don't know if you can hear me, Noah, but I know you aren't gone." It was Samantha with her white eye, her face briefly flickering within the shades of blue mist. "I've been starting to see things ever since my eye was hurt. Spirits—dead things, I guess, and other creatures I've got no name for. One that looks like its made of stone except for its yellow eyes is prowling my street every night, rummaging through the trash cans, searching for something. I don't know if it's the same one that attacked me, but I keep pretending that I don't see it and it hasn't bothered me yet. Am I safe? Please—if you can hear me—please help me understand."

"What a pretty eye you have, girl," Professor Salice said softly.

Samantha's whisper was already growing fainter as another one rose to drown it out. Claire's face was in the mist now. She seemed to be praying. "Dear Noah, please take care of Mrs. Robinson for me. It was hard at first thinking she wandered off and didn't want to stay with me, but now I'm glad that she has a friend over there. Don't forget about us—Samantha talks about you all the time, and I know she won't forget about you…"

Next a three year old child—it was Lewis, but only for a moment, his image distorted and blurry. "Noah…" he said. "I'm hungry, where are you?" Then he too was gone.

There were other whispers—fainter ones from the man driving the jeep, or the people in the ambulance who took him away. There was the echo of phone calls made between relatives, and the gossip between neighbors. These too gradually faded into silence though, and the mist was beginning to dissipate. Just when he thought it was over, his daughter's face finally appeared within the mist.

Mandy's hair was messier than ever, and her face was red and puffy with tears. "Not dead…" she mumbled. "He's with Lewis and they're playing a game. They're playing a trick on me, but I'm not going to be fooled. Oh no, not me. I'm the one who invented fooling people, don't you know?"

Mandy pinched the bridge of her nose and closed her eyes as though trying to concentrate.

Noah's fingers tingled. He looked down to see his hands clenched so tightly that they trembled. He took a deep breath and forced himself to relax.

"I don't want to hear anymore," Noah said. "Make them go away."

Mandy opened her eyes, her gaze darting this way and that —searching for something.

"She can't see me, can she?"

"Of course not," Professor Salice said. "Not unless—"

His words cut short as Mandy's gaze focused deliberately on Noah's face. "I knew it! Noah, I knew—but you're just a boy. Where did my father go? I want my father back! Those horrid girls lied about him. The police—the hospital—they were all part of the game. My father is still here though, isn't he? Tell me he's still here!"

"Oh Mandy, I'll always be there with you," Noah spoke with difficulty, forcing the air out of his throat which seemed to have closed to a pinhole. "I'm not the same as I used to be, but I still remember everything. I need you not to look at the spirits you see though. There's a stony thing with yellow eyes that is looking—"

"Dispersus!" Professor Salice commanded. The word had an unnatural metallic echo to it, and the echo grew louder with each iteration instead of softer as it ought to. Within a few seconds the word 'dispersus' pummeled Noah with a physical force, assaulting him from all directions as it ricocheted off the walls. Noah stumbled out of the circle with his hands clutched over his ears. The mist around him evaporated as the last echoes blasted through the room, now at last growing softer until the last reverberation had disappeared completely.

Noah rushed back to the circle and stepped inside, but the mist was no longer bleeding from the cracks and his daughter was gone.

"What did you do?" Noah shouted, scraping the marble floor with a furious swipe of his hand.

"Why didn't you tell me your daughter was a Chainer too?" Salice hissed. Noah felt his own bluster vanish as that tight skin contorted into a snarl overhead.

"I didn't know—" Noah stammered impulsively, bewildered.

"Liar! You knew how important Chainers were, and still you hid her from me. What were you going to tell her, hm? Come on now, out with it."

The professor's black dog leapt to its feet from where it had been been silently sitting at Salice's side. The flare of tentacles flew from its mouth and a low growl rose in its throat.

"Nothing! I was only warning her—" Noah began, backing away from the creature.

"The gargoyle. Which she could only see if she was a Chainer too. Which means you knew she could see spirits—of course, how could you not, your own daughter. But to have her detect your presence through the Whispering Room—a rare prize indeed."

The dog's growl turned into a wet, squelching howl. It began to advance on Noah with its head low as though stalking its prey. Noah pressed himself against the wall to get as far away from it as he could.

"Visoloth, down," Salice commanded.

The dog sat instantly as though its rear end was magnetized to the floor. The swiping tentacles slowly receded back into its mouth, though they still occasionally snapped through the air like a shadow-boxer.

Salice began to strum his fingers upon his cheek, pinning Noah with his gaze. Then he took a long breath and Noah could see the individual muscles in his face relaxing one by one. "Your grandson. Does he see spirits as well?"

Noah hesitated. "I don't know. He's only three and wouldn't know a spirit if he saw one."

Professor Salice finally succeeded in relaxing his face, except for a single muscle at the corner of his eye which continued to twitch. "Allow me to apologize. I have been rude to you." To Noah's shock, the Professor swept into a low bow at Noah's feet. "I allowed the excitement of my discovery to overpower my manners. Chainers are just so useful and I… but no, I was rash and unpleasant. Please take this key as a token of my apology. You are welcome to use the Whispering Room whenever you'd like."

Noah accepted the metal key in silence, suspicious of the sudden change in behavior.

"Of course, you might still have trouble getting a message across if she isn't thinking about you while you're in the room," Salice continued, his words slow and measured as though he was dictating something to an unseen scribe. "I would be better service to you if I arrange to have your message personally delivered."

"Very well…" Noah said, guarded. "You will have to give me time to write something though."

Salice nodded rapidly—almost eagerly. "Of course, of course—as long as you need. And where will I be sending it?"

Noah felt more unsure than ever. It seemed that Salice wanted to know where his daughter lived for a reason completely apart from delivering a message. Refusing him outright seemed like a mistake though, and Noah didn't want to enrage the man again.

"I'll write the address on the letter when it's done," Noah said. "Thank you."

The muscle just above Salice's top lip curled independent of the rest of his face, then released. The Professor then smiled broadly, although the smile never made it as far up as his eyes. "That will do nicely. Well I can't keep you all day, as much as I would like to. Your imp should be waiting for you on the ground floor with your books and school supplies. Don't wait for me; I plan to remain here a little while."

"I thought you couldn't hear anything anymore?" Noah asked, scolding himself for being nosy.

Professor Salice wasn't angry though. He smiled a sad little smile and said, "Silence sometimes has more to say than words, if you know how to listen. Go along, I will be seeing you again Wednesday for our first class. Do bring the letter you've written then."

Noah was only too happy to exit the room. He wasted no time darting back across the bridge and didn't even look down until he'd gotten to the other side. Then up the stairs, taking them three at a time all the way back to the ground floor.

All the students he passed were now wearing the same gray t-shirt and pants that he was wearing, which apparently was some sort of uniform. None of them were wearing shoes though, which by now had ceased to seem nearly so odd.

Noah found the imp immediately upon exiting the tree. It was on the other side of the bridge sitting atop a pile of books within a cheerfully bright red wooden cart, snarling and baring its teeth at anyone who got too close. This seemed to have unfortunately encouraged some of the students to make a game out of trying to steal its treasure without being bitten.

"You sneak around on the left," Brandon instructed Teresa. "Try and pull its tail, and then when it looks away I can grab the stuff."

"You awful brat!" Jamie scolded. "What could you possibly do with two sets of books?"

"I'd like to see how long it takes for them to hit the bottom of the pit," he replied casually. Several on-looking students snickered at this.

"Watch who you call brat," Teresa huffed, "unless you'd

rather be tossed over instead. It might be easier to tell how deep the pit is by listening to you scream all the way down."

"Leave off!" Noah shouted as he began racing across the bridge. "I need those!"

"Go!" Brandon hissed. Teresa dove for the imp and snatched its tail. The creature wailed pitifully but refused to turn away from Brandon. The boy shied away, pacing the perimeter of its reach. As soon as it became clear that he was hesitating, the imp spun around and took a bite out of Teresa's hand. She let go and stumbled backward, swearing bitterly which sounded all the worse coming from a child. Brandon dove forward and managed to knock over the cart and scatter the books to the ground. He then retreated as soon as the imp refocused its attention on him.

Noah burst through the circle of gawking students to arrive beside the imp. He snatched the fallen books and things indiscriminately, dropping some again in the process as he tried to keep one eye on Brandon.

"First day and you already can't keep up." Brandon scoffed. "Better hurry before the Daymare leaves. I don't think they allow murderers to resurrect anyway."

"Leave him alone." It was Walter, blocking Brandon's route to the imp. "He's not the one you should feel sorry for."

"What's that supposed to mean?" Brandon demanded. Despite the bluster, he seemed less sure of himself now that he was outnumbered.

"It's bad enough having a clingy child without it following you after death," Walter said. "I bet your mom can't wait to start over without you."

Brandon made a lunge toward the imp as though he was going to smash it straight into the wall behind. Walter dove between them and pushed Brandon back. The imp clutched its claws together and gazed up with wonder at Walter as though he was its salvation.

Noah took the opportunity to hurriedly stack his books back in the cart. Teresa hadn't taken Walter's comment well though, and she was scowling wickedly, about to reply when —*SCREECH*—an earsplitting scream exploded overhead. Great gray feathered wings wider across than Noah was tall beat the air, prompting students to hurl themselves to the ground left and right. Talons like scimitars curled around the brass railing, and brilliant green eyes skewered each student in turn with their baleful glare.

"Professor Humstrum. First year class. Fifteen minutes. Third floor!" screeched the creature in short bursts with a voice that sounded like fingernails on a chalkboard. Her face was remarkably smooth and feminine apart from the blazing eyes, although the rest of her torso was covered in a sporadic layer of feathers that looked more like they had been stabbed into her skin than naturally grown.

A hushed whisper passed up and down the gawking students. Noah clearly heard the word 'Harpy'. This distraction gave Noah ample time to right his cart. The imp was reluctant to give up the: *Twelve Signs Your Imp Might Be Plotting To Kill You* book, but Noah managed to wrestle it away without Brandon or Teresa interfering.

"I never noticed—there must be dozens of them," Dolly Miller breathed nearby. "Look up at the tree top!"

More gray shapes were swirling through the boughs of the massive tree. They must be just waking up though, because Noah was sure he would have noticed their screeching the first time he passed through. Noah squinted and thought that he could even make out a number of small ramshackle houses balanced among the higher branches.

The Harpy continued to glare at the students who wasted no time in hustling across the bridge to the central stairway.

"Thanks for that," Noah said to Walter.

Walter grunted in reply, focused on trying to keep his own cart upright with all the other students jostling against it. "Don't get used to it," he said. "I just hate seeing someone teamed up on, that's all."

"Aren't you still worried that I'm going to murder you?" Noah asked, keeping his voice light.

Walter looked him up and down and shrugged. "Just remember I stuck up for you next time you start killing."

"Deal. I'll get you last, and if I'm feeling tired then I'll skip you completely," Noah said, relieved to see Walter grin in reply.

The carts didn't bump down the stairs like Noah expected. In fact they were surprisingly light from the start, but as soon as they were pushed down the first step they continued to glide as though rolling down an invisible ramp. This was especially convenient for the animals who couldn't hope to carry their own books. Elizabeth Washent, the rabbit, had already figured out how to steer her cart and make it propel itself while she sat inside.

There was a commotion as they went down the stairs however. Bowser the dog had pushed his cart ahead only for it to sail off through the air without him. The cart kept going straight ahead until it smashed into one of the curved walls of the tree. Despite this example, several others were beginning to experiment with gliding their own carts, causing even more collisions and accidents and blocking up the stairway terribly. Some of the older students howled with laughter at the fumbling first years, but they were all having such a good time learning to drive their books around that they hardly minded.

The students exited onto the third floor and marveled at the stunning vegetation which existed there. Long tendrils like vines grew from the tree to wrap around the brass railings, and from them bloomed magnificent and alien flowers. The vines spread out along the entirety of the floor, dividing over and over into entirely new plants. Tall ferns, thick bushes, even complete trees were growing straight up from the floor with their long roots interweaving with the branches of the tree.

"Transhumanism and reincarnation studies!" boomed an unseen orator. "Welcome to your first class at The Mortuary."

QARI OLANDESCA ILLUSTRATIONS

TRANSHUMANISM

⚜

"Drat, now how many were there supposed to be again? It seems like there are more every year."

The fair, high voice sounded like it was coming from a student at first, but it was Professor Humstrum himself. The ape was scratching its back with the tip of its staff as it leaned against the wall, almost invisible beneath the broad leafed ivy hanging around the door frame. The students were still chattering loudly to one another, and it seemed that most didn't notice him at all until the antelope head on his staff began to bray.

"Shh, shh, don't startle them Hazel," the Professor said, stroking the side of its head. "Just because you haven't met them yet doesn't mean they aren't your friends."

The students quieted down immediately to watch this odd spectacle. Professor Humstrum continued to pet his staff, mumbling soft words of reassurance to it that Noah couldn't hear. The orangutan waited until the last of the students had exited the stairway onto the bridge before setting his staff aside and rearing to its full height which appeared to be about five feet, only slightly taller than the students.

"Welcome, young Transhumanists!" Professor Humstrum announced. He grinned broadly revealing a pair of deadly sharp fangs, and a small bird stuck its head out of its shoulder fur to see what was going on. "Don't give me those faces. No tests—no essays—I'm not here to try to trick you into learning anything. If your heart has a true fondness for what lies ahead then you will remember my lessons, and if your heart lets go then you will find something else to love. I do hope you all brought your copy of *Don't Be A Cow, Man*... Oh no, you won't be needing your stuffed animal quite yet. Right then, follow me."

Noah counted eight rooms around the circular floor, each numbered with the appropriate number of brilliant red flowers. As he was turning he caught the eye of Jamie who had found her way behind him in the crowd. Her gray t-shirt was bulging, and there was a black tail sticking out below the bottom, swishing with distemper. Jamie's face was almost glowing from the sheer force of how hard she was smiling. Noah grinned and turned back to the front to see the students following the Professor into the first room.

The classroom was entirely organic, from the chairs and desks which grew from the floor to the florescent mushrooms dangling from the ceiling like a chandelier. The Professor nodded and bobbed merrily like an enthusiastic waiter ushering diners to their table.

"I know a lot of you must feel pretty overwhelmed by this point in your death, so let's get the basics out of the way first," the Professor spoke as he waddled toward his wooden pedestal with branches shaped like cupholders. "Our modern understanding of the spirit world is really quite simple. You are a soul, here and there, now and always. If you're a soul with a corporal body, then you're considered 'alive'. If you have no physical body, then your soul projects a spiritual body until you can find a new one. Which body you'll be able to pick will be largely determined by how much you learn in this class. I, myself, spent a life as a lion before giving orangutan a try."

Professor Humstrum puffed out his hairy chest in pride at this declaration as he beamed around the classroom. Hazel, the antelope head, snorted derisively.

"A lion in a zoo. Don't forget to tell them you lived in a zoo," it said.

Professor Humstrum deflated a bit, but he rallied immediately. "I would have told them if it mattered. It's not like that made me any less of a lion."

"'Course not," Hazel said. "Just like I don't need legs to be just as fast as the other antelope."

"Any questions so far? I know it can all be rather overwhelming at first," the Professor asked suddenly, prompting giggles from the class at his overt attempt at changing the subject. "Yes, you, the little blonde dog. Did you have something to ask?"

Bowser put his front paw back down on his desk. "What happens if your spirit body is killed?"

"First you must remember that a spirit body is more than arms and legs," the Professor answered. "You've got a spirit brain too, with memories and thoughts and habits and personality, and all those things about you make you feel like you," Humstrum replied, his voice kind and patient. "If that is destroyed, you will lose all that, but that doesn't mean everything is gone. Your soul is a hard seed at the center that can never be harmed. In time it will grow a new body and a new mind, and although you won't remember the person you used to be, the cycle of life will begin again."

Bowser' paw went up again, and he continued before the Professor had a chance to call on him. "But what if you get really old and you keep spending your last months? Or you get ripped to little pieces and scattered over the oceans? Will you still come back?"

"Every thinking being that has ever lived is either on this side or the other, in one form or another. Does anyone else have questions?"

"Ouch, let go!" squealed Jamie abruptly. Mrs. Robinson dropped from beneath her shirt and made a mad dash for the door. The kitten clawed desperately at the wood, lifting itself off the ground before collapsing in sullen defeat.

"How'd she get in there?" Jamie asked, her voice very small and self-conscious. The class seemed uncertain how to react until Professor Humstrum burst out laughing, and guttural oohs were so warm and heartfelt that the students couldn't help but to follow suit. Humstrum knelt down beside the kitten and whispered something inaudible, and Mrs. Robinson's raised fur and tail settled at once. The Professor cupped his hands to carry the kitten back to his pedestal.

"What is your name, child?" Professor Humstrum asked. There was a brief confusion before it became apparent that he was speaking to Mrs. Robinson.

"I don't have a name," she replied. "I don't want to be here anymore. I want to go home."

"But you *are* home," the Professor said soothingly. "Haven't you gotten your books or anything yet?"

"No," Mrs. Robinson said stubbornly, "and I don't want to read or do human things. I want to be a cat forever."

"Her name is Mrs. Robinson," Jamie peeped up. She immediately slapped her hands over her mouth, apparently startled by her own words.

"Wouldn't you prefer to be a living cat though?"

"No, I don't care," Mrs. Robinson replied. "I miss my Claire. She'll be all grown up by the time I finish school and get back."

Professor Humstrum closed his eyes and ran his hand down Mrs. Robinson's back. A zigzagging sapphire-blue spark raced up his staff, through his body, around his cumbersome knuckles, and in an instant danced across the cat to burst into the air like a tiny firework.

"You used to be a human. Did you know that, Mrs. Robinson?"

The cat looked distrustfully at the staff and didn't say anything.

"It's quite natural for souls to have an affinity toward things they used to be. As for you…" Professor Humstrum strode across the room and placed his hand on Jamie's forehead. "What is your name, girl?"

Jamie told him, and as she did a similar blue spark raced up the staff again and danced through her hair.

"You were once a cat," the Professor said confidently. Then returning to his podium where Mrs. Robinson still sat, he continued. "As I have already said, I have no intention to force anyone to learn against his will. I simply wish that all who attend my class are aware that life is so much bigger than the taste they've had, no matter how rich that experience was," he nodded at Mrs. Robinson, "or how many lives they have already led," and another nod toward Noah, who pretended not to notice.

"It is natural for the freshly dead to obsess over the life they've already lived, because that life and life itself are synonymous to them. Some are never able to let go of that life, and they spend the rest of time dreaming about how it used to be. I would be failing as an instructor if I did not acknowledge this possibility, but so too would I be failing if I did not encourage you to see what *could be* as well as what *was*. Will you consider staying with us, Mrs. Robinson, at least until you better understand what your options really are?"

Mrs. Robinson looked so tiny and alone sitting there on the podium with the whole class staring at her. In the big scheme of things though, Noah decided they were all in the same boat.

"For a little while," Mrs. Robinson conceded. "I'll share a book with Jamie until I get my own."

"Is that alright with you, Jamie?" Professor Humstrum asked. He puffed out his chest and beaming with pride as the cat hopped onto the ground and made her way to Jamie's desk.

"Of course she can. I love her." Jamie said shyly, clearly embarrassed by all the attention. More giggling erupted around her.

"Ah, love," Humstrum said, stroking his orange beard. "A passenger of the soul, so closely entwined that it gets carried along from one world to the next. No doubt you have all experienced an inexplicable attraction or fascination in your life. The glimpse of a stranger with the familiar eyes—kindred spirits—yes, I'm talking about soul mates. When you have loved another soul in a previous life, you can't help but love them again, sometimes without knowing why. Some famous lovers in history—Paris and Helen of Troy, Cleopatra of Egypt and Mark Antony, Amal and George Clooney—have loved one another for a thousand years. Such feelings should always be trusted, because you would have never loved them so long without them being worthy of it. Yes, in the back?"

"Teresa Hides," the girl stated her name in clear, clipped tones as though terrified someone would misspell it. "I noticed everyone has started over as a child here, but not as a baby. What happens when a baby dies?"

"The souls of young children haven't finished crossing from the spiritual world to the corporal world," Humstrum replied. "That is to say, they are still a lot of who they were and very little of who they will be, and the whole process leaves them very confused. An early death will send them back to the spirit world where they will be ready to try again in the form of their previous life. Now please take out you textbooks, and let us begin with *Chapter 1: The First Soul.*"

The remainder of the class was spent learning about the tree of life with its great bloom from which new souls grew like seeds. Such a bloom was theorized to occur every few millennia, but there was a prominent disclaimer that read that seed theory was merely a mathematical proof consistent with the findings of modern spiritology. The fact that no one has yet found this legendary tree does not, however, mean that there isn't strong evidence that it exists.

"Before our next class, you will visit the bestiary, marked by the stained-glass lion, where you will try to determine which animal you have an affinity toward. You are also welcome to use the library, marked by the camel, at any time, although you will only be permitted up to the floor equivalent with your grade level. You may now stash your books in the mausoleum except for *Understanding Undead: The Spirit's Guide to the Other Side.* You will need that for Professor Wilst when the harpy announces it's time. Class dismissed."

Most of the students hadn't gotten the hang of their self-propelling carts yet, and there were multiple collisions as the students pressed for the exit. Noah waited until the traffic jam had subsided, causing him to be near the back of the crowd as they made their way toward the central stairs.

Walter too was straggling behind the others, because every few steps he would turn around and swear at something. Noah had to get closer to reveal the offending pursuer to be an imp trotting along at his heels.

"Get the hell away from me," Walter said, "or get to hell—whatever you do. I've got no business with you."

"Not afraid of an imp, are you? He looks like he only wants to play," Bowser said, surfing by gracefully in his cart.

"He won't leave me alone," Walter whined, "and look, he's holding something. I think he's trying to stick me."

"I don't think so," Noah said. "Isn't that the imp you defended before?"

"I was defending your books, not him. And how am I supposed to know—they all look the same, don't they?"

"This one's got kind of a long nose," Noah said.

The imp made a little charge toward Walter who dodged out of the way and let it tumble past.

"I think he's trying to give you a present," Jamie said, hurrying to catch up. Mrs. Robinson lazed comfortably in her arms, apparently accepting her fate. "I bet he wants to thank you."

"I don't want anything he's got, thanks anyway," Walter said. He shirked around his cart as the imp came round the other way. The imp leapt from the ground onto the rim of the cart, then set a small black stone on top of Walter's books. The imp grinned with all its sharp little teeth, nudging the stone closer. Walter picked up the stone and inspected it distastefully before chucking it across the ground. The imp chittered crossly before scampering after it as it clattered across the floor.

"He doesn't mean it!" Jamie called after the imp. Then, to Walter, "There's no reason to be so rude. You know they're intelligent, so they must have feelings."

Mrs. Robinson failed the temptation and bounded away to chase after the imp. The pair darted through the legs of one student after another, causing a ripple of confusion and counterbalance to spread throughout the whole group. This led to even more collisions from the already unstable drivers, some of which veered dangerously close to the edge of the pit.

"Now look what you've done!" Jamie scolded.

"That's all Mrs. Robinson!" Walter protested. "It's not my fault I don't want to be friends with those nasty little things. If it wants to thank me, it can deliver a message back home. Otherwise it's no good to me." He slid his cart angrily through the air and started climbing the stairs.

"The people you left are going to be okay," Jamie said, keeping up. "Your girlfriend will know you love her without you having to say it—"

"No she won't! Not after how we left things…" He pushed his cart ahead, not looking at her. He seemed like he was about to say more, but his jaw tightened and he shook his head.

"This isn't quite a message, but I know how you can hear what she's thinking about you," Noah said. Walter stopped abruptly and turned around. Several other students glanced at them too. Noah wasn't sure how Professor Salice would react to him making this public knowledge, so he leaned in closer to continue in a hushed voice.

"The Whispering Room, fifth floor. Professor Salice gave me a key."

Relieved to have a chance to talk about it and try to figure out what happened, Noah told Walter and Jamie about his experience with Salice. Walter became excited as soon as Noah explained what the Whispering Room could do, and he turned around to cross the nearest junction of the double-helix stairway to head in the descending direction instead.

"Why do you think he was so interested in Chainers?" Jamie asked.

"I don't know, but it made me uncomfortable just to be near him," Noah said.

"I wouldn't worry about your daughter," Walter said. "They're in a completely different world now."

"That's what I'm worried about though," Noah said. "If he's so enthusiastic about having Chainers around, don't you think he'd be happy if Mandy died?

"So what if she does?" Walter asked. "She'll just show up here, right? Then you could go to school together."

"That's just callous." Jammie sniffed indignantly. "Who would look after the baby then? And anyway, life is precious even if you do have a chance to do it again. You never know which one will be your last."

"Exactly," Noah said, "and Salice could send a demon or something there. Or maybe he already has—there was a gargoyle that got me killed."

"I think demons are only in this world," Jamie said. "Otherwise people would know about them, don't you think?"

Noah explained the monstrous thing that had attacked Samantha before chasing them to his death.

"He's a *Professor* though, Noah," Jamie insisted. "He's already delaying his own rebirth to pass on his knowledge, which seems like a pretty noble thing to me. I think you're worrying over nothing."

"I don't know, that guy gave me the creeps on the Daymare," Walter said. "If I were you, I wouldn't tell him where you lived. Give him a wrong address on the letter."

"Yeah? Then what if some other innocent person gets killed?" Noah countered. After checking to make sure the fifth floor was empty, Noah unlocked the Whispering Room. "I think I'll just keep stalling."

Jamie hesitated outside the room. "I'll just wait out here then. Let him have a private moment."

"Actually, if it doesn't bother you... I wouldn't mind the company," Walter said, sounding embarrassed.

"Well, I should be there to show you how it works," Noah mused.

"Yeah, that's the reason," Walter agreed readily.

"And I should be there to see, in case I want to use it!" Jamie volunteered.

Walter grinned in appreciation and they all went inside. The mist bleeding through the circle was definitely more of a pale green than the blue Noah remembered last time. Noah didn't see that it mattered though, and he instructed Walter to stand in the circle, describing his first experience with seeing the faces appear in the mist. Almost immediately upon entering the circle, tears begun to swell in Walter's eyes.

"Is she saying anything?" Jamie asked. "I can't hear it."

"Neither can I," Noah said. "Salice saw and heard my daughter when they were talking though, so we should be able to."

"I'm sorry," Water mumbled as he turned in slow circles. "Baby, I'm so sorry."

"Well he's clearly talking to her," Jamie said. "You know what that means, don't you?"

"Yeah... No. Actually no."

"It means Salice was doing something special to listen in!" Jamie said. "He brought you here for a reason, then he eavesdropped to learn something from it."

"Last time the mist was more blue than green," Noah conceded. "So you're saying my theory about him wanting to get my daughter isn't so far off after-all?"

"I wouldn't go that far," Jamie said, "but it is suspicious. I guess I'm just saying it wouldn't hurt to be careful."

Walter staggered out of the circle, breathing heavily. His brow was damp, either with perspiration or from the mist, and he wiped it with the bottom of his t-shirt.

"Are you okay?" Jamie asked. "Was she—"

Walter closed his eyes and took a deep breath. Then nodded. "Yeah. She'll be okay. With or without me."

"Oh, that's a relief—" she started.

"We can't just focus on our previous lives, right?" he blurted out, the words all competing to be the first out of his mouth. "I mean we've got to look forward too, right? No point dwelling on—" he took another deep breath, then weakly added, "aren't you going to listen too?"

Jamie shook her head slowly. "I don't know if we'll hear the harpy down here, so we should probably go now."

"It only takes a minute," Noah said. "You shouldn't feel like you have to though. I know it can be hard."

Jamie shook her head, resolutely this time. "I've lived my life, and I don't have any regrets to linger on."

"I want to try again then," Noah said, mounting the dais, "This time without Salice interrupting."

Noah stood in the circle once more and saw his daughter's image appear in the mist. She noticed him immediately this time, but she closed her eyes and slapped her hands across her ears.

"He's not real," Mandy said before Noah could speak. She prattled in a sing-song voice which sounded like it had been repeated so many times as to become a practiced mantra. "I know he's not real. I see things that aren't real all the time. Barnes told me so, and he's real. I'm real, but they're not real. And if a real thing thinks too much about not-real things, then the real thing becomes not so real herself. We can't have that, now can we? Stupid, horrible woman. Who will ever love you if they find out you're crazy?"

"Mandy I am real..." Noah said, but he could tell she couldn't hear.

"Sad? Why should I be sad?" Mandy asked herself, clenching her eyes more tightly shut than ever. "I shouldn't feel sad about something that isn't real. I *mustn't* feel sad."

Noah couldn't bear to watch anymore. He leapt down from the dais and waved his hands through the mist to clear her face away.

"Did you hear what she said?" Noah asked the others, perhaps more sharply than he'd intended.

Walter and Jamie shook their heads. Jamie was about to speak, but Noah cut her off.

"Jamie is right! We won't hear the harpy down here. We should be upstairs now." Noah was halfway out the door before either of them could say a word. They took the hint and did not press him for an answer. That was fortunate because Noah had no answer to give, not even to himself.

There weren't any students left in the stairway, but Noah remembered that necromancy studies were on the second floor. If he could get there fast enough, then he wouldn't have to think about what Mandy was going through. How could she tell herself he wasn't real? She'd been seeing spirits her whole life, although perhaps not as vividly as he did. Of course it might be more convenient to pretend, but why did she have to erase him to do it?

Noah found the distraction he was looking for when he emerged onto the second floor, although the atmosphere here was considerably less inviting than the jungles on the third. As soon as Noah opened the door from the tree, his nostrils were assaulted by a powerfully sterile smell like an insecure hospital.

"Beats the smell of rot, I guess," Walter said, covering his nose.

"Can you not smell the rot?" Jamie whined. "It's definitely under there."

The vertical safeguards on this bridge were primarily composed of rib bones. Long femurs on top formed the railing, some of which were much too large to be human.

"Feels just like home," Noah said, pushing his cart across the bridge.

"What, seriously?!" Walter asked.

"Yeah, whenever I murdered people I'd bring them back to the cave I lived in," Noah said conversationally. "This is how I decorated."

"He's *obviously* pulling your leg-bone," Jamie said.

Walter didn't look so sure, but at least the conversation kept them busy long enough to cross the unwholesome bridge.

"Which room do you think they're in?" Walter asked.

Jamie moved ahead to listen at the first of the eight doors which was identified by a skull mounted overhead with a single remaining tooth. Jamie shrugged, apparently unable to hear anything inside.

"It has to be number one, doesn't it?" Noah asked. "We're first years, it's our first class."

"Yeah but what if it's not?" Walter asked. "It could be a changing room for ghouls for all we know. There could be a vampire just waking up from its nap."

"What exactly would a vampire do to you?" Noah asked. "You haven't got any blood."

Jamie opened the door, revealing little as it was so dim inside. "Hello?" she called. "Is this Professor Wilst's class?"

Walter and Noah huddled behind her to peer down the long, round hallway. The rays of will-o-wisp light reflected from a thousand glinting diamonds embedded every few inches along the wall and ceiling like so many stars. It might have been beautiful apart from the oppressively hot and humid air. Jamie took another step inside.

"He wouldn't be teaching a class in the dark," Noah said. "Let's try another one."

"How do you know?" Walter asked. "Maybe Necromancy only works when it's dark. Hello, is there anyone here?" Jamie stopped suddenly a few feet ahead, her stance rigid.

"Let's get out of here," Jamie said carefully. "Slowly—well not that slowly—go!"

Without seeing what she had seen, both boys beat a hasty retreat. Jamie backed out right behind them, not taking her eyes off what she had seen until the door slammed shut.

"What was it?" Walter asked. "The room looked empty to me."

"It was empty," Jamie said, heaving a sigh of relief. "It wasn't a room though. Didn't you see the walls? They were *breathing*."

"No they weren't," Walter said, unconvinced.

"Go ahead. Open it and look," Jamie replied.

Walter didn't think much of that suggestion. The door in the tree stairway presently flew open though, and a mass of first year students came pouring through. Most of the human children weren't pushing their carts anymore and were instead carrying a single book in their arms. At their lead strode Professor Wilst who looked quite at home with his own foot bones clattering along the skeletal bridge.

"Are they in trouble for sneaking down here early?" Brandon asked hopefully. "They probably stole something. You should—"

Professor Wilst pivoted without a word and moved to the door marked by the skull with two teeth. He opened it and vanished inside, prompting the perplexed students to hurry and catch up. Brandon gave Noah and Walter a wicked grin as he passed, shortly followed up by Teresa's signature stink eye.

"Necromancy," the dry voice from the darkness within said. "Your one true path to resurrection begins now."

QARI OLANDESCA ILLUSTRATIONS

NECROMANCY

"What is an animal to man? Limited, weak, stupid, unable to recall yesterday or ponder tomorrow with more than a dim glimmer. So is man to the undead, lost and isolated in his single life without memory or foreshadowing of who he was before or what he will return to after."

The powerfully sterile and pickled stench was coming from this classroom, although a morgue might be a more fitting name for the space. There were no desks or chairs, but rather evenly spaced metal slabs each occupied by a naked human body. Their eyes were closed and they drew no breath, yet they were so immaculately preserved that they looked more asleep than dead. The walls were lined with jars on shelves containing hands, eyeballs, brains, and other assorted body parts preserved in a syrupy liquid.

The students filed uneasily into the room. "You could have at least put a sheet over them," Dolly Miller said, averting her eyes from the naked bodies.

"Or some underwear," Elizabeth Washent mumbled, crinkling her rabbit nose.

"Why?" Professor Wilst asked. "You are not your organic body, and need feel no shame. You are not bound by death, and need feel no fear. One student per body, spread out."

Noah chose the body of a very fat man with a long drooping mustache to stand beside. He seemed comical enough to rob some of the unpleasantness from the situation. Jamie took an old woman nearby with skin that sagged so much it looked like it might drip right off the table, and Walter stood by what once might have been an attractive woman, if you could get by the bullet hole in the side of her head. Mrs. Robinson never showed up at all.

All the students kept a healthy distance from their bodies except for the blonde boy, Sandy, who found it enormously entertaining trying to open and close the mouth of his corpse as if it were speaking. He quickly gave up though when his hands kept passing through the body as if it was just an illusion.

"These are corporal bodies, and you have no physical force with which to move them," the Professor said. Then in a commanding voice, he added, "Excieo."

Bright yellow light ran up his metal staff, running through his hand and radiating out through his body before bursting into the air. Radiant yellow sparks rained down softly like rain throughout the whole classroom. Students either dove to get out of the way or actively reached out to try and grab them. As the sparks settled amongst the bodies, they all opened their eyes simultaneously to stare vacantly at the ceiling. There was a loud scuffle as curious students quickly backpedaled away from their tables, bumping into one another as they did.

"Consurgo," the Professor commanded. The bodies all sat fluidly upright, their arms hanging limply at their sides. "By the end of the semester, I'll expect all of you to be able to awaken and command your own zombie. Incapable of independent thoughts or feelings, these spiritual puppets grant us a corporal servant to influence the living world. While a living person is a single spirit within a single body, the animation of objects or corpses is the process of dividing the necromancer's spirit amongst the things he wishes to control. This can leave the necromancer weak and vulnerable. When you are ready to return your spirit, you must put the objects under your control to sleep with the spell: Somnus."

At this command the bodies uniformly collapsed back to the table, their eyes closed once more.

"Notebooks out," the Professor commanded in the same authoritative tone he used to animate the bodies. The bones of his toes clattered with each step as he paced between the dormant corpses. "Zombies are the simplest form of undead. Some, such as myself, have chosen to escape the endless cycle of rebirth by choosing to permanently inhabit a corpse. My own corpse, in fact. This is known as a lich. All spirits can focus their power using a bit of their corporal remains, which is what you will be using your stuffed animals for.

"Other notable undead you will become familiar with include the poltergeist, spirits which can interact with the corporal world, vampires, whose corporal bodies use living blood to strengthen their connection to the other side, and the dwellers, which overpower the spirit of living beings to control them. The process of becoming a dweller will not be taught in this class, and they are not welcome in polite society."

"Why does it feel like we're getting career counseling?" Walter whispered.

"Is that what this is?" Noah whispered back. "I thought it sounded more like a retirement plan."

"Textbooks out," barked Professor Wilst. "You should all have a copy of *Understanding Undead: The Spirit's Guide to the Other Side* by Salvadore Frann. Please open to *Chapter 1: You're Only As Dead As You Act.*"

Noah was surprised to find himself disappointed that they did not get to use the bodies for anything yet, but he still quite enjoyed the rest of the lesson which elaborated on the four types of undead creatures. He felt somehow uncomfortable reading the definition of life though, which read only, *'Life: The short duration in which a spirit borrows a biological body and fights everybody and everything to avoid returning it to the biological system it was taken from.'*

"I don't think necromancy is for me," Jamie said as they were leaving the class. "I'd much rather be a rabbit or a bird than any of those grizzly things."

"I would have thought you'd want to be a cat again," Noah said.

"Maybe," Jamie replied in contemplation, "but oh, there are so many more things to try. And what if I can't keep finding my way back to life? We can't all be Chainers."

"We could though, couldn't we?" Noah asked as they ascended the stairs. "Didn't the book on Transhumanism say that souls were only created every few millennia? So the rest of you must have been doing something this whole time."

"I wish we could find out what," Jamie said. "I'd rather be learning about that than all these supernatural encounters we have to read. What do I care whether it was a vampire or a ghoul that bit her? She's just as dead either way, isn't she?"

There was a hub of activity on the ground floor of The Mortuary. An energetic fiddle was accompanied by a lively drumbeat. Colorful pamphlets were exchanging hands, and students were chatting with excitement as they rushed to exit the front doors. A line of large tree stumps were arranged outside, each decorated with posters and stacks of cards, as well as the occasional dismembered hand, crystal ball, tarot deck, and doll. Noah recognized some of the same villagers who had greeted them now sitting behind the stumps.

"They can bury you, but they can't keep you down," shouted an olive-skinned woman with long, curly, black hair and fingers so filled with rings that it was a wonder she could still bend them. "Two apprenticeships remaining. Get Cassandra's Kill Counseling Certificate here and start helping people cope with the rope."

Dolly Miller slipped past Noah and approached the stump to speak with Cassandra.

"Help the right spirits reach the right mediums," announced a tall thin man with yellow vertical stripes along his suit. "Single apprenticeship available, easy to fit in after class. First years welcome." His sign read: 'Spiritual Operator'.

"You there—girl with the ginger head," an ample woman wearing a bright orange dress and a large black belt called to Jamie. Jamie pointed at herself in surprise, and the large woman nodded enthusiastically. "Yes you, darling. You remind me of the babe."

"What babe?" Jamie asked, allowing herself to be drawn in.

"The babe with the power," the woman replied in the hushed tone of a conspiracy.

"What power?" Jamie asked again, quite mystified.

"The power of voodoo!" the woman shouted, barely able to contain herself. "Don't tell me you've never wanted to pay somebody back for the horrible things they've done. A pretty girl like you must have broken some hearts and made some enemies in her life."

"I should hope not!" Jamie said. "No thank you, I don't want to hurt anyone."

"How about doll stitching?" the woman called. "They won't feel the needle yet, what do you say?"

Jamie hurried away, but Teresa swooped into her place to take one of the pamphlets. The sign read 'Ungela Granka's Voodoo. A nearby sign read 'Miss Thatchers Witchery: Curses and Broom Delivery.'

"What's going on?" Noah asked, turning in wonder.

"Oh that's right, you weren't in the village so you must have missed it," Jamie replied. "We all have to work an apprenticeship alongside our classwork. That way we'll have career options if we aren't able to resurrect right away, plus the work covers the tuition of the school. Any idea what you're going to do?"

Noah spotted Walter speaking with the Spiritual Operator.

"Hey—Chainer kid," Bowser barked, wagging ferociously. He was sitting by a sign which read, 'Supernautical Activity'.

"It's Noah," he replied, approaching.

"Okay Noah. This guy is looking for a Chainer to help power his underwater expedition. They're researching sea spirits—want in?"

The grizzled seaman tipped an end of his white captain's hat toward Noah. There was a lull in the general conversation as multiple villagers turned their attention on the Chainer in their midst. The ensuing wave of noise assaulted Noah from every direction.

"Don't settle for him, I've got—"

"A Chainer would be wasted on—"

"Why don't you give back and do some good—"

And a dozen other calls which jumbled over one another. As soon as they'd begun, the calls all cut short as the attention was diverted directly behind Noah. He felt a very human chill run down his spine as a hard, cold hand closed around his shoulder, one curling finger at a time.

"There is no need for such commotion," Professor Salice said from behind Noah's ear. "The Chainer boy will already be working as my apprentice this semester. Isn't that right, Noah Tellaver?"

Noah thought quickly whether he'd told Professor Salice his last name before deciding that he definitely had not. Did he already know something about Mandy? If so, then Salice's words sounded like a threat.

"Yeah," Noah mumbled. "Yeah I said I'd..." and his voice trailed off. He turned around to look at Professor Salice whose tight smile was putting unnatural stress upon his face which peeled back around the ears.

"Tuesday at nightfall then, before our first class on Wednesday," Salice said. "Don't forget to bring your letter." With that he turned to go back inside The Mortuary, not giving Noah the least chance to respond or change his mind.

"Demons are my favorite thing, Professor," Brandon called, hurrying to intercept Salice. "I'd make a much better apprentice than him—"

"Absolutely he would," Noah agreed readily. "I'd probably summon a fairy by mistake, klutz that I am."

Professor Salice didn't slow his pace or turn his head in the least. "You disgraced yourself on the bus already," he replied. "Don't waste my time."

Brandon was at his ugliest wearing the mean, spiteful look he now possessed upon his face. It was almost as if he had wanted to be rejected just so he could have something to be angry about. Noah had never seen someone look so pleased to be furious.

"What's your problem? I agreed with you," Noah said.

"Of course. After-all, you're so much better than me," Brandon said.

Noah wouldn't have minded if Brandon had yelled at him. This clearly fake, goading voice was far more sinister. Noah said nothing and turned to look for his friends. Jamie was speaking to Professor Humstrum, although the ape didn't have any kind of booth or table.

"You're better than everyone here, aren't you?" Brandon pressed, stepping closer. "You don't need us. You already know how to go back to life, don't you? So what are you doing?"

"I don't remember how I did it before," Noah replied. "I'm not any better than anyone."

"Yes you are," Brandon said, his voice lowering to a hiss as he got nearer. "But when I was alive, I was twice the man you ever were. People worshiped the ground I walked on, and I'm going to get that power again. And when I do—"

Brandon lurched toward Noah, forcing him to flinch and stumble backward. Brandon caught himself halfway and laughed at Noah for retreating. Noah was ready to throw the first real punch when Professor Humstrum passed by with Jamie tagging along at his heels.

"Hey, Noah!" she called. "I'm going to help Professor Humstrum take care of the bestiary this semester. Do you want to come with us to do your tranhumanism assignment?"

Noah readily agreed, grateful for a chance to slip away from Brandon. He followed the Professor along the stone path which was flanked by rows of tall juniper trees toward The Mortuary tower with the lion on it. Before the door had even opened, he could hear the stirrings of massive feet and a graveled roar which shook the dust from stones.

~

"Go ahead and put out your hand then—palm facing down, just let him sniff you," Professor Humstrum said. "That's right, he's not going to hurt you. Everything needs a reason to fight, but getting along is its own reason."

Jamie closed her eyes and stuck out her hand a little farther. A black tongue half the length of her arm curled over her wrist, slithering its way up round and round as if tasting her.

"This doesn't feel like sniffing!" Jamie said, still clenching her eyes shut.

"Hold very still now. If you squirm too much he's going to feel threatened," the Professor said.

"He's going to feel threatened!" Jamie exclaimed. "I'm the one being eaten by a —"

"A baku," Professor said cheerfully. "The dream eater. Cassandra has several of them working in her counseling facility. Some spirits will keep having nightmares about their death, but a baku doesn't mind the taste."

The tongue slackened in pressure enough for Jamie to politely disentangle herself. The baku—which could have almost passed for a dog until it turned around to reveal its elephantine tusks and trunk—fell back onto its haunches and blinked its vacant white eyes. Jamie discreetly turned around before furiously wiping her arm on her t-shirt.

"This place is wonderful," Jamie sighed, turning in a slow circle to take in the tower.

The entire building was a single massive room which was

flooded with the light of thousands of will-o-wisps which flew together in a massed swarm, giving the appearance of a fiery sun which floated throughout the space. Trees and plants were growing everywhere like a greenhouse, although the room was divided into distinct biospheres. Snow fell softly from the arched ceiling, icing the tops of the trees where furry animals slid and chased one another. An open stream gurgled from a hole in one of the walls, creating a waterfall which fed into a pristine tundra formed entirely on another layer of branches.

From there the water drained down through the leaves as a heavy rain, creating a tropical rainforest a little further down. There was hardly a dribble of water left by the time it made it all the way to the ground, where stretches of sandy desert and grassy savanna gave ample space to walk around.

"The baku is not the only myth based on reality," the Professor said, turning to stroll through the desert sand. "You'd be amazed at how often a Chainer or a psychic of some sort sees a spiritual creature and then tells everybody who will listen, whether they can see it or not. You'll be looking after the baku's schedule now, making sure he's gotten a walk through the graveyard every morning before people wake up so he can get a nice breakfast in. Oh, and when it comes to cleaning up after him, I should warn you that sometimes when he eats an especially foul nightmare he can leave a rather unpleasant... oh, well, you'll figure it out, don't you worry."

Jamie gave Noah a beseeching 'help me', sort of look.

"You'll be fine," Noah replied, grinning. The prospect of being Salice's assistant didn't seem half as bad anymore, at least assuming imps could clean up after themselves.

There must have been a lot of creatures living here

because the odor was thick enough to taste. It wasn't a necessarily a bad odor—something like sweet curry—but the prevalence and potency would have surely been sickening if Noah's digestive system still whirred.

Noah and Jamie followed the Professor toward the back of the room, pointing out key aspects of the facility such as feed cabinets, medical supplies, and a dauntingly large shovel caked with something pink that smelled like frosting.

"Don't let the smell fool you," the Professor said, gesturing at the shovel. "You don't want to touch anything that comes out of the jinn."

An angular green face with long, pointed, overlapping teeth leered out of a hole in the sand. Noah recognized a few of the animals, such as the restlessly pacing manticore with its scorpion tail flicking over its back, as well as the cyclops at least twice his height who was shaking a fig tree to knock all the fruits onto the ground.

The vast majority were like nothing Noah had ever seen before though. Many looked like conventional wild animals until they turned to reveal part of them as something else entirely, and those with human faces were especially disconcerting as they turned and watched them pass. There were small scaly creatures and giant eyeballs with a dozen irises, and even two-dimensional things which disappeared at the wrong angle. Despite this maddening variety, it was apparent that most of the life was still hidden and rustling through the higher biospheres in the trees.

"The harpys do most of the work mind you, although they spend a disproportionate amount of time with the birds in the upper floors," the Professor said. "If any of the critters ever give you trouble, a harpy is always only a screech away." Then turning back to Noah, he added, "Find any affinitys yet? A Chainer is likely to have been all sorts of creatures before."

Noah was staring at an iridescent turtle shell which not only reflected Noah's image, but actually morphed into a replica of his face to stare back at him until he turned away. "I don't think so," Noah said.

"Ah, well, no need to bother yourself then," the Professor sighed. "I always hope we'll get a real animal Chainer one day, but maybe you were just human all the way back. Nothing wrong with humans, not most of them anyway. Nothing to feel ashamed about."

"Thanks," Noah said. "I'll try not to let it bother me."

In fact he was doing a very good job of not minding in the least, but the Professor still circled back to clap a sympathetic hand against the middle of Noah's back. The antelope staff stuck out its tongue at Noah in what he could only assume to be an insult.

"If you aren't sure you can always touch one of them," the Professor said. "I've left a spell in here to help the students. An affinity will be clearly seen by the scarlet sparks—"

"Sorry, no need," Noah said firmly. "I'm pretty sure about this one."

"So be it, so be it. How about you, Jamie? Maybe there's a little fire in you from an efreet that never went out?" he asked, hopeful.

"Just the cat, I think," she replied. "They are happy here, aren't they? Wouldn't they prefer to be taking classes too?"

"An excellent question! Just what I'd expect from my apprentice. Spiritual creatures who have no counterpart in the corporal world are not the same as spiritual animals who do. The beings who exist entirely in the spirit world often do not speak our language, although some like the harpy are sharp enough to learn a few words and phrases. Bestiary's like this may be thought of like a conservatory. They exist all over the world to protect and study these marvelous creatures, as well as utilize their fantastic properties. Not to mention keeping them out of trouble, as many can interact directly with the corporal world."

"Do you have any gargoyles?" Noah asked.

Humstrum's face crinkled like he'd just witnessed clumps pour out of his milk carton. "You won't find any of those in a bestiary. The T.D.D. has them all employed."

"But there must be wild ones. Or some that have gone rogue and attack people."

The Professor shrugged and his antelope head Hazel snorted loudly. "I wouldn't think so, but anything is possible. You see gargoyles aren't natural like the other animals are—the T.D.D. makes them from scratch. No one outside of the department knows exactly how it's done, but I can't imagine there's anything wholesome about it."

A chittering snicker sounded from one of the jinn, which was swiftly followed by a series of protesting honks, growls, barks, hisses, and all manner of other sounds from the agitated spirits.

An imp who had been stealthily clinging to the back of a tree dropped to the ground, likely realizing its cover had been blown. It looked around in a wild panic at all the protesting spirits.

"What is a demon doing here?" Professor Humstrum asked sternly, his voice boiling with a barely contained rage that Noah had never heard from him before. "Unnatural creature —you do not belong in this sacred space!"

The imp cast a quick glance at Noah before attempting to creep back toward the door, crouching and slinking despite being in plain sight. Noah scanned the surrounding trees, trying to spot if there were any more. He had the unnerving feeling that the imp had been sent to spy on him.

"Did someone send you?" Noah asked, hurrying after the demon. "Was it Professor Salice?"

The imp left all covert pretensions and leaped wildly for the door. Crawling up the wood to pull on the heavy metal handle, it struggled and gasped as it heaved against the indomitable door.

"Hey—I'm asking you a question!" Noah demanded. He flung out a hand to seize the imp by its shoulder. A jolt of electricity shot through Noah's hand, and scarlet sparks hissed and smoldered into the air. He withdrew his hand at once, and that was all the time the imp needed. With a last surge of strength the demon yanked the door open a crack—just enough for it to slip through and disappear. Noah was left nursing his scalded hand, staring at the smoldering sparks which continued to burn sporadically in the air like tiny fireworks.

"You've found your affinity after all," Professor Humstrum said with a tense, hushed voice. "You used to be a demon, boy."

"I didn't know demons could even become human," Noah said. The severity of Humstrum's tone made him feel that he had done something wrong, although he couldn't see what.

"No," Humstrum said after a pause. "Neither did I. Nor anyone else I've ever taught, and believe you me there's enough of them to sink the island if they ever had a reunion."

"I bet that imp is going to run straight back to Professor Salice," Jamie said. "He's going to know too."

"Is that okay?" Noah asked. "I mean, does it matter? People have been loads of stuff."

"Elizabeth told me she used to be a slug before she was a rabbit," Jamie said cheerfully. "She says now she finally knows why her nose is always runny, although I don't think that's really how it works, is it Professor—"

But the Professor wasn't listening. He was having a hurried and whispered conversation with the antelope head on his staff. The antelope kept glancing at Noah every few seconds.

"Please excuse me," Professor Humstrum said. "I've just forgotten that I was supposed to have tea with—never mind with whom, I'm already late. Jamie, please join me tomorrow evening for the rest of your bestiary instructions. Noah..." The Professor paused, chewing on his lip. The orangutang reached out a hesitant hand and patted Noah on his back, rather tentatively as though he was afraid the contact would burn him. Humstrum then turned suddenly and made for the door.

"Professor?" Noah asked, his voice higher pitched and more strained than he'd intended. "Please don't tell anyone."

Professor Humstrum forced a shallow smile over his shoulder, although the bird did not emerge from his beard as usual. "You're human now, eh? Just the same as the rest of us. Our past is only our own burden to bear, and I won't breathe a word."

Neither the Professor's farewell nor his speedy departure did anything to reassure Noah, who was by now feeling a little nauseous. He meekly followed the Professor back toward the courtyard and the rest of the students who were still milling about the remainder of the apprenticeship stalls.

"So nothing to worry about," Jamie said meekly. "There's nothing wrong with imps, and nothing for you to be ashamed of. Anyway, you got over the murderer thing pretty quickly, and I think that would have been much harder for me—"

"You don't think they're related?" Noah asked glumly. "What if I was a rampaging, murderous demon?"

"Oh," Jamie said. "I hadn't thought about that. Well even if you were, you aren't now, right? Have you had any urges or anything... you haven't, have you?"

The more Noah heard about it, the more murder sounded like a perfectly practical solution to get everybody to shut up. Even his thoughts were only joking though, something to try to lighten the pit he felt in his stomach. He never would have...

Couldn't have...

Could he?

QARI OLANDESCA ILLUSTRATIONS

DEMONOLOGY

Noah took his next chance to visit the library to search for more information about his affinity. The third tower marked by the camel reminded Noah of the Daymare because of all the floating platforms which contained reading tables both above and below. A spidery web of stairs branched haphazardly from one platform to the next, but none of the platforms were devoted to the actual bookshelves, which didn't exist.

The books themselves were spread open and glided through the air like flocks of fat, lazy birds. Whenever a book was needed, a student would simply announce what he was looking for and the book would sail over to land on his table. There was a rumor going around that one of the students made the mistake of simply asking for 'books about reincarnation', and his failure to be specific caused multiple flocks of books to swarm him from every direction and bury him completely.

The librarian, a bespectacled vampire named Mrs. Vanderlooth, vehemently denied such a rumor. Her denial was hardly credible though, as she insisted that it's best to be as specific as possible and warned that students should hide underneath the table when a vague statement was unavoidable. Mrs. Vanderlooth was an elegant creature with long purple robes and a prominent beauty mark at the corner of each of her voluptuous red lips.

Noah vastly preferred spending time in the library to studying in the tight mausoleum quarters with Brandon. This suited Brandon just fine, who had responded by scattering his clothes and books across both sides of the room. Noah's coffin now served as storage for Brandon's maps, rope, life vest (the name stamped across the breast without the slightest sense of irony), and other equipment that Brandon had received from the supernautical man.

None of the books Noah could find about affinity gave him the least resolution to his quandary. Some books didn't even consider demons to have souls, while others spoke of them as having their own, distinct type of soul that allowed them to be reborn as another demon, but not as anything else. Noah couldn't even ask Mrs. Vanderlooth for help, considering Humstrum's reaction. He felt it was best to keep his affinity a secret, and her ability to amplify a rumor while pretending to deny it would only make matters worse.

"It's time to earn your keep," Professor Salice's voice spoke directly into Noah's ear. Noah nearly fell backward from his chair, only catching himself just in time before he tumbled off the platform altogether.

"Fourth floor, second room, ten minutes. Don't be late."

Noah spun in circles trying to find the orator. It quickly became apparent that he was alone. He briefly considered ignoring the request and pretending he hadn't heard, or perhaps even hiding here to avoid the meeting. There still existed the possibility that Salice had some leverage over his family though, and in any case even normal teachers couldn't be disobeyed without repercussions. There's no telling what kind of foul thing Salice could do to him, or how powerless Noah was to resist. Shivering involuntarily, Noah climbed down from the spidery stairway and headed for the main tower.

Noah expected the demonology floor to be the most unpleasant of them all, and he felt somewhat dissatisfied in discovering he was incorrect. The railings on the bridge and around the pit were composed of thick red lines that looked more like beams of light than any solid material. They were arranged artfully into perfectly interlocking geometrical shapes and patterns. The floor itself was clean white tile, and the doors were iron portals engraved with the same dizzying array of patterns. Some of the shapes glowed with a soft red light, while others blinked or lit sporadically as though they were having a conversation with each other.

Noah knocked upon the second room, which was distinguished by Roman numerals prominently embedded within the designs. Several of the other symbols flashed in silent unison as soon as his fist touched the iron, although there was no other discernible effect.

Professor Salice opened the door to loom over Noah. If the imp really had told Professor Salice about Noah's affinity, then the Professor showed no immediate sign of it.

"The letter?" Salice asked immediately, his hand outstretched.

"You said I had until our class," Noah protested.

"Ah. I would have thought you'd be eager to contact your relatives," Salice replied, disappointed. "Or have you already found another way?"

"I don't know, Professor. Is there another way?" Noah asked.

Salice gave a thin, lipless smile, then stepped aside to allow Noah to enter. "Do not touch anything that you have not been invited to touch. Do not say anything unless you are invited to speak. And if you are invited to speak," Salice paused to glance pointedly at Noah, "you shall speak to me no lies. Do you understand?"

"Yes, Professor," Noah replied.

The room they were in looked a bit like a police lineup: a large transparent, frosted plane divided two spaces. The walls and ceiling of this side were tiled, while those of the other were overlapping slabs of corrugated iron. The side of the room Noah had entered contained half-a-dozen plain wooden chairs, as well as a filing cabinet and a desk. The other side was completely empty except for a large pentagram within a circle drawn onto the ground. The design seemed to radiate the same beams of light that comprised the railings. Salice's demon, Visoloth, was lying on its back on a dog bed in the corner, revealing its strange, scaly underbelly.

"The cost of your attendance is being covered by the labor of your work as my apprentice this semester," Salice said. "Do you know what that means?"

"No," Noah replied, as much to be difficult as he was confused about the direction this was going.

"Of course not," Salice said. "It means that your presence at The Mortuary is conditional on my approval of your work. It means I have the power to dismiss you from this school if I ever find reason to do so."

"I could always get another apprenticeship," Noah said. "The supernautical man offered—"

"Did I ask you a question?" Salice snapped.

"No, Professor," Noah replied.

"And yet you spoke," he drawled.

Noah bit his tongue to avoid agreeing with Salice out of pure stubbornness.

"That's better. I would like us to be friends, and that can only happen so long as you don't fight me. I will have different tasks for you on different occasions, but you will be spending the majority of your time in my service in this room. Please stand against the glass."

Noah did as he was instructed.

"Closer," Salice prompted. "All the way. Feet against the glass, forehead against the glass."

As soon as Noah had done so, Professor Salice placed one hand against the back of Noah's head and pressed him against the barrier. The cold flat surface immediately gave way to a freezing mist. Noah tumbled directly through the glass, barely catching himself on the other side. He spun around and tried to regain his previous position, only to smack head-first against the pane which had grown solid once more.

"Demonic summoning requires at least two demonologists," Professor Salice said, his voice distant and muffled from the other side. "One to sign the contract, and a second to serve as the vessel for the demon. Today I will be bringing..." the Professor produced a black leather notebook from his pocket and began to flip through it. "...two imps for The Matriarch, replacing gardeners who have expired. One Peruvian Blue Scale for cleaning the Daymare, one Lava Salamander to stoke the fires of Mrs. Thatcher's witchery, and three Gobbler's to polish Francisco Pintilo's gemstones. That's seven total, so you will be out of here before midnight."

Noah raised his hand to ask a question, feeling silly as he

did so. The humiliation increased as Salice glanced up, then looked back to his notebook as though he'd seen nothing.

"Sit in the center of the pentagram with your legs crossed and your eyes closed. All extremities should be within the innermost lines. Once you are seated, you are not to move until the ceremony is complete, or risk part of your body being banished to the netherworld during the exchange. That happened to one of my apprentices once—it only took him a few minutes to find his hand in the nether, but by then the demons had already stripped it to the bone."

The beams of light marking the pentagram were warm as Noah passed through them. The sensation might have been pleasant if it weren't for the looming dread for what was about to occur. Surely it couldn't be worse than risking his chance to come back to life though... could it?

Professor Salice described the summoning process as three distinct steps. First Salice would read aloud one of the contracts which he had already prepared. That would bridge the connection between Noah, the "host", and the demon in the netherworld. The second step was for the demon to be summoned here, and the third step was for the demon to be bound by the contract.

The words Salice read were meaningless to Noah; they sounded more like the chittering, cackling sounds the imps made than any human tongue. As Salice read the image of the demon grew gradually clearer in Noah's mind.

The long snout appeared in his thoughts first, just as though he'd consciously conjured the image. Then two beady black eyes, then a lithe, thin body like a snake. Four legs ending in sharp claws gradually resolved themselves from the darkness, and then all at once the skin turned deep blue and cracked like dry mud under a blazing sun.

Noah found it deeply unsettling that he was imagining this creature against his will, and that try as he might he could not force himself to stop thinking about it as the image continued to become more vivid and focused. The cracked skin continued hardening into distinct scales, and quite soon he was picturing what he could only assume to be the Peruvian Bluescale.

"Genitus," Professor Salice said at last. "Hold very still now. Take care not to cross any of the lines on the ground."

The image in Noah's mind vanished, and at the same instant he felt sharp claws sinking into his shoulder. A high pitched screech blasted directly in his ear. Every instinct demanded that he flee. He opened his eyes to stare directly into the long blue snout and beady black eyes he'd imagined a moment before. It would have been bad enough for the demon to simply materialize on top of him, but it was far worse seeing that the full demon hadn't arrived yet. The claws dug more deeply into Noah shoulder for support as the Peruvian Bluescale dragged itself directly out of Noah's forehead.

It didn't feel like his head was being split in two, although he did feel an immense amount of pressure which didn't relieve until the demon had completely pulled itself out of his body. It was only the size of a medium dog, and it didn't take long before the demon had completely tumbled free to land in Noah's lap. The demon tried to flee, but as soon as it began to cross the first beam of light in the pentagram, the light flared and red sparks flew into the air. The demon recoiled as though burned, prompting more high pitched, whistling screeches.

Professor Salice slapped the contract he'd written against the glass and answered the demon with a similar screech, sounding all the more unnatural coming from his human lips.

His other hand held a black stone which he also pressed against the glass. The whole pentagram flared once more, this time burning green. The colorful sparks bled from the air and drifted into the black stone which absorbed the light.

"Sit," Professor Salice ordered, and the demon did so at once, its long body curling several times beneath it.

"Rise," Salice said. The demon stood on its hind legs, lifting its head high into the air. "Dance; on my beat." Salice began a rhythmic clap and the demon swayed, bouncing and hopping about on its hind legs in time with the clapping. After a few moments Professor Salice nodded, content.

"Wait in the corner," he commanded. The demon seemed hesitant to cross the pentagram lines. When it did work up the courage it crossed all at once in a terrified dash without meeting any resistance this time. Noah began to rise as well, but Salice's words were sharp enough to make him drop back at once. "Sit down, boy. We have six more to go before you're finished."

The imps came easily enough, as did the Gobblers who were little more than giant, toothless mouths embedded in a misshapen fleshy lump like melted candle wax. The Lava Salamander was much less pleasant, its purple rubbery skin scalding Noah all the way out. Despite being vaguely shaped like a salamander, the creature moved as though it had no bones in its entire body and propelled itself by stretching parts of itself until they were almost transparently thin before snapping the rest of its body into the new location.

"You must remember that a contract with a demon is one of partnership, not servitude," Professor Salice proclaimed after a particularly nervous gobbler seemed reluctant to exit the circle. "The netherworld is a terrifying place, even for those that call it their home. Most demons are eager to work for a chance of freedom in one of the other planes, though it is up to the summoner to help them fulfill that dream once their contract is complete. To abuse their trust or attempt to cheat them would be... unforgivable."

Noah's forehead was burning when Salice invited him to lean against the cool glass once more, thus allowing him to pass. The Professor became preoccupied with instructing the newly summoned demons on their duties and paid little attention to Noah, who was only too relieved to escape.

Despite being told he'd be out by midnight, it must be almost morning by now. Noah was filled with restless energy after sitting for so long though, and he didn't take the stairs up toward his mausoleum to rest. Instead he turned downward, slipping down through the emptiness toward the Whispering Room. He stood and stared at the greenish stone circle for a long time, unable to bring himself to step inside.

Instead he sat with his back against the marble dais and closed his eyes—near enough to hear the whispers, but not so close as to make out exactly what they were saying. He shivered as the cool mist drifted over him, but he didn't suppose it could do any harm now. In that weary state he dreamed of home, so close that he might really be there and dreaming of here, and yet so far that he may never see it again. He dreamed of his daughter, and his grandson, and the taste of hot chocolate fresh from the stove, and softly he cried himself to sleep.

∼

"THE KNOWN universe is divided into three distinct worlds," Professor Salice said in the first demonology class the next day. "The living world, also known as the corporal world, the spirit world, and the netherworld."

This room was much less interesting than the others had been, with nothing but plain white tiles, rigid metal desks and chairs, and a dusty chalkboard at the front.

"Pssst," Jamie leaned over to Noah. "Did you finish the letter to Mandy yet?"

"Yeah," Noah whispered back. "A fake one anyway. It's just addressed to a random government building in a different city."

"The term for a soul passing from the living world to the spirit world is called death, or resurrection in reverse," Salice droned on, sounding so uninterested in his own words that the students were obviously struggling to do otherwise. "A soul going from the spirit world to the netherworld is a banishment, and one going the other way is called a summoning. There is anecdotal evidence of souls transferring directly between the living and nether worlds, although there has yet to be a controlled experiment to replicate those results."

"Aren't you worried that he'll find out?" Jamie whispered.

Noah shrugged. "It'll buy me some time at least."

"I think you should tell The Matriarch," Jamie said. "She defended you during the weighing ceremony, so I think she's taken a special liking to you."

"Tell her what? I don't have any proof that he's up to something. I don't even know what he could possibly want another Chainer for. He's already got me hosting his summonings."

"The diagram on page seven details this process," Professor Salice said, turning the page. "Demonic servants can be useful for all sorts of things because they are comprised of both matter and energy, allowing them to operate equally in all worlds. From protection, to cleaning houses, or even transportation, such as the Daymare... The Mortuary itself was constructed by the demon Morogoth, who planted the great tree from a seed it brought with it from the netherworld. The ceremonies to summon such powerful demons are extremely complicated and require the minds of many dozens of souls to conceive and host them."

"I've got an idea," Jamie whispered, raising her hand. Noah tried to kick her under the table, but she swung her legs away and stretched her hand even higher. "Excuse me, Professor?" she asked.

Professor Salice looked up from *Twelve Signs Your Imp Might Be Plotting To Kill You*. The sour look on his face would have been extremely appropriate on the cover. "What is it, Mrs. Poffin? I presume you do not need to use the bathroom."

"Could a Chainer be used to host more powerful demons than a non-chainer?" she asked. "Even if it's only one soul, it's heavier than normal souls because of how many lives it lived, right? We saw that at the weighing ceremony. Does that mean it's also bigger?"

Noah felt the eyes of the whole classroom fall upon him. He wanted to try and kick Jamie again, but he couldn't manage it now without being seen. Instead, he pretended to be extremely interested in the soul transfer diagram in his textbook.

"Yes," Professor Salice said, his voice barely above a whisper but clearly audible in the suddenly still room. Even the two imps who had been wrestling in the back stopped to listen, their squabble forgotten. Noah looked up and met Salice's gaze for an instant before turning back to his book, a feeling like ice in his veins.

"Professor Humstrum might have told you that all souls

are created equal, and perhaps they were, but that should not be confused to mean that all souls *are* equal," the Professor continued, his voice still low and hushed. He began to pace between the rows of chairs, but Noah kept his eyes firmly on the book in front of him. "An animal that lives its life in a cage before being slaughtered has had little chance to expand its soul. It has little experience of new things, new feelings, or new thoughts. And if it were to never live again, its soul would remain small and cheap, disposable and useless for any greater purpose. But one who has lived many lives, who has learned and grown from each, and loved and lost so many times…"

His voice trailed off as he stood directly over Noah, who stubbornly refused to look up.

"Pain," the Professor said, almost purring the word. "Suffering, loss. Like the accumulation of scar tissue, it may harden the soul against future injury. Such a soul can endure and be used for many useful things."

"You're bonkers," Walter whispered, perhaps louder than he'd intended in the quiet room. He winced immediately as other students suppressed quiet laughter around him. To their surprise, Professor Salice only smiled and returned to the front of the class.

"If death has taught you anything, it should be this," Salice replied, "that sanity, morality, and our fragile cultural beliefs are nothing but the current whims of those who happen to be alive at the same time and place. Reality does not care whether or not it is popular. Page eight, you will find descriptions of the different stones used for sealing contracts. The unique attributes of each stone will determine whether it is best suited to add duration, fine control, or protection in case the demon rebels, etc. You will each be required to memorize the twenty four most common forms of opal and be able to recite their strengths and weaknesses."

The lecturing drone continued through the rest of the period, although there was an interruption near the end that jolted Noah back to alertness.

"Professor?" Brandon asked, his voice high and ingratiating with artificial respect. "Can we come back as demons next time?"

Noah watched Brandon out of the corner of his eye. Was he asking out of curiosity, or did he know something about his demonic affinity? Brandon didn't seem to notice Noah and gave no hint as to what he was thinking.

Professor Salice closed the book on his podium with exquisite delicacy. "Some consider such a transformation to be the highest obtainment possible for a soul, something which bridges them with the divine. Would you choose such a path?"

"Of course, Professor!" Brandon said in his whining voice. "I think demons are amazing. I can't think of anything I'd rather be."

"Is that allowed though?"

It was the first time Noah heard that girl speak. He'd always assumed she'd been a boy because of her closely shaved hair, but hearing her voice it was undeniable.

"Hand, Rachelle," the Professor barked.

Rachelle raised her hand and continued, not waiting to be called. "In Chapter 16: Demonic Stigma, it says that human transformation into demons was banned in 1940 by Theodore Oswald, then Magistrate of the Trans Dimensional Department. It says—"

"I do not need to be lectured on the contents of my own textbook, Mrs. Devon," Salice said with a sneer. "If you were listening earlier instead of reading ahead, you would remember that public opinion is as arbitrary as it is inane."

"But didn't that happen right after the purges?" Rachelle persisted. "A lot of people were being killed by—"

"Do not mislead this class with such idle propaganda. We can discuss it after class, if you wish," Salice cut her off. "Noah, perhaps you will stay as well? I believe you have something for me."

The harpies had begun to screech outside, and the students were gathering their things to leave. Noah crumpled his note tightly in his hand while waiting behind Rachelle.

"You are correct that demons perpetrated a good deal of slaughter during the purges," Professor Salice was saying to her, "but your presumption of guilt is unfounded. Magistrate Oswald of the T.D.D. began the conflict by persecuting the large population of liberated demons. They were on the verge of earning voting rights from his progressive rivals, the Elmond twins, when Oswald vilified the movement as nothing short of a demonic uprising in order to stay in power. The escalating tensions led to the mass banishment of free demons at a political rally, which in turn sparked actual demonic attacks. Oswald used these as justification to begin the mass banishment of demons, an unforgivable act known as the purges. You must understand that these are demons who had served their contract faithfully for years on end, only to finally earn their freedom and be banished before they could make use of it."

Professor Salice was powerfully animated by the conversation, the topic obviously close to his heart. He seemed to have forgotten Noah was even there.

"But I heard that the demons attacked first. Did Oswald get rid of all the free demons then?" Rachelle pressed.

"Most of them," Salice said, his eyes wandering over the girl's shoulder to Noah. "It was rumored that the Elmond Twins helped a few of them transform into humans to escape the purges, but again this is the type of political fear mongering that has never been proven. His ban on human transformation was not meant as an actual policy, rather a mean-spirited attempt at convincing his followers that former demons could be hiding anywhere. If you really want to learn more, I recommend the book *Those Teeth Are For Smiling: The Misunderstood Demon*. Now Noah—where was that letter?"

Noah wordlessly handed over his note and turned sharply from the room.

"Not even a thank you?" Salice called after him in a sardonic tone. "I am doing you a favor, boy. Best remember that."

Noah couldn't get away fast enough. Demons... who killed people... who became human to escape punishment. If only he could outrun the implications of that thought as well.

QARI OLANDESCA ILLUSTRATIONS

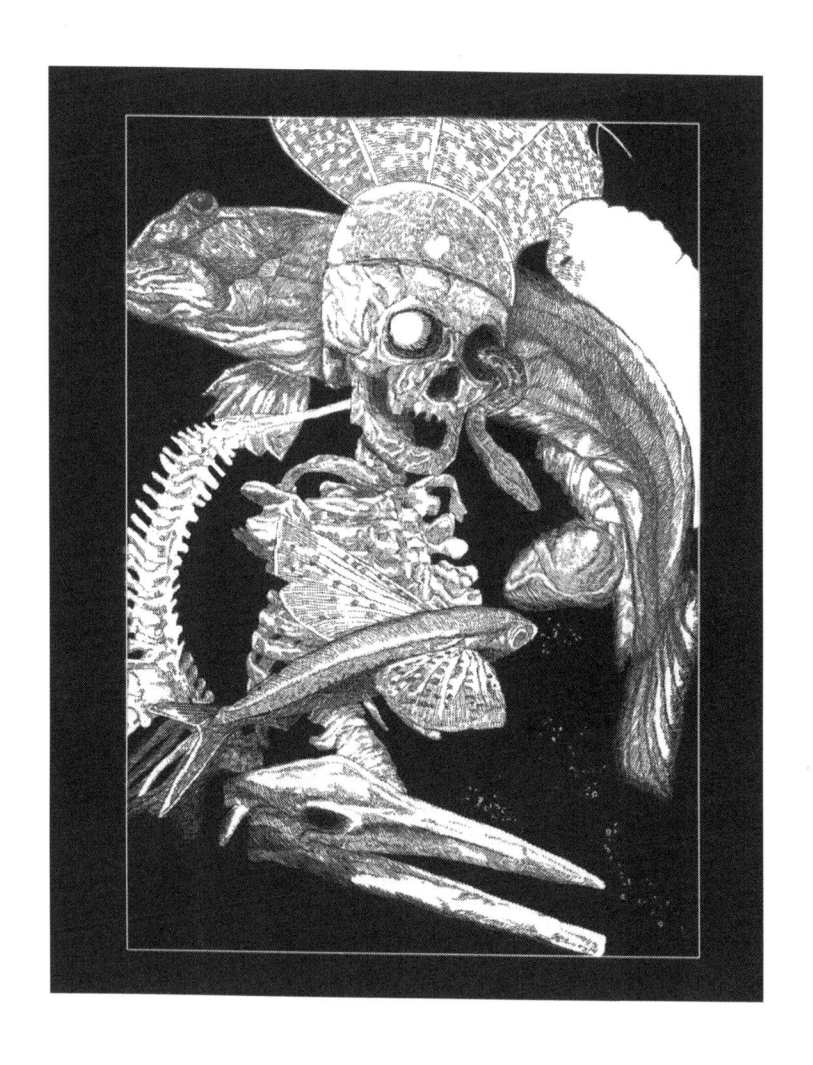

HALLOWEEN

THE THRILL OF NEW DISCOVERIES DID NOT COME WITHOUT THE burden of learning, and Noah had hardly any free time. Besides the main subjects of Necromancy, Demonology, and Transhumanism, there was a never-ending stream of guest lectures that Noah was forced to attend. These were intended to broaden the student's perspective on life and death.

Noah had never stopped to consider what it must be like to live a hundred generations as a turtle before spending one as a bird, but Ikella, the finch, explained at length. On a different occasion, an old man named Barosca who wore his beard like a belt said that he spent all his years gambling five hundred years ago. Fearing he would disappear completely, he swore a death of austerity. After that he hasn't spent a day since, and he swears he couldn't be happier, although admittedly he'd wished he wouldn't have minded being twenty five again.

The Necromancy class consisted of a lot more anatomy than Noah expected, and they were required to learn the names of every bone and muscle fiber for them to weave magic into. Noah would have expected his medical knowledge from his previous life to serve him well here, but despite his proficiency in naming the muscles he always had trouble getting them to respond.

Professor Wilst said that lurching zombies were an unfortunate stereotype caused by amateur Necromancers who made sweeping commands like 'Kill them all' without telling the poor confused zombies how to do it. The studying was exhausting, but it was all worth it when Noah was able to get his corpse to raise its hand and wave for the rest of the class. That was at least as well as Jamie or Walter could do, and considerably better than Mrs. Robinson who hardly ever bothered to show up for class at all.

Despite the experience of his previous life not helping much, there were bits and pieces which did come to him as sudden revelations. The more he read, the more it felt like he was reviewing long forgotten information rather than learning something new. When Professor Humstrum asked the class whether plants had souls, Noah knew at once that they possessed something similar but distinct which spiritologists have named the life-force, which instead of having a unique soul meant that their essence was returned to fuel the cosmic tree and its millennial bloom.

When Noah was asked how he knew since it was not in the required reading, he made up an excuse about Professor Salice mentioning it during his apprenticeship to hide the fact that he didn't know how he knew. Noah could only assume that one of his previous selves knew the fact, and that somehow all those experiences were still buried inside him somehow.

Despite Noah's aversion toward Salice, he confided in Jamie and Walter that Denomology was actually his favorite class. He still hadn't told Walter about his demonic affinity—being a murderer seemed like more than enough to test their friendship—but it was demonology more than anything that caused these feelings of deja vu. As soon as Professor Salice mentioned that the full moon can make it easier for the host to find demons in the netherworld, Noah not only remembered that different phases of the moon can help find different demons, but he also remembered that the Boar-headed Thimbler could only be found during a solar eclipse.

If Professor Salice had realized that Noah gave him the wrong address yet, then he didn't mention it. Their relationship had even improved on account of how much additional time Noah spent with the Professor as his apprentice. Salice responded to Noah's interest with encouragement, and he spent as much time receiving private guidance and tutoring as he did actually working on Salice's behalf.

There were only two things about this period at the school that Noah did not enjoy. He didn't like how Brandon and Teresa treated the imps, which was almost as bad as how they treated him whenever he tried to defend them. And he didn't like that he couldn't stop thinking about the Whispering Room.

Noah couldn't bear to enter again after the morning he'd fallen asleep there, and for several nights afterward all he could dream about was his daughter's tormented whispering. At the same time he blamed himself for allowing that fear to prevent him from checking on them. Not to mention poor Samantha who must be so frightened by the spirits she sees, and Claire who would have loved to know how well Jamie was taking care of Mrs. Robinson.

Their first real opportunity to interact with the living world came sooner than anyone was expecting though. Noah was playing a game of knucklebones on the grass with Walter and Dolly Miller when Elizabeth Washent came bounding through the high grass in the graveyard.

"We're going to have a Halloween surprise!" she exclaimed, bouncing vertically on the spot, "and I'm going to spoil it! Who wants to know what it is? I heard it straight from The Matriarch's own mouth."

Elizabeth was quickly surrounded by students who came scrambling out of their mausoleums from all around to hear. Everybody knew that The Matriarch had taken Elizabeth as a personal apprentice because Elizabeth had made sure to tell everyone that very same day. She had never been very clear how exactly a rabbit was able to fulfill that duty, or what the duty even consisted of, but it was hard not to be swept up in her contagious enthusiasm.

"We're each going to have our own imp for the day!" she squealed, unable to contain her excitement.

"What would we want an imp for?" Walter asked in disappointment. "The ones we have don't do anyone any good."

"Well that's because they're stuck here on the island," Elizabeth said smugly. "We're going with our imps to the mainland to make mischief in the living world!"

"Why would we want to cause mischief?" Jamie asked, appearing from the graveyard gate with Mrs. Robinson on her shoulder.

"That's what's expected on Halloween!" Elizabeth said in exasperation. "*The Matriarch* said people would be disappointed if they *didn't* have their laundry all died pink or have toilet paper thrown over their house."

The more they thought about it, the more sensible Elizabeth's excitement became. Walter's apprenticeship with the Spiritual Operator hadn't given him the chance to make any calls, so he decided this would be his chance to finally send his girlfriend a letter. Bowser also wanted to check in on his family, although he was only planning to use the imp to terrify the superstitious father of his household who had never once given him a treat or called him a good boy. Noah overheard Brandon making a list of all the people he wanted to get revenge on, but he'd be hard pressed getting to every name in that notebook in a single day.

By the time The Matriarch arrived at the graveyard gate everyone was already massed about the entrance in anticipation. She stood in her customary red hat and coat with her hands on her hips, wearing a coy smile which suggested she knew perfectly well that the news of her 'surprise' had already spread.

"How are we all this fine autumn night?" The Matriarch asked, taking her time to draw out each syllable. "If I didn't know that this was a perfectly ordinary Tuesday, I would have thought you were all expecting something."

"Does it have to be an imp?" Jason Parson shouted, breaking his poorly concealed mask of ignorance. "I think gobblers would be much more fun for stealing candy."

And then everyone was talking at once, about where they were going and how long they'd be and whether the imps were allowed to bring anything back with them, and a hundred other questions which washed over The Matriarch like waves breaking against the implacable cliffs below.

"I don't suppose there is any use pretending then," she said, pouting her bottom lip. "But it *does* seem that one part of the surprise has been exaggerated. The imps will be going to where they're directed in the living world, but our class will not be leaving the island. We will all be going down to Montgomery Wolf, the Spiritual Operator who lives in Teraville, where we will be monitoring our imps through scrying crystals."

There was a collective wave of small disappointed groans, but The Matriarch waved it into silence with a flick of her wrist. "And yes, your imps *will* be able to bring you back a souvenir. Although I wouldn't recommend candy because you won't be able to eat it. If anyone has a problem with that, then they can sit in their coffins all day for all I care. Who is with me?"

This time the response sounded with unabated enthusiasm. The Matriarch waited at the gate while the students streamed out onto the grassy hillside. The moment Noah had passed her however, The Matriarch left her position and merged with the crowd by his side.

"How is our little Chainer doing?" she asked him. "I imagine you'll be excited to send the imp to visit your family."

Noah had already dismissed the possibility. The imp might be obeying him for the day, but it was Salice they had the contract with and he had no doubt that they would report where his family lived directly back to him. For all he knew this entire holiday could have been planned around that fact.

"I don't want to scare them," Noah replied. "I'd rather just have it go trick-or-treating in a friendly neighborhood."

"Very sensible, you never know when demons will try to pull something horrible," she said, looking about her in a conspiratorial fashion. The surrounding students were gradually spreading over the grassy hillside. "You know, if it were up to me, I wouldn't let the little beasties anywhere near my school. We've got the T.D.D. to blame for that—requiring a 'full curriculum' to qualify for department funding. It's a disgrace if you ask me. I've had more than my share of problems with them in the past, and even when they aren't fighting each other or playing tricks on people, they're still the ugliest little monsters I've ever seen."

Noah said nothing, wondering whether Professor Humstrum really had rushed off to tell The Matriarch about his affinity. Noah glanced behind him and met Brandon's beady eyes for an instant. He'd been whispering with Teresa, and both of them were staring at him with undisguised loathing. Noah wasn't sure whether they could overhear him, but this wasn't a conversation he wanted to be having regardless.

"I'm going to catch up with my friends now, hope you have a happy Halloween, Mrs. Matriarch."

"Elanore Barrow," The Matriarch said. "You may call me Elanore, and if you ever want to discuss anything that has been troubling you, my office is the first door on the first floor. I think you'll find me a very attentive listener."

Noah thanked her and hurried forward, making a show of joining Walter and Jamie as though they had been expecting him. To The Matriarch's credit—Noah didn't think he'd ever be able to call her Elanore—she hadn't pushed him on visiting Mandy or sharing more than he was comfortable with. It was a welcome contrast with the constant pressure he'd grown accustomed to from Salice, and it was almost enough for him to want to tell her everything and ask for her help. On the other hand, she clearly saw the same significance in being a Chainer that Salice did, and Noah didn't want to expose his family to a whole new avenue of risk.

"I think you can trust her," Jamie said once Noah had explained his doubts. "She's been teaching at the school for so long that I'm sure she's come across loads of Chainers before. Someone like that wouldn't think of interfering with the living."

"I'm not so sure," Walter said, "You were all for trusting Salice too, and one look at him will tell you he's up to no good."

"We still don't know he's not!" Jamie said. "You'd think someone who just shed their body and is on the way to find a new one would know not to judge someone on their appearances."

"How about their personality? That whole 'I'm better than you just because I can summon a demon that can melt your face' attitude? Is that fair game?"

Noah was eager to drop the subject and instead asked Walter about the Spiritual Operator they were approaching. Walter pointed out Montgomery Wolf's house, a stone tower that was so twisted it looked like someone trying to wring out a wet towel. The whole tower was completely engulfed in climbing ivy, and there was a large glass room on the top which glowed beneath the moon like a lighthouse.

"That's where Mr. Wolf—and you have to call him that or he gets really mad—that's where he keeps the Netherball which he uses to look into the demon world. I'm not allowed to touch that one," Walter said. "Mostly, the place is just filled with crystal balls for spying on living people. They're enchanted so people who can see and hear spirits like mediums light up. Once he's found one, he can send messages to them and ask for them to relay that onto the nearby people. Some of the stronger psychics learn how to call him back, and then he's the one who is supposed to go find the spirit."

"That's really good of him, helping people find their families again," Jamie said.

"Not really," Walter sighed. "He charges six months to find the right person, and he won't even give me a discount for being his apprentice. I'd still have done it if it weren't for The Matriarch's stupid restriction per semester."

"I might be able to buy it," Noah said. "Professor Salice had an imp pick up my school supplies, and I never had to pay for any of them."

"Would you really?" Walter asked. "I've still got two months left this semester, and I'll pay you the rest back after Christmas."

"You shouldn't take his time. I thought the imp was going to deliver it," Jamie said reproachfully.

"Well I've thought about it, but any message I wrote down would be on spiritual paper. I'd have to get the imp to write down the message on material paper, but I don't think they can even write."

"How do you know they can't write?" Jamie said, frowning. "They're very—"

"Not this again. Did you know that imp Brandon has it out for won't leave me alone? I think it's trying to haunt me."

"Aha!" she exclaimed. "So you *can* tell them apart now. And don't think I don't recognize the necklace you've started wearing. That's the rock the imp gave you," she added triumphantly.

Walter clutched at the string around his neck self-consciously. "I didn't want it," he mumbled. "He just seemed so hurt and I thought it would shut him up…"

Soon the entire class was gathered outside Mr. Wolf's tower where he stood waiting to greet them. He pulled the knees of his long striped legs past his waist as he stepped through the children, walking with a haughty disdain as though he was afraid of getting one of them on his feet.

"Are there supposed to be so many, Matriarch?" Mr. Wolf asked in a long-suffering voice. "Might as well open the bestiary and let them all run amok inside. Scrying crystals are very fragile, you know, and if anything breaks—"

"Nothing is going to break, my dear, silly man," The Matriarch replied. "I know how much the T.D.D. is paying you for the day, so do play nice. If it's really too much of a burden on you, then I'm sure the students will have just as much fun spending the holiday turning into frogs and riding broomsticks at Miss Thatcher's Witchery."

"Miss Thatcher? She has a broomstick so far up her backside that she —"

"Mr. Wolf!" The Matriarch interrupted sternly.

"—lifts off every time she farts. There, you made me say it. Come along then children, one at a time. Yes, yes the crystal balls are very pretty, but they aren't for touching. Or licking, Mrs. Horlow! Why on Earth—"

The inside of the tower was dazzlingly bright. Hundreds of thin silver chains suspended from perfectly smooth crystal balls of every imaginable color, as well as at least two colors that Noah had never seen before and couldn't even imagine when he wasn't looking directly at them. Some crystal balls were barely the size of marbles, while others must have weighed a ton and required four supporting chains securely anchored to the walls and ceiling.

"It's all very simple really—not the business, that's more complicated than any of you could manage—but what you'll be doing today," Mr. Wolf said. "Two people per ball, it doesn't really matter which, they've all been configured for you already. All you must do is look into your reflection and tell it where you'd like to see. Once the scene has resolved itself, look around until you find your imp—you do not need to touch the crystal to do this, Mr. Parson—simply walk around to view the scene from another angle. Do look where you're going though—it's as crowded as a mass grave in here."

Noah found a pale creamy crystal a little smaller than a globe, and Walter spoke the name and neighborhood of an unfamiliar city. Tall dark buildings huddled together deep within the glass as though it was a snow globe.

"Your imp will automatically travel through the nether to the chosen location," Mr. Wolf continued, prowling incessantly through the room. "Look for him now. He'll be easy to recognize because he lights up."

Walter raised his hand which prompted Mr. Wolf to strut over to them. They explained that they would rather find a medium, which Mr. Wolf was happy to oblige as soon as he realized he would be paid in full.

"You won't tell The Matriarch, will you?" Mr. Wolf asked, bending low. "I won't be giving any refunds for the simple scrying she's already ordered."

"Not a word," Walter agreed. "There is a medium who is close by then?"

Mr. Wolf reached inside his mouth as though he was fishing for something. Noah winced as the man plucked one of his own teeth out, which was actually an aquamarine stone shaped like a tooth. He grinned to reveal the gaping hole which remained.

"Can never be too safe with these," Mr. Wolf said. "Go on then, grab hold. Six months it is, that's the deal, take it or leave it. No discounts, no bartering, and definitely no backsies."

"I'll be giving two months, he's got the rest," Walter said. "Thanks again, Noah. You don't know how much this means to me."

They both paid the transaction, and Noah was surprised to realize he didn't even mind holding the tooth when it was his turn. This whole place was so macabre that nothing that used to bother him had any real horror left. The groggy, dizzying feeling was more pronounced this time, and he was sure he could distinctly feel his hair and fingernails growing. His shins suddenly became extremely sore and tender. He was sure Walter had been taller than him a moment ago, but now they were the same size.

Mr. Wolf meanwhile grabbed the crystal between his hands and began dancing a complex pattern with his fingers. The image spun smoothly in response, the viewpoint soaring upward before swooping between the tall dark buildings like a bird. The view whirled straight through walls, catching one man on a toilet and others sitting in their living rooms or eating dinner at the table. The only indication that they were noticed was that people tended to shiver briefly as the viewpoint passed through them.

"Margret Vintilo?" Mr. Wolf mused, his brow furrowed with concentration. "No, she stopped doing business after that gobbler got her fluffy little dog. Pedflam Grasowitch? Now I'm sure nothing would have stopped old Pedflam."

The viewpoint in the crystal shifted sharply to the right, breaking free of the apartment buildings and speeding down the street.

"Although he did have that run in with the police when he started selling amulets," Mr. Wolf continued thoughtfully. "'Course, it was the boy's own fault when he thought it would stop a bullet, but that's what you get when you think you're too good for disclaimers. Are you in there, Pedflam? Come out come out, or I'm coming in."

The scene in the crystal paused briefly before a crumbling stone cottage. It looked like it had been built a hundred years ago and had only been maintained by dry wind and the occasional tornado. A moment later and they were through the door within a living room that was stacked from floor to ceiling with old magazines, newspapers, and casually discarded books.

A fat middle-aged man with thick glasses, greasy hair, and an uneven beard sat in an armchair which was the only furniture in the room. He grunted in surprise and swiftly shut his bathrobe, or at least closed the part that wasn't being obstructed by his low-hanging stomach.

"Get off then!" he shouted. "No spooks allowed, not in here. Out, out, or I'll—"

"You'll what, Pedflam?" Mr. Wolf asked. "Who you gonna call?"

Pedflam was still glowering, but his face softened with recognition. "I'll call your daughter, if she's still alive. What is it this time, Montgomery?"

"A message for Mrs. Natasha Cortico of 324 Browsly Street. It shouldn't take you more than an hour, a little more if you'd like to make yourself presentable."

"Make myself present—hmph," Pedflam said. "That's what I've got a lock on the door for. What's in it for me then?"

"A week. An hour for a week, you can't say no to that."

"A week?" Walter asked incredulously. "You charged us six months."

"Shh, quiet," Mr. Wolf hissed. "There are conversion rates to account for... it's not easy sending time over, you know. It gets all compressed and... it doesn't matter, just stay out of this."

"Who is there?" Pedflam asked suspiciously. He stood up and waddled over to open the curtains, although the window was so dirty that this did little to bring in more light.

"Just the client, a poor lost soul missing his love. Ten days, that's my best offer."

"Get off then, I'll take it," Pedflam grumbled, "but only because it's in the name of love. Give me a few minutes and I'll meet you there." He began stomping across the room toward an adjoining bathroom which looked dirty enough as to instantly negate the effect of a shower as soon as he got out. "And don't follow me in here!" he bellowed, snapping the door shut behind him.

"As if," Walter said. "Is he really the best we can do? I think Natasha would laugh him straight out the door."

"It's hard finding a reliable medium, especially this far south," Mr. Wolf replied indignantly. "Something about warm weather makes it harder to concentrate. Besides, you should have learned by now not to judge a soul by its shell. Mr. Grasowitch is doing very well for being over eighty years old. He's been officially licensed by the T.D.D., and he's been paid handsomely by the looks of it."

The crystal view whirled out of the house and began meandering down the moonlit street.

"Do you recognize the area?" Noah asked.

"Yeah, sure," Walter said, barely glancing at the crystal before averting his eyes to gaze around at the other students.

"Aren't you excited to be seeing her again?" Noah pressed. "What are you going to say?"

"I don't... It doesn't matter," Walter said. Noah had the impression that Walter wasn't really seeing anything, least of all the crystal which he was purposely avoiding. "I don't think she'll want to hear from me," he added quietly.

"Of course she will," Noah said reassuringly. "And it won't be any pressure, because Pedflam will be doing all the talking."

Walter was fidgeting so bad that he couldn't stand still. He darted outside for a bit of fresh air while waiting for the medium to be ready, and Noah could see him out the window pacing in agitation. Noah took the chance to track down his imp and had just begun having it howl below people's windows when Walter returned, as pale as Noah had ever seen him.

"Ready then? Pedflam should be there soon," Mr. Wolf said, swiping the crystal ball so that the image spun. "324 Browsly Street? Could that be her?"

The crystal viewpoint zoomed in on an elegant dark skinned lady with a soft, curly afro. There wasn't a straight line in her entire body, as was abundantly evident from her red dress which flowed along her curves as tightly and smoothly as a second skin. She sat on the front steps of a clean white house with a leather purse between her legs, her attention focused on her phone.

"Walter?" Mr. Wolf asked. "I've spent quite enough time on you two already, and The Matriarch would complain mightily if I didn't make sure the imps weren't getting into too much trouble."

"Yeah," Walter breathed, his eyes fixed on the woman. "It's her alright."

"She's quite charming," Mr. Wolf said rather nasally. "I'm glad that I was able to give you this opportunity. Just wait here until Pedflam catches up. I'll check in with you again before—hey! Little fat boy! What's going on over there?"

Mr. Wolf hurried away to where Brandon had begun to shout into his orb. Noah caught a glimpse of an imp chasing a group of costumed trick-or-treaters, its sharp teeth flashing in the crystal. Despite the commotion, Walter didn't turn to look or even blink.

Noah couldn't help but think back to his own wife, a

cheery English woman named Olivia Wells. They'd had a brief but fulfilling affair, but it was undeniable that his awareness of spirits had put a strain on the relationship. They were fighting all the time by the point of Mandy being born, and when the child began seeing spirits as well it was too much for Olivia to bear and she was never to be seen again. This sent his thoughts spiraling back to Mandy once more, and what she must be going through trying to raise Lewis on her own. It was no wonder that she'd prefer not to see the things she did, but denying them didn't seem like any solution at all...

Had Noah ever truly fallen in love? He'd loved the idea of love, from books and movies and all the ways it could have been if life hadn't gotten in the way. He had no doubt that he loved his parents, and his daughter, and his grandson, but that wasn't the same as falling in love with a stranger. There had been a few times in his life when he thought he'd found the one, but it always seemed like the more he got to know her, the less he knew himself, and in the end he'd be alone again. Perhaps he'd been too selfish to ever lose himself in someone else.

Noah studied Walter's face, how he had barely moved a muscle this whole time. It hardly seemed worthwhile to fall in love if it hurt so badly when it was over. Even now that Walter had found her again, it didn't seem to make him happy. If anything he looked like he was about to cry. Slowly, tenderly, with trembling hand, Walter reached out to touch the crystal ball. At almost the same instant Natasha looked up from her phone, her deep, brown eyes lighting up the stone.

"Oh, there you are, I've been waiting almost an hour," she said, her voice low and smooth.

"I'm sorry, baby," a husky voice replied. "Next time you can take two hours getting ready and we'll call it even."

She laughed and smiled, allowing herself to be swept into the arms of a man in a suit that looked so new that it bent rather than folded. Noah thought it was only decent to turn away when they kissed, but Walter still didn't blink.

"We should hurry though," Natasha said, nestling against the man. "The curtain is going to open before we even get there."

"Fine with me," he replied. "The only show I'm interested in will be going on in the back of the theatre."

Natasha laughed again and drew away teasingly, leading the man away from the house. They were approaching a sleek black town car parked on the street when another car driving much too fast swerved to drift into an uneven park nearby.

Pedflam squeezed himself out at once, and Noah would have laughed to see him if it weren't for the severity of Walter's stare. The medium had dressed in flowing robes of red satin, his ample neck almost invisible beneath a mass of silver and gold chains attached to amulets, mystic symbols, and what appeared to be the lower jaw of a human skull whose teeth were entirely gold.

"324 Browsly Street? Natasha?" he shouted before Natasha had a chance to enter her car.

"Who wants to know?" she asked uneasily.

The man in the suit looked highly amused. "A friend of yours?" he asked.

"No," Walter said. "It's not her. Get back in the car."

"What do you mean it's not her?" Pedflam asked, turning to meet Walter's gaze in a huff. "Of course it's her. You think this is my first transmittance?"

"Who are you talking to?" Natasha asked. "I'm sorry but we really have to go—"

"Just a moment," Pedflam told her, turning his attention back on Walter, which to her must appear that he was speaking into the empty air. "Montgomery doesn't offer refunds, and you're not going to get another chance at this. If you have something to say, then say it. If not, then I'm going home. It's all the same to me."

The man in the suit opened the passenger side door of the town car and gestured for Natasha to get in. Then to Pedflam, he said, "Whatever you're selling, we aren't buying. Happy Halloween man... whatever you're dressed as."

"This," Pedflam replied magnanimously, sweeping his hands down the length of his satin robes, "This is no costume, sir. This robe represents the highest trust and honor that the Trans Dimensional Department may bestow upon a living mortal. And the only thing I'm selling you is the truth, unless of course you were interested in a protection amulet..."

"It wasn't supposed to go like this," Walter moaned. "Just tell her—tell her to be happy, okay?"

Natasha's door was already swinging shut when Pedflam spluttered, "Walter wants you to be happy."

The door halted so suddenly that time might as well have stopped. Walter was speaking quickly now, and Pedflam hurried to repeat every word.

"He says he's sorry he didn't show you how important you are when he still had the chance, but he wants to say it now. He wants you to not take any of it too seriously, because it'll all be over too soon and none of it can follow you where you're going. That it doesn't have to all be done right the first time round, because you'll get to try again and everything will be easier next time. He wants you to know that there's no feeling so heavy that your soul can't carry, and whether it's good or bad it doesn't matter so long as you can feel something that makes you feel alive. Walter wants you to know that he loved you while he was alive, that he still loves you now that he's gone, and that he'll continue loving you in the next life too. Even if you're a hawk and he's a rabbit, because it's your soul that he loves, and you don't have to belong to him for him to see its light."

Natasha didn't have words to respond with, but her mouth parted and her eyes glistened, and to Walter that must have been enough. Not even waiting for a reply, Walter turned away from the crystal globe and stumbled blindly through the room, nearly tripping over Elizabeth and pushing past Rachelle on his way out. They giggled at him as he passed, but he didn't seem to hear. It's probably best he left when he did, because Pedflam had appended the speech with a well rehearsed sales pitch for his amulets.

"… and I'm sure he would have wanted you to stay safe with one of these harpy claws, hand-calcified to be in the physical world, of course."

Noah turned away from the crystal as well. Everyone else was still playing with their imps, but such games lost their appeal in the face of the heavy wistfulness filling his heart. Love didn't seem quite as silly to Noah as it had a moment before, although he still had a hard time believing that it was worth it.

"Is Walter okay?" Jamie asked from a nearby orb which she shared with a tall, thin girl named Jennifer Alaski. Jamie's imp was in a kitchen washing dishes, looking glum.

"Go and find out, why don't you," Jennifer snapped. "You're not using your imp right anyway."

"They needed the help!" Jamie insisted. "All those kids

running around and making a mess already, it's the least I could do."

"He'll be okay," Noah said, watching Walter exit the building. "I think he just wants to be alone."

"I understand," Jamie said. "It's funny, but for years and years I was afraid of dying alone, but now that I'm dead I have more friends than I ever did alive. Do you feel that way too, Noah?"

Noah wasn't listening anymore though. He'd gone to the window to watch Walter walking a few unsteady steps outside, then tipping over to land on his back in the grass and stare up at the moon. How odd that it was the same moon that stirred such feelings in the living. Would they look at it any differently if they knew the dead were watching too?

QARI OLANDESCA ILLUSTRATIONS

ZOMBIES

There must have been a secret pact among the professors to all begin increasing the workload at the same time. Demonology remained Noah's easiest subject as he kept remembering things he never thought he knew, but even so there were long histories to learn that he knew nothing about. Professor Salice had an extremely sympathetic view of demons and lectured at length about how they were persecuted throughout the ages. He seemed to think they were a universal scapegoat for everything that went wrong, and tended to gloss over the 'historically insignificant' massacres which they caused every few decades.

Professor Humstrum's class had moved onto communicating with living animals. He'd setup a scrying crystal in the middle of the class which went on a tour from house to house looking for cats to speak with. Noah could never seem to get the cat's attention, although the Professor admitted that sometimes cats prefer to feign disinterest even when they're perfectly aware of the spirit's presence. Mrs. Robinson was a regular feature of the class now, although her attendance for the other classes was sporadic at best. She never attended necromancy at all, saying she couldn't stand their smell.

Humstrum did seem to act more cooly toward Noah since the incident in the Bestiary, however. The ape maintained a constant air of being politely unimpressed by Noah's work, saying that Chainers are often weak at transhumanism because they're 'so busy with the cycle that they don't stop to appreciate the beauty of individual lives'. Noah thought that sounded made up.

Necromancy was even worse though. Despite zombies not having spirits of their own, Noah was convinced that his was being deliberately obstinate as it never seemed to do what it was told. Brandon was the star pupil in this class, which only served to frustrate Noah more. His zombie was practically tap-dancing while Noah struggled to get his own to stop chewing on its arm long enough to listen.

While Professor Humstrum never gave tests, Professor Wilst was an endless source of pop-quizzes, chapter evaluations, and a looming final exam. Wilst threatened that the worst performing student would have their body exhumed, while the best performer would be allowed to use it for the next semester. It was almost impossible to tell whether the dry, skeletal voice was speaking sarcastically, but the thought of Brandon being able to use his body like a puppet would have been nauseating if Noah still felt that sort of thing.

Help came from the most unlikely place one November afternoon class where Noah was performing abysmally. The students had taken their zombies out to practice walking up the stairs, but Noah's zombie had somehow gotten scared of the pit and refused to cross the bridge. Noah grew so frustrated that he shouted at it, causing it to collapse and flop violently on the ground like a fish out of water.

"You're going to fail, you know," Teresa told Noah conversationally. She stayed back with him while the other students went ahead to cross. "I wouldn't be surprised if you've already lived your last life."

Noah ignored her and began reciting commands from the textbook once more. The zombie flopped onto its back and rocked from side to side, unable to stand up.

"Do you want to know how Brandon does it?" she asked coyly.

"No, I don't," Noah replied sharply. "Of course he gets along with zombies. They're both braindead."

Noah expected her to become outraged at any slight against her precious son, but to his surprise she only giggled.

"He's got a mermaid skull from Nepon Vasolich, the supernautical sailor. It translates his commands into a smooth music that only the dead can hear, and it helps them understand."

"So he's cheating," Noah said bluntly.

Teresa's face crinkled into a sneer, but an instant later it was gone. She was smiling now. "No more cheating than being a Chainer. Anyway, it's not even cheating, because Professor Wilst never said it wasn't allowed. Would you like to use it?"

Noah hated the idea of needing help at all, but as things were he was at risk of being the very bottom of the class. Noah kicked his zombie, his foot making contact as its animation imbued it with spiritual energy.

"Why do you care?" he asked at last.

"I don't," she said curtly, spreading her fingers to look at her glistening white nails. "It's all the same to me if you never get to the advanced classes or come back to life at all. Rumor has it that you have a key to the Whispering Room though…"

"Says who?" Noah asked, as stubborn as his useless zombie.

"I want it," Teresa said. "I know you don't use it. The mermaid skull would do you more good."

"How do you know I don't use it? Who has been talking about me?"

"Words have wings of their own," Teresa replied cryptically. "I want to use it tonight. You'll take me there and show me how it works, okay?"

"Let me see the skull then," Noah said.

Teresa only smirked. "I'll give it to you in the Whispering Room." She turned to her zombie which had been standing motionless behind her the whole while. "Consurgo!" she barked. The zombie lurched forward to follow her across the bridge.

Noah spent the rest of the class trying and failing to get his fat zombie to even stand up again. It rolled back and forth and moaned most piteously, and at one point it began humming loudly to itself to prevent any commands from being heard. Noah hadn't made any conscious decision yet, but part of him already knew that he wanted to make the deal.

Noah asked Walter afterward whether he was the one who told Teresa about the whispering room, but he denied it vehemently. Walter called her a snake and said not to trust her, but Jamie was quick to disagree.

"Do you know how she died?" Jamie asked.

"No, but I can guess," Walter said. "My money is on being shot by the police after trying to kick a puppy."

"I bet Brandon killed her," Noah said. "Spoiled brat didn't want to die alone, so he took her with him."

"Close, but no," Jamie said. "She did die trying to save Brandon though. They were on a boat when he went over, and she went after him. They both drowned in each other's arms."

"How do you know?" Noah asked suspiciously. "Were you the one to tell her about the Whispering Room?"

"So what if I did?" Jamie asked, turning up her nose. "She's got loved ones like anyone else. Doesn't she deserve to hear them too?"

"No," Walter and Noah said in unison.

"You murdered people," Jamie reminded Noah sharply. "So what if she hasn't always been the most pleasant person? We've all got a chance to leave ourselves behind and start again. If she wants to say goodbye before she can have a fresh start, then she deserves that."

After some bickering, Noah decided that he would meet Teresa for the exchange, although Walter insisted he and Jamie accompany as backup to make sure she wasn't trying to play a trick on him.

The fifth floor which contained the Whispering Room was empty as usual when the three arrived. Noah could still hear the speech and laughter of jostling students above, but it was muffled and tinny like they were only hearing an echo. It might have been his imagination, but even the will-o-wisps seemed to be burning lower than usual, their normally warm red light muted into pale orange.

"I was wondering when you'd show up," Teresa said. She was standing outside the Whispering Room with her arms crossed. She didn't seem surprised to see Walter and Jamie, giving them no more attention than a swift, contemptuous glance.

"Let's get this over with then," Noah said. "Do you have the skull?"

Teresa nodded and produced a round object covered in a

piece of lavender cloth. The air seemed to grow colder and more brittle for an instant, and Noah shivered involuntarily. Mrs. Robinson, who had taken to sitting on Jamie's shoulder, hissed softly at the bundle and flattened her ears against her head.

"Disgusting creature," Teresa said, stepping back from the cat. "I don't know why anyone would choose that over being human."

"How do we know the skull works?" Walter asked. "You could be trying to cheat us with a piece of rubbish."

"How do I know the key works?" she countered. "Show me how to use the Whispering Room, and I'll show you how to use the skull."

Walter looked like he was ready to argue again, but he held himself back when Noah approached the door. Noah slid the key inside and pushed it open, not taking his eyes off Teresa the whole time. She smirked, her dark eyes twinkling in anticipation.

"After you, murderer," she quipped sweetly.

Noah rolled his eyes and pushed open the door. The room was deserted with pools of green mist floating along the floor, just as Noah had seen it last.

"Where are they?" Teresa asked.

"Where are who?" Noah said.

"All the people. Everyone I used to know."

"That's not how it works," Noah said. "You've got to stand in the circle and listen. Sometimes you can see them if the connection is strong enough, but mostly it's just whispers like the room says."

Teresa looked suspiciously at Noah for a moment before mounting the raised dais. She was still clutching the bundle in her arms, and Mrs. Robinson's attention was still fixed on it.

The cat had crept along behind her, stopping a few feet away, still crouched and ready to spring.

"Gentle now, Mrs. Robinson," Jamie said. "We're all on the same team, okay?"

"Can I talk to them?" Teresa asked.

"Not unless they're a psychic or a Chainer," Noah said. "Then it's more like a two-way window."

Mist was beginning to billow upward and swirl around Teresa's feet.

"There's nothing to be frightened of," Jamie said, prompting a sharp glance from Teresa.

"I'm not frightened," Teresa snapped. "I just don't like being watched."

"Don't worry about us," Jamie said reassuringly. "I was in the room when the others used it and I couldn't hear anything the living said."

Teresa took a deep breath and nodded rigidly. "Thank you," she said, her faint smile seeming more genuine this time. "I needed this. Did you look inside too?"

Jamie shook her head. "I think we often need something until we get it," Jamie said, "but some things are better not to have."

Teresa's top lip pulled tight into the beginning of her customary sneer, but her face relaxed quickly. She nodded and, taking a final deep breath, plunged her face into the swelling green mist. "Now what do I—" she began, the words strangled in her throat as the mist began to flow around her and obscure her face.

Teresa's face was invisible for several minutes before she jolted out of the circle and gasped for air. Her hair was damp from the mist and her eyes glistened with tears.

"I hate it!" she screamed, the sound painfully sharp and piercing in the silence. "It's a lie, and I hate it!"

"Your own fault I bet," Walter said. "Did you think people would miss someone who treated them so nastily?"

"Deal is off," Teresa said, wiping her face with the back of her sleeve. "I don't want your stupid key anymore."

"You can't do that!" Noah protested. "I did my part, now let's see the skull."

"Not happening," she spat, shoving past Noah to make her way toward the door.

Walter leapt in front of her to block the way. "I knew you were going to try and cheat," he said. "You're not leaving with the skull."

"Brandon!" Teresa screamed in her piercing voice. "They're attacking me, Brandon! Help your mother!"

"I didn't touch you, you horrible hag," Walter shouted back. "Now give us the skull or—" he snatched at the lavender bundle in her arms, but whisking away the cover revealed only her stuffed Whale underneath.

Something slammed violently against the outside of the door, powerful enough to shake it in its frame. It sounded like claws were dragging along the wood, then another shuddering boom as the force drove in again. A shower of dust and splinters rained upon them, but the door remained standing.

"There's no way Brandon is doing that," Jamie said.

"His zombie wouldn't have claws either," Walter said. "Maybe a demon?"

"Get out of my way," Teresa screamed, diving for the door.

Walter tried to snatch away her stuffed Whale, but at the same instant the door behind him was assaulted again. The jolt knocked Walter off balance, giving Teresa the chance to evade his sweeping arms. She pushed the door from the inside and the lock clicked open. By then Walter had regained his balance and grabbed Teresa by the shoulders.

Noah meanwhile tried to scramble past both of them to close the door again. He drove his weight against it to slam it shut, but it didn't close all the way. A long bony foot was wedged into the crack, each nail a deadly curved point like the talons on a bird of prey.

As they stared, more curved claws slipped through the crack and folded around the door. Walter shoved Teresa out of the way so he could join Noah in trying to press the door shut again. An irresistible pressure swelled from the other side however—it felt like bracing against a car to prevent it from starting. There was nothing they could do but leap out of the way as the door swung outward.

"He's got a ghoul!" Jamie shouted, identifying the lithe corpse which loomed in the doorway. Its tongue lolled all the way past its chin, and a sloppy grin bristled with teeth which overlapped and forced each other to jut out at odd angles.

Jamie snatched up Mrs. Robinson who was cowering against the dais, and all three friends retreated onto the raised ground. The ghoul fell onto all fours and sauntered into the room, its movements so fluid that it almost seemed to be dancing, completely unlike the rigid zombies they'd grown accustomed to.

"Do you like it?" Brandon asked, now entering the room. Both of his hands were clutched around an elongated but almost-human looking skull whose eyes glowed with soft yellow light. "I picked it up loping around the graveyard last night. Puts those zombies to shame, doesn't it?"

"I told you not to wait so far back," Teresa scolded her son. "Let's get out of here."

"Already?" Brandon said, his grin vanishing. "We haven't

even had any fun yet." The ghoul matched its master's agitation and began shuffling back and forth along the floor, its gruesome face locked on Noah and the others.

"Ghouls are corporal, right?" Walter whispered hurriedly. "It can't really attack us, can it?"

"It absolutely can," Jamie said, "don't you ever pay attention?"

"We can try to control it then," Walter said nervously. "There's three of us and only two of them."

"Yeah, but we don't have a mermaid skull," Noah countered. "And I'm no good at undead anyway, so they'd win for sure."

"That's enough," Teresa said. "The deal is off, so we're leaving. As much as they deserve to be punished for trying to cheat me, it's not worth getting kicked out of school."

"Just the cat then?" Brandon asked. The ghoul turned its head toward Mrs. Robinson so sharply that it looked like something snapped inside its neck. Mrs. Robinson spat and hissed, all hair raised. "Cats disappear all the time, and no-one could prove anything."

Teresa sighed, giving into her petulant child. "Very well, just the cat. But leave the rest alone."

"Thank you, mother," Brandon said in a breathy gush.

"I won't let you have her!" Jamie shouted. She grabbed Mrs. Robinson just as the ghoul lunged up the dais toward them. Long claws shredded the air where the cat had been an instant before. Mrs. Robinson made a long, low growl of warning, now from within the circle etched into the stone. Fresh mist was bleeding from the circle—blue again this time. It quickly reduced the ghoul to a silhouette, which only made it even more frightening as it was difficult to tell when it was preparing to lunge.

"Mrs. Robinson?" a faint voice called, as light as wind with the cool of mist. "Is that you?"

"Who said that? Who is here?" Brandon snarled, drawing back upon the skull and causing the ghoul to stumble. The ghoul jerked unevenly backward as though a rope around its waist had snapped taunt. It turned without apparent instruction to glare at Brandon, annoyed at being deprived of its prey.

Inspired by Brandon's hesitation, Noah grabbed Walter and Jamie by the arms and dragged them to cluster inside the circle as well.

The blue light was becoming more intense around the lines, even more than when Noah had entered the first time with Professor Salice. The stone carving was beginning to move, the lines snaking and twisting and scribbling themselves into new patterns. The mist was flooding more powerfully than ever, growing deeper and darker until it was almost purple. The whole room swam with ghastly shadows as the lines altered and the new light shined upon the ghoul.

"Mrs. Robinson?" the voice said again, louder this time and almost as clear as if it were spoken from within the room.

"That's Claire's voice," Noah said. "It was her cat, and she must have been thinking of her, but I don't know why we can hear too."

"What's the light? What's going on?" Brandon demanded.

Noah shrugged helplessly, but Jamie was quick to interject. "He's casting a spell, that's what. He's going to melt your faces off if you don't get out of here."

"Yeah?" Brandon asked, stepping back uneasily. "How's he going to do that?"

"She's lying!" Teresa said, trepidatious. "Where would he learn to do something like that?"

"He's a Chainer, stupid," Jamie replied. "He learned it in another life—I've seen him do it. Just you watch."

The mist was so thick that they could barely see the silhouettes anymore, but they could tell from their shadows that they were hesitating.

"There's something else out here," Walter said. "Something in the mist that wasn't there a second ago."

"He's still got the key!" Teresa insisted. "Take it from him!" Her voice was fainter now, little more than a shouted whisper.

"I'll leave the window open, okay?" Claire's voice came again, so close and real it made them all jump. "Just in case."

The purple light at their feet vanished, as did the circle. They were left blind in the mist which had begun to whip around them as if they stood in the eye of a hurricane. It was dissipating though, blowing off in every direction as it went.

"...and don't worry, because I won't be mad that you've been gone all this time," Claire said. "I won't even ask where you've been. I'll just be happy to see you again, okay? So please, if you can hear me... Please, come home."

Noah, Walter, Jamie, and Mrs. Robinson were now standing in a tight huddle in the center of a bedroom. The last of the mist vanished to reveal yellow sheets, curtains, and a bright blue carpet. Claire, dressed in a white night gown was staring out the open window, apparently oblivious to the whole scene which was unfolding right behind her.

"Claire?" Noah asked in disbelief.

She turned from the window and seemed to look straight at him for a moment. The instant was insubstantial though, and a moment later she'd climbed back into her bed. She didn't see them after-all. Neither did she notice Mrs. Robinson who had leapt onto her bed and curled on the pillow beside her. The cat's fur had settled along its back, and a contented purr was rising from deep within it.

"Where are we?" Walter asked, stepping away from the others to explore the surroundings.

"A long way from The Mortuary," Noah said. "The Daymare departed not far from here."

"That was over a seven hour drive!" Jamie protested. "Or walk, or scuttle, or whatever the Daymare did. But that's a long way!"

"How do we get back?" Walter asked, sounding so disheartened that it was hard to believe he'd just escaped a ravenous ghoul.

"Look, the circle is still there!" Jamie said, pointing at the faint outline indented within the carpet. "You never told us the Whispering Room could send us to where people were thinking about us too."

"I had no idea," Noah said. "Professor Salice! What if he cursed the room to transport me so he can find my family?" Noah spun in rapid circles, checking for imps in all the dark corners of the room. "The blue mist was something he did before—I'm sure of it. What if he's here too?"

"Calm down, Noah" Jamie said. "Professor Salice didn't even know we were in the room."

"Unless Brandon told him," Walter said, inspecting the board games stacked on a chair beside Claire's bed.

"It's not going to work," Noah said, pacing in agitation. "I'm not going to visit them. I'm not even going to look at them. He's never going to know which ones are Chainers."

Noah stopped suddenly mid-stride, then turned to walk straight through the bedroom door.

"Where are you going?" Walter called. "We need to figure out how to use this circle to get back."

Even as he spoke though, the circle had continued to fade. The subtle imprint was almost completely gone.

"I know someone who we can talk to, and she might be able to help," Noah said. "Her name is Samantha. She's not a Chainer, but she got attacked by a gargoyle and now she can see spirits."

"What about Mrs. Robinson?" Jamie asked in dismay. The cat was nestled against Claire and showed no inclination to follow.

"What about Claire?" Mrs. Robinson asked. "She's been looking for me this whole time. I'm not going to leave her again."

"You have too," Jamie said. "You need to go to school."

"I don't *have to* do anything. It never felt right, being in school. Everything I want is already here."

"But she can't see you! Please come with us," Jamie insisted, distraught. "She won't even know you're there."

"I'll know," Mrs. Robinson said matter-of-factly.

As if in response, Claire cuddled closer to the cat, her arms passing straight through it without seeming to notice.

"I'll make sure Samantha tells Claire that you're back," Noah said.

"We can't just leave her though!" Jamie pouted. "I'll miss her so much."

Mrs. Robinson didn't reply though. She was only purring.

"It's where she belongs," Noah said reassuringly. "I understand because part of me doesn't want to go back either. Sometimes it's hard to tell the difference between what is familiar and where we belong though, and I don't think the rest of us will find that until we're alive again."

QARI OLANDESCA ILLUSTRATIONS

THE NETHERWORLD

"I thought I might see you again," Samantha said, "though I liked you better as an old man. You're too skinny and weird looking now."

Noah jumped. He thought he was going to be the one to surprise her, but he hadn't seen her standing outside her house in the darkness. She was dressed in pajama bottoms and a purple sweatshirt which was drawn tight against the sharp night air.

"What are you doing out here? It must be past midnight!" Noah exclaimed.

"Does it matter? Were you worried about me?" she asked innocently.

"Why would I be worried about you?" he asked. "I'm the one who is dead. I just mean that most little girls wouldn't be standing alone on the street after midnight."

"Thank you," she replied, even though Noah hadn't intended it as a compliment. Her milky white eye almost glowed in the moonlight as though drawing focus to the fact that she was not a typical girl after-all. "You're being rude though. I know you aren't used to having any friends so you might not know how it goes. You're supposed to introduce me."

"Right, sorry," Noah said. "This is Walter and Jamie, and we've all gotten sent back here by accident and —"

"Oh, I know," Samantha interrupted. "That's why I was waiting here for you."

"Hello, Samantha," Jamie waved.

"What happened to your eye?" Walter asked. Jamie elbowed him in the ribs and he muttered something indistinct under his breath.

"What happened to your body?" Samantha shot back without losing a beat. "Hello, Jamie. Hello, Walter. Let's all go inside, or else someone will drive by and try to kidnap me."

She turned smartly and opened her door, leading them in.

"But how did you know we would be here? We didn't even know we'd be here," Noah said, hurrying to keep up.

"Mr. Hampton told me," Samantha said. "We've become good friends, although my parents don't like it when I talk to the spirits. They think I'm going crazy. I tried to reassure them by telling them I was crazy long before the incident with my eye, but that only seemed to make matters worse."

"Hello Noah! How has your death been treating you?" George Hampton was sitting at the kitchen table with a cup of deliciously steaming cocoa in his hands, although closer inspection revealed that his fingers were overlapping with the corporal cup. He wore the same waistcoat and pinstriped hat as Noah had seen him last, although that was hardly a surprise as laundry was one of the burdens that spirits have left behind.

"Fine, thank you," Noah said guardedly. "How did you know I was coming tonight?"

"A little bird told me," George said, trying to lift his cocoa mug, then scowling as it remained on the table. "Well, not exactly a bird. Quite a lot uglier, in fact."

Something bumped under the table. The scratching of little claws along the edge, followed by an imp's leering face poking into view.

"He's been keeping an eye on you for me," George added.

"I told you not to let those in the house!" Samantha scolded. "The last one tore up my mother's under clothes and she blamed me for it. If she catches that thing in here I'm going to—"

"You'll what, exactly?" George asked mildly. "Make me wish I was deader?"

"I'll catch a thousand spirit spiders and drop them down your back," Samantha declared ferociously.

"Oh dear," George sighed. "We do need him though. He'll be leading our friends back to school through the netherworld. Better be quick about it too."

The imp disappeared beneath the table once more, and Walter squatted down to watch it chew on the base of the wooden table.

"Salice really did send us here then?" Walter asked. "And you knew?"

"Clever lad," George said, a touch of pride in his voice. "The Whispering Room is a nexus where the three worlds meet. It's typically restricted to verbal communication, but it would seem your Professor altered it to allow travel as well. Do you have any of his possessions with you?"

"I don't think so…" Noah began.

"The key!" Jamie said. "You never gave it to Teresa, did you?"

"Quickly now, let me have it," George said, extending his hand. Noah obliged. "Dissipati," George declared, causing the key to glow red hot. The metal bubbled and ran into a silvery liquid which trickled through George's fingers. Just before it vanished completely, a small puff of blue smoke separated itself to dissipate into the air.

"Hey! I might have wanted to use that," Walter protested.

"As I thought, the blue you just witnessed was a tracking charm. Destroying it is necessary to prevent him from tracking you further, although we were too late to stop him from knowing where you are now. There won't be any living people here thinking of Salice, so he won't be able to establish a link through the Whispering Room either. That means he will be making his own journey through the netherworld to join you here. If he left shortly after you, then he should be here..." George casually checked his golden wristwatch, "in about ten minutes."

"But but—" Noah spluttered, unable to decide which of his thousand questions to ask first. "How do *you* know that Salice is trying to find my family? How do you know any of this?"

"Ca'akan here," George gestured to the imp. "Your professor isn't the only one who can summon them. He's been looking after you for a while.

The imp bowed sheepishly, his tiny claws interlocking behind his back. He garbled something in his own language.

"He'd also like Walter to know that he's glad he started wearing the stone he gave him. He says he was scared going undercover with the rest of the school imps, but Walter made him feel welcomed."

The imp covered its face with its claws and ran around behind the table to hide.

"I've been suspicious ever since the gargoyle attack, and Ca'akan has been helping me to understand," George Hampton continued, tapping his nose. "I nose all sorts of things, and my gut guesses many more. I found it interesting that the gargoyle went after Samantha rather than you, although it makes sense when you consider that she was the one looking at it while Noah purposefully averted his gaze. That makes me think that the gargoyles are hunting psychics and Chainers and only got Samantha by mistake."

"Is the gargoyle still looking for them?" Noah asked.

"Your daughter was smart enough not to stare at spirits, and the gargoyle never figured out that she was a Chainer. I haven't seen it in some time so I presume it has continued its search elsewhere. Did you ever tell Salice when or how you died though?"

"No, I don't think so..." Noah said.

"Good," George continued rapidly, his fingers dancing a silent but erratic rhythm on the table. "In that case he only knows that someone was thinking about you somewhere around here. That's plenty of obscurity to shield them. Enough dawdling, you must be off."

George stood and vanished straight through the wall. The imp followed at his heels, running face-first into the kitchen cabinets. George leapt back through the wall and turned for the door instead.

"Enough to shield them?" Noah asked. "Do you mean—"

"Quite so," George replied, vanishing through the door. Samantha opened it and they all chased him back onto the lawn. "If he is the one sending the gargoyles, then the reasonable thing for him to do is kill your daughter and her son.

Well, maybe not the *reasonable* thing, but certainly the likely thing."

"But why?" Noah demanded. "What does he need Chainers for?"

George stopped suddenly to consider this, and the imp following him rammed against his legs. "An excellent question. Rest assured I will be investigating. Oh, and one more thing…"

George's hands were rhythmically weaving through the air as he spoke, leaving soft trails of light wherever they went. Noah recognized his white ring which radiated the light, now understanding it to be the bone of George's physical remains.

"My imp told me about the affinity," George said quietly out of the corner of his mouth. "I'd keep that a secret if I were you."

"That was your imp too!" Noah exclaimed. "So, Professor Salice doesn't know."

"He might," George conceded. "Professor Humstrum may have told The Matriarch, and she might have discussed the matter with him. But it's more important that the other students don't know. I daresay you already have enough trouble fitting in being a Chainer."

"And a murderer," Walter added.

"I knew it!" Samantha declared happily. "Well I didn't *know* know, but that's pretty cool all the same."

"You think so?" Noah asked.

"As long it's a people murderer," Samantha said. "I wouldn't even mind being friends when you come back to life. Of course, you'll be a baby though, but I can be your teacher or something. Won't that be fun?"

"How come you can hear us?" Walter asked, looking as

confused and flustered as the rest of them. "If it was just your eye—"

"You notice all kinds of things when you start paying attention," Samantha cut him off. "Do you want to know how spirits smell?"

"Now, if you please," George Hampton said. The light from his hands blew outward into a nova to suspend an erratic circle in the air. The space surrounding the circle seemed to shimmer and melt, while the area within had darkened to black. Walter walked around the floating circle suspiciously, peering at it from every side.

"Follow the imp back to the school," George said, "and make sure it's the same imp, mind you. Ca'akan is missing one of the ridges on his back just below his head. Follow the wrong imp and you could very well end up all sorts of nasty places. Oh! and one more thing," he added, blocking the hole with his arm as Ca'akan tried to crawl inside. "Try not to touch anything in the netherworld. Even if it touches you first."

George removed his arm to open the way. The imp chittered something which sounded like it would have been mortally insulting if Noah could have understood, The imp crawled inside and continued crawling as though it had entered a tunnel, not emerging on the other side of the hole.

"What do you mean 'even if it touches you first'?" Walter grumbled, although no-one paid him much mind.

"Can I come too?" Samantha asked.

"The netherworld is dangerous enough for spirits, but a living body would be killed almost immediately," George Hampton dismissed.

Samantha shrugged. "That's okay. I don't mind."

"Well, your parents would," George said.

"They'd get over it," she quipped.

Noah put his hand through the hole and recoiled immediately. It felt like he'd just stuck his hand into a pool of cold jello, and his fingers still tingled after he'd removed them.

"Well, come and visit again soon then," Samantha said. "George and I will keep an eye on your daughter for you, so you've got nothing to worry about."

"Thanks," Noah said. "Tell Claire that Mrs. Robinson is back with us. We left her sleeping on her pillow."

"Do we really have to leave Mrs. Robinson here?" Jamie asked. "Claire won't even be able to pet her!"

"You don't really have to do anything, because it's not really your choice," Samantha replied. "Mrs. Robinson has made her own decision."

Noah took a deep breath, closed his eyes, and plunged headfirst into the cool abyss, leaving the two girls glaring at each other behind. There was an initial shock as he slid into the gelatinous space, but almost immediately it became an incredibly comfortable feeling. Every movement felt controlled and deliberate, and the soft pressure around him seemed to mold around his body like a perfectly fitted wet suit. It was completely dark with his eyes closed, and Noah spent several lazy seconds floating through the timeless space before he heard the first sounds.

Chittering, slurping, smacking lips. It was the same type of sound he'd grown accustomed to from the imps, but it was greatly magnified as it traveled through the gelatinous space. The sound reminded Noah of a time he went snorkeling and heard the echo of dolphins communicating through the water, only this was much more powerful and emanated from every direction at once. The next shock was realizing that even though his eyes were closed, he could still see Ca'akan waiting just ahead, as well as Walter and Jamie crawling along behind.

Noah's first impression of the netherworld was that it wasn't his first impression at all. His second impression was that it was the most magnificent sight he'd ever not seen.

What at first appeared as empty darkness now resolved itself into an infinitely textured space filled with overlapping layers and shades. He felt like he was on the inside of a giant paper origami that was folded and twisted upon itself into maddening abstraction, yet he also had the sense that if he could only see the place from the right angle it would be clear that it wasn't abstract at all and that every line and crease was exactly where it needed to be.

"Where's the light coming from?" Jamie asked, close behind. "One second it feels like it's pitch black, and the next it's all lit up, and then it's black again without anything even changing."

Jamie's voice sounded thick and slow and incredibly low pitched here. No wonder the imps chittered, Noah thought, as those sounds seemed to carry more easily.

"There is no light," Noah replied, unsure of his words until he said them, "but you don't need light to see here. The part of your brain that processes the seeing is interacting directly with the environment. Try and 'see' something behind you and you'll understand what I mean."

"That doesn't make any sense," Walter complained, his voice even more thick and syrupy.

"It does to me," Noah said, effortlessly turning and flipping while the others struggled to swim and catchup. It was difficult to distinguish directions in this vacuous world, but Noah had the distinct feeling that they were going upward.

"I hate it," Walter moaned. "I feel like a soggy vegetable floating in soup."

"The soup isn't so bad," Jamie said, turning in a slow circle. "It's the noises that bother me. I can't tell how close they are or what's making them."

Noah concentrated on the sounds, and gradually he became aware of dark shapes slipping through the nether around them. None came close enough to be clearly distinguished from the textured background, and he decided his friends would be happier if he never mentioned them at all. He contented himself to study his surroundings in silence.

Flocks of small shapes that could be imps pulsed in rhythmic motion to an unfelt beat like schools of fish riding the tides. Other serpentine things circled around them, so long that they completely encircled the travelers despite seeming a long way off. There were other solitary creatures that followed them curiously for a while, but most soon lost interest and swam away.

Walking, crawling, and swimming all seemed to have a similar effect in the netherworld. The three students alternated between different forms of movements as they struggled to follow Ca'akan. Progress was slow and the imp often looked back impatiently at them, but at least it provided ample time to get used to the new environment and the altered sense of blind perception.

Most interesting of all were the subtle shifts in the textured background at the edge of awareness, like distant mountains which briefly reared or sighed, changing the landscape with the slightest change of position. Noah tried to imagine something like that in the living world, but it was difficult to guess their true scale in this place where perspective and distance were so hard to judge.

A much closer chittering caused Walter to make a little gurgling yelp, but it was only Ca'akan who had paused to wait for them.

"Hold still," Noah said automatically.

"Not happening," Walter said. "I'm not spending a minute longer here than I have to."

Ca'akan made a short, sharp squeak.

"Don't talk either," Noah said softly. "Not until it passes."

The nether had gone silent. The demons had stopped chittering, the flocks of imps dispersed, the long serpentine shapes breaking their circles to flee. The silence had a force of its own, uninterrupted even by the draw of breath or a beating heart that would accompany any such living encounter. Embedded in that silence was the unmistakable sense that they were not alone.

It was difficult to understand what was approaching because there was nothing to see and nothing to hear. If Noah's mind really was interacting directly with the environment, then it wouldn't have been any of his known senses which tracked the being. It was a deeper part of his mind, the activation of an animalistic impulse that he'd forgotten was even there. This feeling was not an interpretation of a sensation, nor a conscious realization of danger, nor even a reaction to an imagined outcome—this was the raw fear of a screaming mind, and here in the netherworld it had a life of its own.

Walter opened his mouth, but Jamie slapped a hand across his face. A moment later something like a shadow passed over the group. Noah could only associate the feeling with swimming with a sea monster slowly rising from the depths.

Noah's body prickled with a thousand freezing needles. It felt like his brain was replaced by a block of ice, and his thoughts felt rigid and immovable. He had the most unnerving instinct that if he tried to force himself to think in that moment then his entire mind would shatter into a thousand pieces and trickle out through his ears.

Noah was vaguely aware that Walter and Jamie were shivering uncontrollably behind him. He had to reassure them that everything was going to be okay, but he couldn't make sense of the words in his head, let alone work his locked and rigid mouth.

The feeling continued to grow more intense for the next few seconds, until Noah was so numb that he couldn't tell whether he was awake or asleep. The pressure of a suppressed scream was building in his chest, but he couldn't let it out even if he wanted to. The pressure became so great that he felt he would be ripped apart if he had to hold it any longer, but a moment later it began to subside once more.

The shadow was lifting, slowly swimming away from them. Already Noah's mind was beginning to sluggishly stir back to life. Jamie had calmed considerably—she might even be unconscious as she floated peacefully with her eyes closed. Walter did not share the same tranquility, and even though the chill was fading he was trembling worse than ever. Walter's head was flopping back and forth as though his neck had no bones in it at all, and his fingers were convulsing as though his life depended on clutching onto something that wasn't there.

"It's almost over. It won't hurt you," Noah said quietly as soon as he was able. At least, that's what his mind had instructed his mouth to say. Somehow the message was scrambled in transit though, and what he actually said was a burst of short, harsh, grating syllables that sounded like metal saw blades clashing against one another.

Jamie jolted suddenly as though just waking. "You can speak demon?" she asked.

"Of course not, it's gibberish," Noah tried to say. The sound that came out was comparable to a brick in a clothes dryer. He clamped his mouth shut and covered it with his hands.

Jamie wasn't the only one to notice either. The shadow which had almost completely passed was now stopped, and the icy needles were beginning to intensify once more. It was aware of them for the first time.

Ca'akan squealed in the universal language of terror and hurled itself through the nether. Jamie needed no translation. Walter had gone completely limp however, except for his head which continued to thrash from side to side. Noah surged back through the nether to grab a dangling arm, and Jamie snatched the other to drag him along.

"Wait for us, Ca'akan!" Jamie gurgled with as much strength as she could muster. The imp was barely more than a silhouette scrambling away from them as fast as it could.

The nether parted smoothly before Noah as he bent his entire body into pursuing the imp. Jamie was struggling mightily to match his pace, and it didn't take long before Noah had to drag both her and Walter behind him. All the while the icy feeling was growing once more, threatening to sap what remained of his strength, his will, and the very instinct which begged him haste.

"Where's he gone?" Jamie slurred, her pace slackening once more.

"This way," Noah said. "Ca'akan is just ahead, don't stop now."

The truth was that Noah couldn't sense Ca'akan either though. The imp had completely vanished, and it was all he could do to follow where it had been and not allow Jamie to give in to despair. If they stopped for even a moment, that would be enough to realize they were lost in an alien world with no way of finding their way out again. Just a moment, and the shadow would pass over them and freeze their bodies and minds into surrender. Already these thoughts were beginning to slow as Noah's brain stiffened with cold, when—

A short squeal, just on the other side of a great gray wall which loomed ahead. Noah shot forward dragging Walter and Jamie behind, prepared to slam straight into the barricade if there was no other way to escape their silent pursuer. The distant chirping and chittering from the demons rose in a feverish pitch as Noah sped forward, each sound closer with more intent than the last. Straight into the gray mass, and then through as if it were no more than a soap bubble.

Noah tumbled straight onto a stone floor and sprawled out on the raised dais inside the Whispering Room. One of his hands was still firmly clutched around Walter's limp wrist, and he had to laboriously drag his friend up through the stone floor with Jamie scrambling after him. The circle below their feet was blazing with light, its interior a dark tunnel like the one they'd entered from the living world.

Ca'akan shrieked like mad, flinging itself around the empty room like a child having a tantrum. The hole in the ground was constricting rapidly after they had all exited, but Noah couldn't resist dropping to his hands and knees to peer back inside one last time. That was the first time he got a good look at the shadow.

He was surprised to see that it was not much larger than himself, since its presence had seemed like a looming leviathan beside them in the nether. It bore a generally humanoid shape, although the gray rubbery skin looked like it would be more at home on a seal than a person. The most striking feature was its face though, which was long and sharply angled. There were no eyes or nose, only a single fleshy toothless mouth which the chill seemed to be emanating from.

Noah braced, half-expecting it to make a final lunge and drag its way into this world before the hole had closed. The creature drew itself all the way up the ground, but it never went any farther. The mouth made a few wet smacks, then gave Noah a wide and sloppy grin. Next Noah knew, he was staring into the hard stone floor and the light from the circle had faded.

"Shut up, you little monster," Walter growled at Ca'akan who was still throwing itself around the room. "You tried to leave us behind!"

Jamie began to scold him, insisting that he be grateful to the imp who had, in her opinion, saved their lives.

Noah shivered involuntarily and pulled himself off the floor.

"Are you okay, Noah?" Jamie asked, eyeing him critically.

"Yeah," he said, relieved to hear human words coming from his mouth once more. "Just rattled, that's all."

"Did it say anything to you?" Walter asked. "Right before the hole closed up, it sounded like it was talking."

Noah furrowed his brow, unable to get the wet smacking out of his head even if he wanted to. "Yes," he said at last, forming the word deliberately with his mouth.

Jamie and Walter looked at one another, then back at Noah. They waited several seconds, but he didn't say anything more.

"Noah?" Jamie asked, tentatively. "You understood Ca'akan

when he was warning us. You never told us you could speak demon. What did it say?"

But Noah shook his head, unsure himself. "I couldn't speak demon. I still can't, I only understood Ca'akan while I was in the netherworld. I'd already exited by the time that cold thing spoke though, and it didn't make any sense to me either. Probably just an idle threat or something though."

Noah didn't believe that though, even as he was saying it. He felt that the creature had been trying to say something specific, and that it had been directed at him. The thought alone was enough to make him start shivering again.

QARI OLANDESCA ILLUSTRATIONS

VISOLOTH

Professor Salice was not pleased with Noah the next time they met. He wouldn't allow him to ask questions anymore during his time as his apprentice, and he kept Noah in that small glass summoning room for hours. There were so many more demons that needed summoning than usual, but Salice was never willing to explain what they were being summoned for. The ones who appeared rarely satisfied him, and he always blamed Noah for catching such weak, scrawny demons.

Noah now realized that his mind was floating in the netherworld when he played host for the new demons. Sometimes when he sat in the circle and the demonic images flooded his mind he would hear them chittering and understood isolated words and phrases, but the moment they were summoned away from the nether he was unable to comprehend anything but the vaguest intention. Despite searching his textbook thoroughly for an explanation, he couldn't find any mention of anyone understanding demons at all, and Salice refused to comment on his own ability.

Professor Humstrum's class became considerably more enjoyable as it neared the end of the semester as he held true to his promise not to test the students. While necromancy and demonology were filled with tables to memorize and cram sessions for the finals, transhumanism had moved to the bestiary where the students were allowed to directly interact with the spiritual creatures.

The whole class was jealous of Jamie who was the only one allowed to ride the temperamental manticore. She stroked its mane tenderly and attributed their bond to her affinity for cats, although Walter thought it was more likely that she was only tolerated because she fed it and cleaned up the environmental disasters it left in the sane. None of the spiritual creatures consumed corporal bodies, but that didn't stop it from draining a small bucket of aquamarine stones every night. Professor Humstrum proudly declared that it ate almost an entire month every single day, but the trans-dimensional department gladly paid its salary in case they ever needed it in war.

More than any class or test, what was first in everyone's mind was the upcoming Christmas break. The Matriarch had announced that the Daymare would be back to bring everyone to the living world so they could spend the holiday with their families. She warned that it wasn't easy to celebrate Christmas with a family that was still mourning their loss, but most of the students were excited all the same.

Walter decided that he would rather not go back to watch Natasha and her new boyfriend, although he was still looking forward to seeing his parents and his two brothers once more. Jamie remained adamant that there was nothing left for her to return to though, and Noah was glad to have the company as he had no intention to give Professor Salice another chance to follow him anywhere.

"You think you're being a hero or something?" Jamie asked when Noah told her his intentions to stay.

"What's that supposed to mean?" Noah asked, ripping up a fistful of fresh grass to scatter to the wind. They were sitting together on one of the hillocks overlooking the other students who boarded the Daymare below. It would have been a dark, moonless night but for the whirling will-o-wisps. The Daymare lazily swatted at them with its numerous legs.

"By staying away from Mandy," Jamie continued. "You think they're really better off if they never see you again? If your daughter can see spirits, then she's going to wonder why she can see all of them except you. She's going think you don't love her."

"You're one to talk," Noah grunted. "I don't see you making much effort."

"I'm not a Chainer," she countered, leaning back onto her elbows to look up at the sky.

"What's that supposed to mean?"

"I mean my family and I had just met," Jamie said. "We were a couple of random souls who found each other then went our separate ways. If Chainers are so rare, do you really think it's a coincidence that there could be two or three in one family?"

"I hadn't really thought about that," Noah said, shrugging. He wanted to change the subject, but he couldn't find the words. Talking about his family just left him with a great, empty pit inside.

"Well, I have," Jamie said matter-of-factly. "I think you've been helping each other come back to life through the years. When one of you is dead, you protect the other ones. Then the dead one comes back as a child, and it's the other one's turn to protect them."

"I'm not coming back as my daughter's son," Noah said decisively. "That would be too weird."

"How so? When did your mother die?"

Noah fell back onto the grass as well. The way the dark clouds were layered reminded him of the netherworld, which was never far from his thoughts anymore.

"Before your daughter was born, I bet," Jamie continued, "about six years before."

"Six and a half," Noah said after a moment to do the math. "How'd you know?"

"It takes six years to graduate from The Mortuary," Jamie said. "Did she die around March?"

Noah sat rigidly upright, looking down at Jamie suspiciously. "March 10th."

"There you go then," Jamie said, as though that proved everything.

"There I go what?"

"It took six months to wait for a new semester in August, then six years in school before she graduated. Mandy isn't just your daughter, she's your mother too. And what about her son, Lewis?"

"Lewis isn't a Chainer," Noah said cautiously, his mind spinning as he double-checked the numbers.

"As far as you know," Jamie said. "When did your father die?"

"About ten years ago," Noah said. "A little less."

"Six years for school, plus... how old is the boy now?"

"I haven't always been human," Noah replied, feeling flustered. "Whatever family line you're imagining isn't real. If you're trying to convince me to go visit them, then it's not going to work. Even if we did share multiple lives together, then that's even more reason not to put them in danger now."

"They're already in danger," Jamie said gravely. "How long do you think it will really take Salice to figure it out? There will have only been so many people who have died in your area within the last year. He can do the math, same as me, and sooner or later he's going to narrow it down. If you really want to protect them, you're going to need to do more than pretend they don't exist."

"I'm not going back," Noah repeated stubbornly. "I can't do anything for them there."

"Then do something for them here," Jamie insisted. "We can tell The Matriarch —"

"That her star teacher who revolutionized demonology is secretly plotting to kill my family? Fat chance she'll believe me."

Jamie leapt to her feet and began rapidly brushing the loose grass from her clothes. "If not, then we need to *make her* believe you. We need to find out what Salice wants more Chainers for so we can have proof, and I know how to get it."

Noah was on his feet too—Jamie's excitement was contagious.

"The only question is, how are we going to get Visoloth alone in the nether where you can understand him?"

～

"THAT WAS A STUPID THING TO DO," Professor Salice said with a crisp voice like thin ice. "I wish I could say that I was surprised." He leaned back in his leather chair (which was stitched together from at least a dozen different kinds of skin), and steepled his thin fingers together in contemplation.

This was the first time Noah had been in Salice's office, and the demonology professor seemed even more menacing in his own element. The will-o-wisp here was locked in a small wire bird cage where it darted back and forth in restless agitation, causing the thick shadows of the room to constantly shift. Noah tried not to look at the cruel array of nameless bladed devices lining his shelves, or listen to the ceaseless whispering which emanated from stacks of hefty books. Visoloth was curled in apparent sleep beneath Salice's desk, looking almost like a normal dog now that its mouth was closed.

"You're right, I'm sorry," Noah said, forcing a tremor into his voice. "I thought visiting my daughter would only be hard on us both, but this will be her first Christmas alone and..." he allowed his voice to trail off, half-surprised to feel how naturally his voice cracked. Was he really doing this for Mandy? Or was he putting her in even greater danger to satisfy his own suspicions?

"The Daymare won't be coming back," Salice said, studying Noah's face intently. "You're sure the Whispering Room is quiet?"

Noah hoped his face was inscrutable as he replied, "Yeah, it's been quiet for a while. That's part of why I'm so worried. There was only a connection last time because Claire was calling for Mrs. Robinson, but Mrs. Robinson didn't come back with us after we fell through. So I was hoping Visoloth would take me through the nether to let me visit my family that way."

Professor Salice's already tight face strained further in a motion Noah had come to recognize as a smile. "Passages through the nether are not pleasant affairs, even for seasoned demonologists. You may have traveled that way in ignorance before, but you must be desperate to attempt it again."

"Please, sir," Noah said. "I'll do anything to spend Christmas with my little girl again. I thought that maybe because I was your apprentice, and you've been kind enough to help me before that…"

Salice's face slackened. The will-o-wisp darted backward once more, casting him into deeper shadow so that only the slits of his red eyes colored the darkness. Had Noah gone too far? Salice wasn't known for his kindness anywhere in the school, and their tense relationship in the past would only heighten his suspicions. The wisp was back to the front of the cage though, and Salice was smiling once more.

"Today is your lucky day," Professor Salice replied. "It has always been my intention that you should see your family again, and I'm not disappointed even though it has taken you so long to come to your senses. Visoloth!"

The demon dog opened one eye which focused laser-like on Noah. He had the unnerving feeling that it had only been pretending to be asleep this whole time. A single inquisitive tentacle poked from its mouth to taste the air.

"You know the way, don't you Visoloth?" Salice asked, stroking the dog's rough hide with his foot.

Of course, he does, Noah thought. *You were tracking me the whole way there, weren't you?*

Visoloth made a wet, slurping sound as the tentacle retracted into its mouth. Salice nodded, finding this satisfactory. "Very good. You will take him through the nether to see his family for Christmas. You will then wait until he's ready to return, no later than the resumption of the new term, and then you will lead him back again."

Visoloth cocked its head to the side, listening intently.

Then it looked at Noah, letting its mouth hang loose to let its full dozen tentacles slide out and twist through the air. It let out a long, gurgling howl.

"Those are your instructions," Salice said cooly. "If I need them to be altered, I will tell you as such. Now stand."

Noah was only too happy to slide his chair back, eager to be away from his professor. He knew that Visoloth could not break its contract and disobey a direct order, but that wouldn't be a problem. Even if he had to travel all the way back to his hometown, he could still say he was ready to return immediately without interfering with the directive.

Salice was already drawing a circle of light into the air, opening the way into the nether. Noah couldn't help but notice that the lines Salice conjured were considerably cleaner than George's had been, and that the circle was large enough that Noah wouldn't have to crawl this time. The light seemed to be focusing on his professor's cufflinks—small bones that must have once been part of his long-discarded corpse.

Visoloth sat upright to attention, its eyes still fixed on Noah while the circle was being drawn.

"You're doing the right thing, you know," Professor Salice said as the interior of the circle darkened to black. "Actions have reactions which have their own reactions, and even the wisest have trouble understanding where the final piece will fall. Although today it seems that you are only facing your past, you are facing your future as well, setting a course of history whose ramifications will far outweigh these small steps today. I am pleased that my apprentice has begun the path of his own mastery."

Those words sounded genuine, but they were poison to Noah. Salice was already gloating about his perceived victory.

Even now he might have been imagining Visoloth attacking Mandy and ripping her son from her arms. Noah swallowed hard, refusing to allow himself to react to the image. "Thank you, sir," he replied stiffly. "May I go now?"

Salice waved his hand dismissively and made his way back around his desk to sit down. He looked strangely small and tired as he slumped over the wood. Visoloth paced around the floating circle twice before bounding inside. Noah paused only a moment to consider the weary figure before stepping into the circle to return to the netherworld.

The cool welcome of the nether slid around his body in an encompassing embrace. The dull, chittering echos filtered through his consciousness once more, and as the circle closed behind him he became suspended in the vast nothingness that felt like home.

Visoloth made a gurgling sound which Noah understood to mean "Follow me".

"Not yet," Noah replied. "I didn't come here because of a deal with Salice. I came to make a deal with you, Visoloth."

The dog paused and sat down, despite there being nothing definite to sit on. It twisted its head from side to side. "I already have a contract," Visoloth replied. "Come."

"I'm not talking about a contract. I need to know something about your master."

Visoloth stood and began to pace a circle around Noah, its mouthful of tentacles stopping just short of brushing against him. Noah remained still and fought against his instincts to draw away. It was impossible to read the demon's monstrous face. Was it curious that he could understand it? Would it attack him for his impudence? Was Salice listening through its ears somehow even now?

"I do not make deals with students," Visoloth said slowly.

"I wasn't always a student," Noah replied with more confidence than he felt. "I can understand you, can't I?"

Visoloth was behind Noah now, but he could perceive it as clearly as if it stood in front of him. He felt one of the tentacles slide along the back of his knee and then slither down his leg, leaving his skin tingling as though charged by electricity.

"Does Salice know that you once lived as a demon?" Visoloth asked. "I'm sure he would be interested to know."

Was it a threat? There didn't seem to be any malice in Visoloth's tone. While a human voice might disguise itself with many subtleties, the speech of a demon felt more like a bond between the minds. Noah could only hope that Visoloth felt the same connection and allowed itself to trust him.

"Not unless you tell him," Noah said. "One secret deserves another though, don't you think?"

"What do you want to know?" Visoloth asked.

"He needs hosts to summon something," Noah guessed. "Regular students don't have heavy enough souls though. He needs Chainers, more than one of them. He needs me and my daughter."

"That wasn't a question," Visoloth replied languidly. It began to groom itself with its tentacles.

"That wasn't a denial," Noah shot back. "What does he want to use us for?"

"It wasn't a denial," Visoloth consented. "You mentioned a deal. I'm still listening."

"I can help you become human too," Noah said. "I've done it before; I know how it's done."

There was a long silence between them where only the distant echoes of the nether floated past. Visoloth had stopped grooming itself and was staring at Noah once more.

"You're lying," Visoloth replied.

"I'm not," Noah insisted. "It might still take some time before I've figured it all out, but I used to know, and I'm remembering more all the time. If anyone can do it, it's me."

"Why would I want to bother with being human?" Visoloth asked, turning a lazy backflip through the nether as though to prove how content he was. Noah understood its voice as implicitly as he did his own thoughts though, and he could feel the strain behind the calm it sought to portray.

"Because even when you're set free, you'll never be treated like the other spirits," Noah said. "People don't trust demons. Even if you go back to the nether, there will always be a bigger fish in the pond. You'll always be living scared of whatever else is out there. But once you're human, you can come back as anything. You can be free."

Visoloth didn't reply. Its face was inscrutable, seeming to have already figured out how well Noah could read its speech. The longer the silence stretched on, the more aware Noah was of the magnitude of the gamble he was taking.

If the demon decided not to take his deal, then it could immediately report to Salice and tell him everything it had learned. Salice would know that his game was up, and he'd have to resort to force to learn where Mandy and Lewis were. Noah's mind went unbidden to the many bladed instruments lining Salice's shelves and he tried not to imagine what creative and deranged uses they might have.

"You're cheeky," Visoloth replied at last. "Arrogant, even. You should have stayed a demon. No more sure than Salice though; there is nothing in our contract to forbid me from telling his secrets because it never occurred to him that someone could understand them."

"It's a deal then?" Noah said hopefully. He inwardly cursed himself for sounding so eager, but he was also keenly aware of the vastness of nether around them and didn't want to delay in this place any longer than was necessary.

Visoloth had completely circled Noah several times, but now he had stopped directly in front of him. "What's it like, being human?" he asked. "Is it worth it?"

Of course it is, Noah thought. But the thought of trying to explain exactly how was more daunting than he expected. To explain what it was like to be alive—to feel yourself grow and learn—the warmth of falling in love—the pride of helping someone achieve something they never thought was possible. And yet reconciling that with all the doubt, and regret, and grief of loss that all sounded unpleasant until you lived it, before you realized life wouldn't have been worth living without these things giving life meaning.

"What is so great about being alive?" Visoloth hissed, its words trailing away at the end to leave the heavy thought floating beside them in the nether.

"Do you remember the first time you were summoned into the spirit world?" Noah asked. Visoloth said nothing, so Noah continued. "I guess you were so used to being in the netherworld that you thought that's all there was. Then you set foot in the spirit world and suddenly reality got bigger than you could have ever guessed. There were more things to see, and more to discover, and more spirits and histories and cultures—more than you could have ever guessed existed when you only lived here."

Visoloth cocked his head to the side, silent.

"But you were still a demon—an outsider—and seeing it wasn't good enough, was it?" Noah continued. "No-one could understand you, and you weren't allowed to do all the things that the other spirits were doing. It won't be like that when you're human. When you're human you aren't just watching the show—you are the show. You can do everything that can be done, and learn everything that can be learned—you can spend your whole life finding out more about life, or you can find one thing you love more than anything, or one person you love more than anything, and spend all your days with them. And once you're done you'll get to live again as something else and everything will be new again. Being alive is the best thing there is, because the world is only as big or as small as what we think is possible. And everything is possible only when you're alive."

"I want that..." Visoloth growled. "Very well, I will hold you to our deal. You are correct in your assumption that Salice needs at least two Chainers to host the demon he wishes to summon. The Rasmacht would destroy any single mind which tried to contain it. Even Salice cannot claim to control such a creature."

"The Rasmacht?" Noah prompted hesitantly.

"You've met it once before, on your way back from the living world," Visoloth said. "I watched it chase you back to the Whispering Room. Professor Salice wants to summon it into the spirit world. We best keep moving though, unless you'd like to risk meeting it again. I still received a direct order to take you to the living world, and that's what I intend to do."

"That cold thing?" Noah said, swimming hastily through the nether after Visoloth. "What could Salice possibly want with that?"

"The Rasmacht is only ever summoned for one reason," Visoloth said, "which is why it is better known as 'The Soul Eater'. Those consumed by it are gone forever, not leaving even so much as a shade behind. Every life they've ever lived, every life they ever will live, all erased so that no one will remember they've ever been. The Matriarch will be devoured and all her teachings will be undone. She who has claimed to have lived a thousand lives will cease to exist, and every soul she has ever painted will shed her colors. Now, where was that exit to where your family lives?"

QARI OLANDESCA ILLUSTRATIONS

THE MATRIARCH'S WRATH

When Noah was a child, he used to believe that good and evil existed. There were noble knights and champions of justice who fought the brigands and cheats, always conquering the wicked. Not one of his favorite stories contained a darkness so dark that it could continue to exist when the light was shone through it.

As he grew older, he wasn't so sure anymore. Even good people did things out of pure self-interest, and even evil men had their own principles and people that they loved. He figured that everyone was doing the best that they could in a mixed-up world, and that even when they were cruel to each other, they were only doing so as reflections of their own pain.

Now more than ever he decided that evil must exist, and that its name was Zandu Salice. The Matriarch had devoted her entire existence to helping souls come back to life, yet Salice was planning to destroy her and steal her teachings from the myriad of souls she had touched.

Visoloth didn't know exactly why Salice was set upon this

path, but Noah didn't think such heinous act could ever be justified. Perhaps he was jealous of her power, perhaps he wanted to run the school himself, or even preferred that demonology was the only lesson to be taught. Salice made no effort to hide his disdain for the *'lesser domains'*, especially reincarnation, and it was no great leap of faith to assume he'd abolish them altogether if he was in charge.

"You know he's watching you, right?" Visoloth asked, rousing Noah from his thoughts. They had arrived at a folded corner of nether, a pocket of space that Noah had come to recognize as an opening into the living world.

"Yeah, I figured," Noah said. "You've brought me here, that was your job. You were also ordered to bring me back when I was ready."

"Not even a step into the living world? Not even going to say hello?"

"It's too much of a risk to bring him that close," Noah said. "I want to go back now."

"He won't be happy to see that," Visoloth said. "He'll know something is up."

"He'll know anyway. We need to hurry," Noah said. "You're not afraid of him, are you?"

"I'm not afraid," Visoloth said, pacing restlessly before the folded nether pocket. "Fear is just the anticipation of danger. I have been in danger since I spoke to you, and it is no greater now. We will run together, on my count. We must be well on our way before he realizes what has happened if you ever want to make it back."

"I'm ready," Noah replied, grinning despite himself. It felt good to have his suspicions proven, even though it was to his detriment. A known enemy was so much more reliable than a suspected one.

"Three, two, one," Visoloth said, coiling its body in preparation to spring. "Let the fire in your soul give wings to your flight."

And they were away, the nether flowing against them without dampening their speed. The omnipresent chittering seemed to grow louder, and dark shapes began to curiously orbit their race. It felt so liberating to hasten through this void, and Noah couldn't help but swerve and soar for the pure joy of the infinite feeling.

Visoloth kept a direct course as straight as an arrow. His legs sprang ceaselessly forward as though he ran on solid ground. Watching him, Noah realized that with concentration he too could harden the nether around his feet and thus launch himself more effectively forward. He still preferred a swimming motion though, as that made him feel like he was flying.

"Stay straight," Visoloth called.

"I am! Basically. I'm keeping up with you."

"Our destination is directly ahead. If you are facing even a few degrees off, then you won't find it."

"I've got you to follow," Noah replied stubbornly, twirling dexterously as the nether rushed over him.

"Seven minutes, directly this way," Visoloth said. "The pocket you're looking for will have three folds in a triangular shape, each lighter than the last. That will take you directly to The Matriarch's chambers."

The severity of Visoloth's tone gave Noah pause. "You're coming with me all the way, aren't you? Everything looks the same here, and I don't think I'll find it —"

"He's here," Visoloth interrupted. "I'll take you as far as I can, but I cannot overpower my contract. As soon as he catches up with us you must not trust me anymore."

As if in answer, a booming crack rippled through the space. The nether stirred chaotically, rising up into waves which beat against Noah and disrupted his flight.

Visoloth stopped dead as though rooted in place. Noah slowed too, but Visoloth roared with a ferocity quite unlike his usual calm tone. "Get away from me! As much distance as you can!"

Noah oriented himself against the turbulent waves of nether and pushed onward, aware once more at the enormity of the space around him. If he wasn't going exactly the right way, then it would be only too easy to get lost forever in these endless folds.

"Visoloth!" boomed Salice, his voice deeper and more powerful than it had ever sounded in the spirit world. "The boy is escaping! Hunt him down."

Visoloth's effortless grace which Noah had admired before transformed into a predatory and lethal blur. The demon was lunging and bounding through the nether behind, his tentacles flailing from his mouth in ravenous anticipation. Noah hadn't realized that Visoloth was moving slowly before in order for Noah to keep up, but now the demon was gaining swiftly.

"Three folds, triangle," Visoloth panted. "Don't stop. Don't watch me. You'll never escape if I catch you."

Noah had never gone faster in his life, but it wasn't fast enough. He couldn't help but watch Visoloth closing in as his awareness extended even behind him. Every passing second brought those grasping tentacles closer. Soon one was already brushing against his ankle. Noah surged away from it, snarling in pain as a ragged patch of his skin tore free to remain attached to the suction cup.

"Faster!" Visoloth howled. "I'll have you next time."

"Stop him!" roared Salice. "Rabie!" Again the nether bucked and heaved in response—an underwater storm in an alien sea. The ripples were spreading throughout the nether, smothering the chittering sounds which encompassed them. A moment of terrible silence, then all the sounds came back at once, this time with a screeching intensity that sounded like the whole world had turned against him.

The dark shapes at the periphery of Noah's awareness were now swooping in from every side. Flocks of imps, rubbery Lava Salamanders, fleshy Gobblers, and others of more hideous deformation which Noah couldn't recognize. Serpentine creatures slipped smoothly through the nether, open mouths lined with razor teeth which gnashed their way toward him. All the while screaming, gurgling, bellowing, frothing with frenzy born of the impetus of Salice's command.

Three folds, a triangle, that must be it ahead. But the escape seemed so far that Noah would never reach it in time. Already he could feel the tentacles snaking their way around his ankle once more, this time securing a stronger hold with dozens of suction cups latching against his skin. If he pulled free this time he might have to rip his entire foot off.

He wouldn't stop though. Couldn't. He strained against the implacable grasp, dragging Visoloth's whole body along as he staggered onward. Another tentacle latched hold onto his other calf, dragging him to an almost complete stop. The demons swooped and shrieked in from every direction. Three folds in a triangle—unobtainable far —now blocked from view completely by a thick mass of imps which swarmed over one another and bit each other to be the first to descend upon him.

The sight was too horrendous to bear, but even closing his

eyes did nothing to shield him from the churning madness around him. He was forcibly aware of each grasping claw, each slimy tooth, each razor spine, all converging on him from every direction. Helpless, terrified, and utterly alone, Noah called out for the last thin hope which he could conjure.

"Rasmacht!" Noah called, funneling all the power he had into one desperate shout.

He might as well beg a wild lion to help him against a pack of wolves, but there was no denying that the name had power over these teeming creatures. "Rasmacht, Rasmacht, Rasmacht!" His shouts were obdurate, the word cutting through the frenzy and giving pause to even the most ferocious of the flock. Even Visoloth's vise grip seemed to have slackened for a moment. What was this thing that could inspire such fear with the first mention of its name?

"Seize him!" Salice commanded. "There is no Rasmacht."

The demons shook themselves as though breaking from a spell and began to converge once more. They had barely begun to move again before a familiar numbing chill stole over Noah's senses. Whether summoned by his call or simply curious to the commotion, the Rasmacht was here. No command could overcome the blind panic which set into the teeming masses at the arrival of the soul eater.

The imps broke first, shrieking and scattering in every direction like a flight of startled birds. Demons tore at one another as they crawled over each other to escape, and Noah braced as the swarming things dug into his body to push away. Salice was shouting something, but Noah couldn't make out the words over the commotion. A shock of pressure released as Visoloth relinquished his grip to bound howling back the way he'd come.

In a matter of seconds Professor Salice was clearly visible

turning in an angry circle in the nether, his strained face contorted in anger as he shouted at each fleeing demon. He completed the circle to face Noah once more, his red eyes boring into the boy.

"You don't understand," Salice growled. "Your daughter isn't doing any good in the living world. You must let me kill her."

Three folds, in a triangular shape. Noah had to focus. His mind was already so cold that his thoughts moved as ponderously as a glacier. The Rasmacht had idly floated into view, its toothless mouth gaping like a whale filtering the ocean. Webbed fingers and toes spread luxuriously through the nether to propel its sleekly closer. Noah pushed away and drove his body toward the exit.

"I won't let you!" Salice bellowed. "You are my apprentice, and you will do as I say. I order you not to—"

Noah flew headfirst through the pocket and tumbled onto something hard. A stone floor. His skin prickled with the shock of exiting the nether, and his body wouldn't stop trembling.

"Goodness me," The Matriarch said, quite bewildered. She was sitting on the other side of the room in a generously cushioned armchair with an open book on her desk. Will-o-wisps floated idly around her to illuminate dark wooden bookshelves stuffed with dusty leather volumes, each shelf rising so tall that it curved at the top to meet in an arch without spilling the books. There was a real fireplace in the corner, although it was only inhabited by another pair of wisps which lazily chased each other in slow circles.

Noah jolted upright and turned to see the hole into the nether closing swiftly behind. He barely had time to rise to his feet and leap out of the way before Professor Salice came tumbling after him.

Noah pointed a trembling finger at the Professor. "He's trying to kill my family!" Noah shouted as soon as he could fill his chilled lungs.

"Calm down, you look like you've seen a ghost," The Matriarch replied, her voice warm and patient. "Professor Salice would never—"

"He needs more Chainers to summon the Rasmacht. He wants it to eat *you*!" Noah spluttered, diving away as Salice snatched at his leg from where he lay sprawled on the ground. A moment later and Visoloth bounded through the hole and fell into an immediate crouch, ready to spring.

The Matriarch snapped her mouth shut and narrowed her eyes. She lifted the book from her lap and set it calmly on the desk in front of her. "Is this true, Zandu?"

"Preposterous…" Salice moaned, lifting himself unsteadily to his feet. "Who would believe such a thing—"

His words were interrupted by a loud smacking sound. Just as the hole to the nether was closing, a blank rubbery face rose into view. It continued floating past through the nether, giving everyone a clear look into its toothless mouth before the hole completely closed with a pop.

"Thank you, Noah Tellaver," The Matriarch said softly, not taking her eyes from Salice as she spoke. "I see that you have gone through considerable personal risk to warn me. You will find that I do not forget those who have been loyal to me. *Nor forgive those who have not.*" Her voice completely changed when speaking this last line, twisting into something cold and biting.

Salice scowled ferociously. His fingers began to dance

through the air, a new glowing circle stitching itself into existence.

"I wouldn't do that if I were you," The Matriarch said with iron in her voice. "The Rasmacht will be waiting for you."

Salice's fingers fumbled for a moment, and his circle of light dissipated into a sparkling nova. His eyes darted to The Matriarch before beginning again with redoubled focus. The old woman rose from her chair.

"I'm speaking to you, Zandu," The Matriarch said. A casual flick of her wrist prompted hurricane force wind to lift Salice straight off the floor and slam him into the stone wall behind. He crumpled to the ground like a marionette doll with severed strings. The circle of light he'd been spinning flared briefly with defiance before being extinguished by the torrent.

"Visoloth! Attack her!" Salice demanded, prompting the dog to release its tension and lunge through the air. As soon as his feet left the ground that same wind flared to life and knocked him spinning. Both dog and master collided violently by the force they were helpless to resist.

"You cannot silence us," Salice hissed. "You will not survive another purge." Then to Noah, his stretched eyes wild and pleading. "Don't walk the road from death while that woman is—"

The Matriarch was smiling a thin, shallow smile while he spoke, but she didn't let him finish. She blinked twice, and when she opened her eyes the second time Noah could clearly see the glowing skull beneath her flesh. Dazzling white diamonds rested in place of where her eyes had been. The stones seemed to gather all the light in the room until nothing was visible except their piercing brilliance. Noah heard Salice scream powerfully for a second, but he couldn't see what was happening and the sound cut short a moment later.

One of the diamond eyes flared even more brightly. It flashed blood red in stark contrast to the other shining as a star. Light was returning to the room once more, but Noah still had to blink away the spots as though he'd just been staring into the sun. The Matriarch stuck one of her fingers behind the red diamond and popped it out of her eye socket. She blinked twice more rapidly, this time revealing her old eyes back in place once more as the glowing skull faded from view. When Noah's vision fully returned, he stared in disbelief at the empty stone floor where Salice had lain a moment before.

The Matriarch rolled the red diamond in the palm of her hand and smiled down at it. "There we are," she said with satisfaction. "He won't cause any more trouble in there, now will he?"

"What did you do to him?" Noah asked.

"What *didn't* he do to Mandy and little Lewis?" The Matriarch asked sweetly. "That's the only question that matters, don't you think?"

There was something about the way she asked the question that made Noah think she didn't really require an answer. The Matriarch opened a drawer in her table and dropped the red diamond inside. It might have been Noah's imagination, but he thought he heard the faint echo of Salice's scream as she did so.

"Heel, Visoloth," The Matriarch said without glancing. The demon had just been regaining its feet and a low growl began to rise in its throat. "Heel!"

The wind stirred again and the dog was flattened to the floor. It pulled itself painfully upright once more, but did not rising beyond a sitting position.

"Better. You will be taking orders from me now, do you

understand?" The Matriarch told it. "Salice served at my pleasure, and by extension you and all the other demons will think of me as master. I will not release you from your contracts early."

Visoloth looked expressionless at Noah for a moment before bowing its head. Noah couldn't help but feel as though he'd betrayed it somehow, but shouldn't it be happy that Salice was gone? Being free from his power hungry dominance should be a victory for all of them.

"I suppose I'll be needing a new demonologist," The Matriarch reflected, sighing. "Halfway through the year with no notice, what a shame. I might have to even teach the class myself. Would you like that, Noah?"

"Yes ma'am," Noah said automatically. He gauged that to be the correct answer by The Matriarch's enduring smile.

"Yes indeed," she said, "but then is only a poor man's now. Have you been staying here over Christmas just because you were trying to protect your family?"

"Yes, ma'am," Noah repeated, eyeing the writing desk where Salice's soul was bound.

"You dear suffering soul," The Matriarch sighed again. "Well, you did the right thing, and now you have nothing to worry about. There's no reason for you not to spend Christmas with them anymore, is there?"

"No, ma'am."

But Noah couldn't meet those eyes which had been diamonds a moment before. His gaze found excuses to look everywhere else: the towering books, the drawer with a soul inside, the stained-glass windows now dark without the faintest glimmer of moonlight to give them life. And finally, to the stone gargoyle with the upside-down smile sitting motionless in the corner of the room...

He supposed he should feel like a hero, but heroes must be surer of themselves than Noah felt now.

"You must be worn thin, you poor thing. Why don't you go rest in the graveyard? First thing tomorrow evening, I'll collect you for the journey home. You'll be spending Christmas Eve with your family again, isn't that marvelous? It will be a happy reunion all around."

"Yes ma'am," Noah said, bowing his head and feeling like Visoloth as he did so. He caught the writing desk again out of the corner of his eye—had it just rattled? Or was that only his imagination?

He didn't just feel worn thin. He felt worn away completely, with nothing left inside.

QARI OLANDESCA ILLUSTRATIONS

CHRISTMAS

Noah didn't see Jamie in the graveyard that night. The burden of all he'd seen weighed heavily upon him and he couldn't wait to tell her everything. She must have an opinion about what the gargoyle in The Matriarch's office meant, and why Salice had used his last words to try and warn Noah about the road from death.

Without an easy answer, he forced himself to refocus his thoughts on Mandy and Lewis and how good it would be to see them again. Would his grandson have grown in the months since Noah had last walked the earth? Would his daughter recognize him this time, even though she now appeared old enough to be his mother?

Fortunately, Brandon had left with his mother to check on how their money was being spent so Noah didn't have to worry about another run in with him. The graveyard was almost entirely empty, although he did see Bowser and Elizabeth Washent sitting close in private conversation as he made his way to his mausoleum. It was strange to think that a dog and a rabbit had enough in common to forge a friendship, but it's not like she would have much in the way of family to go home to. Bowser might have visited the family who had owned him, but Noah could only imagine how hard it would have to watch them getting a new puppy on Christmas morning.

Noah climbed on top of his mausoleum where he'd grown used to sleeping to avoid Brandon. It seemed that Noah had barely closed his eyes before the red glow of the setting sun pierced his eyelids.

"Don't you use your coffin?" The Matriarch asked, immediately rousing Noah. It took Noah a few tense seconds before he could locate the origin of her voice as she had been sitting completely still on the moldy gravestone of an alumni. She was wearing a long dress the color of the night speckled with real twinkling stars which looked exactly like someone had taken a cookie-cutter to the sky. How long had she been sitting there watching him?

"I hope you at least use your stuffed tiger," she added. "I make those myself, did you know? Not all the stitching, mind you, but I *did* cut out your jaw and put it inside. It's always tricky figuring out which part of the body to hold onto, but I just had a feeling that you'd feel more comfortable with it. There's nothing like a bit of body for the soul to feel at home, don't you think?"

Noah was very fond of his tiger, but The Matriarch didn't stop talking long enough for him to say so.

"No home like home either though. You are ready, aren't you? Of course, you are, why wouldn't you be? It must be a relief not having to worry about Salice anymore. You'll never understand how sorry I am for bringing him to this school, but I suppose that's what I get for trusting someone who consorts with demons. Shall we be off then?"

"Will we be going through the nether again?" Noah asked with trepidation. The Rasmacht had come so quickly last time that Noah had the unnerving feeling it had been waiting for him. He couldn't even think of the place without remembering what it felt like to be engulfed in all the grasping, clawing, biting...

"Of course not," The Matriarch said disdainfully. She rose from the gravestone and dusted off her already pristine dress. "It is nothing short of abdication of duty to allow a student to travel somewhere so dangerous. No, we will be traveling by Whispering Room, as is the only T.D.D. approved method for teleportation."

Noah expected The Matriarch to explain how the Whispering Room functioned as she led him through The Mortuary, but she either didn't think he needed to know or took it for granted that he already did know. Considering that Professor Salice had been operating behind her back, it was unlikely that he had told her about his previous visits. Considering that Brandon had been terrorizing him with a ghoul at the time, he probably hadn't recounted the expedition either.

"Is it unusual for there to be a whole family of Chainers?" Noah asked as they walked.

The Matriarch didn't turn to look at him as she continued her brisk pace. "Chainers themselves are unusual. However when they are found, it isn't uncommon for them to be found together. It's no easy feat finding your way back so many times without losing yourself in the process, and we all need a little help sometimes."

The cathedral was still dark as most of the wisps were still asleep, but The Matriarch snapped her fingers to prompt a pair of them to leap into the air and begin to orbit her. She held the door to the stairway open for Noah and smiled at him as he passed.

"It's convenient of course for humans to pretend all souls are the same size, but they don't really believe it. Insects are killed without hesitation, chickens and fish are slaughtered in mass, but try and do the same with a dog or a horse and you'll have people up in arms about the sanctity of life. They find it quite acceptable to eat intelligent animals like pigs, but teach that same pig how to paint, how to perform tricks, how to dance—they can learn, you know—and suddenly its soul becomes a little too big to destroy. A genius composer weeping over his music has a doubtlessly heavy soul, but who can even compare that to the drug-addled youth whose mind can barely grasp his own name?

"Mind you, I'm not saying that humans are correct in their imagined hierarchy of souls, merely that they believe it whether they like to admit it or not. The fact is that your average sea sponge can lead a more fulfilling life than a human who is always bitter about one thing or another. You have no idea how many complaints I've received about using the weighing ceremony to turn students away, but even the smallest souls have a chance to grow during their lives. Those which do nothing to add to their weight can hardly justify being alive at all. I'm sure a Chainer such as yourself can appreciate that."

"I haven't really thought about it," Noah replied honestly. "I've never thought of myself as any more important than anyone else."

"But you do still surround yourself with other Chainers," The Matriarch said, opening the door onto the fifth floor.

"Maybe it's just because I love them."

"Ah ah ah, but would you still love them if they had shallow souls?"

"Id love them anyway, all the more because I only had one life with them instead of many," Noah replied defiantly.

The Matriarch looked at him with either pity or disappointment, perhaps both. "This iteration of you is still young. You'll know better when you get back to your old self. Come though, no matter. Let's find out if your daughter is still thinking about you."

Noah followed The Matriarch into the Whispering Room, his brow furrowed in thought. He didn't like the way she had said that, as if there really was a chance that Mandy had forgotten him already.

The sight of the glowing blue circle chased away these bitter thoughts though, and bounding onto the dais he could hardly wait for the whispering to begin. The instant both his feet had crossed the line in the stone he was met by a wave of blue mist and those sweet words.

"My little boy looks so handsome in his new coat. Dad would have been so proud to see him now."

And a moment later, Noah really did. The mist grew thicker and deepened to purple. It twisted sinuously in the air until two little hands were clearly visible. A moment later and Lewis' face resolved from the air, scowling fiercely down at his generously padded winter jacket. Larger hands appeared, a woman—Mandy, it had to be Mandy—stuffing a warm red and black trooper hat lined with thick brown fur onto the boy's head.

"Don't like it," Lewis muttered. "Wanna be cold."

The red light of the circle was pulsing, growing brighter with each cycle. Lewis and the rest of the mist began swirling around Noah, distorting his image. The Matriarch stepped into the circle and laid her hand on Noah's shoulder.

"You're coming with me?" Noah asked, momentarily setback.

"Of course, I am. How else did you plan to get home, my silly bumpkin?" she replied patiently.

Noah had no time to protest. The swirling mist had turned to a storm, flashing around them so wildly that each image was torn apart the moment it had formed. The Matriarch clutched tightly to Noah's shoulder, her long nails digging slightly through his t-shirt into his skin.

"Is Papa coming too?" Lewis asked. There he was in the flesh with bright red pudgy cheeks, right in front of Noah. The rest of the room spun into place as the mist dissipated in every direction.

"Papa isn't..." Mandy began, her voice vaguely trailing off. She had her own winter coat on, caramel colored and padded with large black buttons down the front. A black cap was pressed onto her head that did little to hide her wispy golden hair sprouting out at all angles. She stared vacantly at Noah, her eyes not quite focusing, her brow lightly drawn.

They were standing in an unfamiliar modern house with great glass windows. Shining steel shone with harsh white light in the kitchen behind them, everything looking new and sterile and cold. Mandy turned away from Noah and refocused her attention on putting Lewis' boots on.

"Your father is going to be home any minute, and he'll expect you to be ready," she said. "He doesn't have much time tonight, so we mustn't keep him waiting."

"Mandy?" Noah asked, the word coming out as little more than a breath.

"Papa!" Lewis declared excitedly, seemingly oblivious to

the fact that Noah only appeared to be a boy himself and looked almost nothing like the grandfather the boy once knew. Lewis rushed to Noah and tried to hug his legs, but he sailed straight through and tumbled to the ground.

"Enough with this silliness," Mandy said sternly. She passed through Noah to force the second boot onto Lewis' foot. "Papa is in the happy place, remember? He isn't coming tonight."

The Matriarch meanwhile had peeled off to snoop through the kitchen. Noah caught her eye for a moment, but she quickly looked away as though fascinated by the double oven.

"You can see me, can't you Mandy?" Noah asked, louder this time. "I'm right here. I'm sorry that it's taken me so long to visit and I know I don't look like you remember, but just wait until you hear about…"

Mandy passed straight through Noah a second time on her way to the kitchen counter. She retrieved a sleek black purse with a golden buckle, her hands trembling slightly as she did so. She paused, looking lost as though she'd forgotten what she was doing. Then nodding to herself, she passed through Noah again and joined Lewis by the door.

"He should be here any minute," Mandy said, her voice thin and strained. "Please stop wandering off."

Lewis had been walking toward Noah once more, but Mandy had seized him by the shoulders and turned him back toward the door.

"Papa's coming?" he repeated.

"No, baby," Mandy said. "I want you to stop asking that."

Noah squatted down to Lewis' level and looked him in the eye. "I want you to tell your mother that my spirit is here, alright? I've come to spend Christmas with you both."

"Mommy—" Lewis began.

"I heard him," Mandy said sharply, her attention focused on the door. "He isn't your Papa. Remember what your father said: only crazy people talk to spirits. We aren't crazy, Lewis, and we won't let anyone think that we are. Your father takes such good care of us, but he wouldn't love crazy people. We aren't crazy. We're normal. Perfectly. Perfectly normal."

The door opened and Barnes Horton stepped through smiling. His thick black beard made him look much older than when Noah had seen him last before Lewis was born. His dark hair was short and cleanly cut, and he wore a well fitted dark suit with a deep burgundy tie. Noah had seen zombies with more life in their eyes than his cold grey stare which didn't alter in the least when his mouth smiled.

"Not waiting too long, I hope?" Barnes asked, swooping in to kiss Mandy. He then hoisted Lewis into the air, prompting the boy to giggle madly at his flight.

"We'd wait for you forever, dear," Mandy replied smoothly. "Do lets hurry though. I feel like I've been cooped up in the house all week."

"Forever isn't nearly long enough," Barnes said through his perfect teeth. "I would wait forever and a day."

"Forever and two days!" Lewis squealed.

"I can wait here too," Noah said from behind her. "I won't touch anything—I can't, obviously, but I won't cause any problems. Then when he's not around we can—"

"Enough waiting! Let's all *leave*," Mandy said, putting particular emphasis on the last word. "Please," she added, casting Noah a glance for a fraction of a second.

"But Papa—" Lewis started to whine, barely getting the word out before Mandy gave his arm a tight squeeze. Barnes looked instantly suspicious as his mouth pressed into a hard, thin line.

"Peppa Pig and all your other cartoons can wait until you get home," Mandy interrupted at once. "We're going to enjoy Christmas Dinner with your other grandparents." She avoided Barnes' probing eyes and exited immediately, holding Lewis by the hand. Barnes swept the house with his grey eyes before turning to follow them out the door.

Noah felt like he was watching a dream, powerless to interact or even wake from the sight before him. He wanted to say something more, but by the time his wits had returned the door had already closed. He rushed toward it, but a hand on his shoulder caused him to lurch to a halt.

"Easy there," The Matriarch said, her voice sweet and soothing. "It isn't uncommon for the dead to carry the living longer than the living carry the dead. It isn't your place to force a burden onto those who cannot bear the weight."

"I'm not a weight," Noah said, pulling away from her. "She's still my daughter and—"

"—and her life is with him now—"

"Not by choice," Noah interrupted back. "He left her. She's just afraid, but she doesn't have to be because I'm here and..." his voice trailed into silence.

"...and you're going to take care of her?" The Matriarch prompted. "You're going to build her a house that she can live in? You're going to hold her when she's sick and help her down the stairs when she's old? There's a reason not many of the dead continue dwelling amongst the living."

"She can see me," Noah said, the words sounding flat and useless even as he said them.

"She can see a boy she's never known," The Matriarch replied. "She can see lots of spirits every day. Some of them talk to her, others torment her, others just watch and say nothing. And none of them help her in the least. You must remember what that's like."

"I'm not going back," Noah said. "Even if she doesn't want to talk to me, I can still be here with her. I can get to know her all over again. And I can talk to Lewis when he gets older, and we'll be friends and he'll think we're the same age."

"Do you really think that would make his life easier than if he had living friends? Or is that just something you want for yourself?" The Matriarch asked.

Noah didn't answer. He didn't trust himself to open his mouth without screaming in frustration.

"You're a Chainer, Noah," The Matriarch said gently. "You are destined to live again, but you can't do that here. You must be diligent in your classes and find your way back the right way. By then maybe Lewis will be all grown up, and he'll have a son of his own. You can be part of his life forever and ever, but you must know deep down that it is not yet time."

"I hate Barnes," Noah said. "I can curse him, can't I? Or get that witch to make him into a voodoo doll."

"If that would make you happy," The Matriarch said. "I can't imagine that it would be what's best for Lewis or Mandy though, do you?"

Noah said nothing again, finding more validation from nursing the seething fire within him than anything that could be said.

"Let's go home," The Matriarch said, already drawing a circle of dull yellow light on the ground around them with her cane. "Your new home, for as long as I am the headmistress and you are my student. The past cannot be made more beautiful by the present, but the future can be."

Noah kept his silence as the circle flared into life. Mist was beginning to come from somewhere again, and Noah didn't do anything to resist as The Matriarch laid her hand on his shoulder once more. The mist became a hurricane, and he was swept away back into the Whispering Room. The room of false hope and lies, that Noah swore he would never enter again.

QARI OLANDESCA ILLUSTRATIONS

SPRING SEMESTER

Noah was far from the only one to be disappointed with his Christmas break. It was with considerable satisfaction that Noah witnessed Brandon's despondent return, as it turned out a large portion of his fortune was "wasted" on charitable donations. Grace Horlow wouldn't stop blubbering about how few people attended her funeral, and Jason Parson lamented to everyone who would listen that his lazy son had immediately dropped out of medical school which he'd apparently only attended to please his father.

The only one who seemed to be in really good spirits was Walter who had been to visit his brothers. They had held a Christmas Eve candlelight vigil in his honor, and he was downright boastful about seeing his normally stoic family still in tears over his untimely demise. Jamie, on the other hand, was unusually quiet and self-reflective, although she was briefly animated by Noah's description of how Professor Salice had vanished into a diamond.

On the positive side, the results of last semester's examinations were completely discounted. The Matriarch announced that Professor Salice had chosen to resurrect over the holidays before he'd even graded his tests and that she'd decided to start over with a fresh start.

Likewise, Professor Wilst's exam, for which Noah had been unable to even get his zombie to walk in a straight line without staggering drunkenly into a wall, had been invalidated upon the discovery of contraband in the classroom. An anonymous tipster had disclosed the unfair use of mermaid skulls, and as the Professor could not decipher who was thus aided, had decided to grant everyone a pass. No one's body was to be used for the class' entertainment this time, although Wilst declared earnestly that the same leniency would not be granted next semester.

The next section fortunately required considerably less anatomical percision as it dealt with poltergeists. These beings consisted of a spiritual body that was devoid of a soul and were formed by a deep emotional imprint upon the world.

"Anger is the most common," Professor Wilst told them. The corpses that had once been distributed on the metal tables had been replaced with ceramic urns which had to be tied down to keep them from rattling off the table. "Poltergeists can be formed by any strong emotion though, like an echo which lingers after the soul has departed. In fact, I once met an especially ardent poltergeist which continued making love to the deceased's living wife every night after his death. I was working as an exorcist for the the T.D.D at the time and was dispatched to assist her, but she turned me away insisting things were fine the way they were."

Despite the students being primarily composed of the middle aged and elderly, that didn't stop them from giggling in response like the children they appeared to be. Noah was especially surprised to see Teresa stifling back laughter, although she stopped and coughed as soon as she met Brandon's glare. It seems that she had been in a considerably better mood than her son ever since his return from Christmas.

Professor Humstrum's class had become more enjoyable as well, as it had moved past the theoretical aspect of affinities and moved to the practical implementation of test-driving animals.

"Before you decide which animal you'd like to return as, I highly recommend spending as much time as possible viewing the world through its eyes," Professor Humstrum said, gesturing to the rather confused great horned owl perched on his wooden podium. It kept swiveling its head and staring at each student in turn as though trying to decide whether or not they were real.

"Each week the class will have the company of a different animal," Professor Humstrum continued, occasionally adjusting his orange beard to ensure the finch that lived there remained hidden from the owl. "While it is extremely advanced magic to dominate the mind of an animal as a Dweller might, it is rather simple to enjoy a ride as a passenger. While inside the animal's mind you will not be able to dictate any actions or even read the animal's thoughts and feelings, but you will be able to experience its senses. Only one student will be able to do this at a time to avoid giving the poor creatures headaches, however, so the rest of the class will be continuing from the textbook while waiting their turn."

Noah didn't even have to turn to recognize the squeal of excitement coming from Jamie.

The most expansive change of curriculum doubtlessly came from demonology. The Matriarch made good on her threat to teach the class herself, and waiting beside her were a towering stack of new textbooks which she distributed to the class as they arrived.

"I must say I was most disappointed upon a closer review of Professor Salice's previous lesson plans," The Matriarch said, sighing mightily to reinforce the fact. "I would have thought that a book titled *'Twelve Signs Your Imp Might Be Plotting To Kill You'* would have more appropriately warned of the *dangers* of demonology, but it turns out that the book was as deceptive as he was. I read it cover to cover over break, and there's hardly anything in here about the righteous purges or forced demonic mutations at all!"

The new book was considerably thicker despite its smaller print. The title read: *'The Forbidden Fruit: Demon Do's And Don'ts'.* As soon as Noah sat down and flipped it open to the table of contents it was clear that the *Don'ts* category comprised the much larger portion.

"Let me begin by correcting his teaching as clearly as I can," The Matriarch said. "Demons are not your friends. They are not your pets. They do not have souls. They may seem to have individual personalities, but they are no more their own entities than your arms and your legs are independent creatures. All demons are made from the nether, and to the nether alone they belong. We may borrow them for a time and bend them to our will, but they are all threads from the same fabric. They are not owed any more consideration than a shovel, or a teapot, or any other tools we use for our convenience."

Noah had to bite his tongue to keep from protesting. Of course they had souls—otherwise where was he supposed to have come from? And the way the other demons had scattered when the Rasmacht appeared—they wouldn't have done that if they weren't afraid of their soul being eaten. The Matriarch was looking directly at Noah now, but he turned his eyes away to pretend to study the textbook.

"Yes? The boy with the shaved head?" The Matriarch asked sweetly.

"It's Rachelle," Rachelle Devon responded, unfazed. "Professor Salice said we were going to be taking turns as hosts to summon imps this semester. Is that still going to happen?"

"Goodness, no," The Matriarch said. "We already have more demons than we know what to do with. The late professor seems to have been summoning far more than were required for service in the last stages of his term. Besides, Zandu was the only one here who knew how to write the contracts in demonic. By next semester we might get another so versed in the *profane* art, but contracts typically last for ten years so it's not exactly essential. A much more useful understanding of demons can be derived from a *historical perspective*."

Several more hands appeared in the air, but The Matriarch had already begun reading from the textbook, showing no signs of stopping. One by one the hands dropped, and she spent the rest of the class reading about the purge of 1940. Her account was considerably different than that of Professor Salice, who had said the purge was a politically motivated persecution.

This textbook described the purge as a necessary emergency response to a demonic uprising. The consensus of cited scholars was that this was proof that demons cannot be trusted to ever be free. The innocent victims were certainly in the thousands—tens of thousands by some accounts—and this number only increased as the T.D.D begin to fight back. The whole incident was later disguised as a genocide instigated by humans, and the offending demons were permanently banished so that no summoner could ever bring them out of the nether again.

The effect of The Matriarch's lessons were not limited to the classroom. The imps working at The Mortuary quickly became a favorite scapegoat for every unfinished assignment or lost item. Of course, it didn't help that the naturally mischievous imps really had stolen their fair share of personal effects over the course of the previous semester, and all sorts of things were turning up now that they were being actively pursued.

With each passing class, the harmless pranks the imps once played were seen with more vitriol and the students were beginning to respond in kind. Brandon, who was once scorned for his abusive behavior, had begun to gather a small following of his own. Dolly Miller, the girl who had killed herself, as well as Jennifer Alaska and a tall boy with a Jack'o lantern grin named Kyle Thrope were often seen together now, jeering and laughing as Brandon hurled stones and clods of dirt at the scampering imps.

Noah did his best to stand up for them, but as the weeks wound on he found himself spending more time alone and trying not to get involved. When he'd first attended the school, his mind was scattered with worries about his family and the distractions of this new world, but now more than ever he had a clear goal in mind: to return to life whatever way he could. He studied in the library late into the morning when the rest of the graveyard was heavy with the dreaming dead, resolving not to get distracted in the social dramas and intrigue that kept so many others away from their work.

While the necromancy class advanced with poltergeists, Noah asked for and received special permission to return to his zombie after class. He practiced until he could animate it fluidly enough to pass the physical portion of the field sobriety test administered to drunken drivers. He devoted the time once spent on being Salice's apprentice to studying some of the professor's old contracts, trying to decipher the meaning of the arcane symbols.

Even his transhumanist studies received extra attention. He had no intention to return as an animal, but there was no telling where a hidden insight might be that would aid in his rebirth. Professor Humstrum said that a comprehensive understanding in all fields would provide the very best chance at another life.

The heavy snow of winter had given into the reluctant thaw of spring by the time Noah made his next great breakthrough. He had been sitting in the empty demonology classroom copying one of Salice's contracts when he realized one of the symbols was familiar to him. This wasn't unusual in itself, as he had continued to slowly recall bits and pieces here and there from his previous life, but this particular symbol of the bottom quarter of a sun with a small door inside had appeared on every contract he'd encountered so far.

He flipped through the pile of papers on his desk and located the symbol on each, always on a line of its own. Closer inspection revealed that these were always drawn in a slightly different shade of red than the rest of the contract, indicating to Noah that they were either written at a different time or with a different type of blood entirely.

The Matriarch's new textbook had no translations for demonic, so he brought out Salice's old one and flipped through it for the hundredth time. Even here translations were limited, and no amount of scanning or restless pacing gave him the least satisfaction. The meaning was floating at the back of his brain somewhere, but the more he thought about it the more elusive it seemed. He was sure that it meant something crucial, but additional effort only translated into additional frustration at its secret.

Head in both hands, Noah would still his mind in quiet meditation hoping the answer would shout itself from up high, or down low, or somewhere deep within, but such a shout never came. On one such occasion his concentration was disrupted by a shrill screech. The harpies were going off again, but unlike their usual alarm there were two distinct words clearly audible amidst the noise.

"Noah Tellaver. Noah Tellaver!" they screeched.

Disconcerted, Noah abandoned his work and made his way to the demonology door. He had only just touched the handle when the screech sounded again.

"Matriarch's office. Bring the contracts." *Screech.* "The contracts!"

Noah scanned the room, searching for a sign that he was being watched. The light of the overhead will-o-wisp glittered against something high on the upper reaches of a bookshelf against the wall. Standing on a chair to inspect more closely, it looked like a white diamond, very much like the one The Matriarch had plucked from her eye. The light dimmed for a second as he stared at it—no not dimmed. *It blinked.*

"Noah Tellaver! Noah Tellaver!" the screech began again. Noah hastened to scoop the pile of papers under his arm and ascend the helical staircase toward The Matriarch's office on the first floor.

"Wonderful, just the boy I'd like to see," The Matriarch said from her reading chair. "Be a dear and shut the door behind you." The door had already been standing open as Noah had approached it leaving no doubt that he was expected. He did as he was asked and moved to stand before the old woman.

"Yeah, I heard," Noah said. "Have you been watching me?"

The Matriarch swatted the question out of the air with her hand as though driving away a fly. "How nice, you brought the contracts with you. I'm so glad to see you taking such a keen focus on your studies. Oh, but I'm being rude. Sit, won't you?"

The room contained only a single chair, that which The Matriarch herself occupied. She gestured toward the circular rug at her feet though, and Noah hesitated only briefly before sitting cross legged before her.

There was a slight pause while The Matriarch regarded him critically. Noah opened his mouth to reply, but she immediately cut him off.

"I imagine you're learning a lot. About the contracts, that is. You've been reading them, haven't you?"

"I've been trying," Noah admitted, "but I still don't know what most of the symbols mean."

The Matriarch stood abruptly and puttered over to one of the bookshelves looming over her chair. She ran her fingers across the spines, and in the silence the murmuring from the books was more pronounced than ever. Noah thought he could even make out a few of the words like "secret", "blasphemy", and "death", as well as a good deal of barely audible hissing and other demonic utterings. She selected one, a thick leather volume with golden demonic symbols along the spine.

"I have something that may assist you. A curious Chainer like yourself may unveil many hidden truths that are beyond the most arduous study of a common soul."

She thinks I'm learning demonic because I'm a Chainer, Noah thought. *Does she still not know I have an affinity?* Noah kept his face as uninterested and expressionless as he could to not betray his thoughts. He stretched out his hands to receive the book which The Matriarch was carrying in his direction. At the last second before his fingers closed around the spine, she withdrew it from him and flipped it open.

"Of course, I wouldn't normally encourage an interest in the profane arts—especially not in a first-year student—but I do see a certain benefit from our partnership of minds. You would like to help me, wouldn't you Noah?"

"Help you with what?" Noah asked, weighing his words carefully.

"Wrong answer," she replied curtly, snapping the book shut. "You are a student at my school, of course you will do as you're told. More than a student in fact—now that Professor Salice is no longer here, you will be needing a new apprenticeship to earn your keep, and I can think of no higher honor for a Chainer than to serve the headmistress herself."

"Don't you already have an apprentice, ma'am?" Noah asked. "Elizabeth Washent—"

"Useless," The Matriarch dismissed. "And so nosy! Always going through my personal things, although I suppose that's what I should have expected from an animal soul. All this talk of infinite potential and they tend to forget their place. You will be my new apprentice, do you understand?"

"Yes, ma'am," Noah replied uneasily. The book she was holding continued to murmur, and now that it was close, Noah was sure that it was speaking in demonic. If nothing else it would be worth it to learn from her personal library.

"Better," The Matriarch said, smiling as sweet as artificial sugar. She extended the book once more. Noah grasped it quickly before she could remove it again. The Matriarch allowed him to take it and turned to pace the room. "Your first assignment is to continue your study of demonic from this book. You will do so in my office every other night from civil twilight until dawn. And when does civil twilight begin?"

"When the sun is six degrees below the horizon," Noah replied quickly, a fact he knew from his necromancy class as the prime hours for awakening the undead.

"Very good," she said. "Once you are able to read the contracts fluently, you will be assisting me in making some small... alterations. It would be irresponsible to permit any lingering loyalty to that disgraced man who sought to kill your family, wouldn't you agree?"

"Yes, ma'am," Noah said, already flipping open the book. Each page was intricately illustrated in rich crimson reds, azure blues, and glimmering gold like a medieval manuscript, while all the text was in demonic. The murmurings from the open book were even louder, and Noah had the unnerving sensation that they were less of a dumb recording and more like a living entity trying fervently to speak to him.

"They must answer only to me," The Matriarch said, tracing idle patterns of light in the air as she paced. "The expiration dates must be adjusted too. A free demon is just a disaster waiting to happen. Speaking of, those mischievous harassments they do will have to stop. You will need to add a clause punishing such behavior. How am I to expect the students to behave if I can't even get my minions to obey the rules?"

"They already had a contract when they agreed to be summoned," Noah said. "Changing everything now doesn't seem very fair—"

"Fairness is only relevant between equals," The Matriarch interrupted, pivoting on the spot. "It isn't fair to the tree to cut it down, nor to the animal that is eaten, but it's done without hesitation because they serve a higher being."

"How would you like it if a higher being came along and did the same to you?" Noah asked.

The Matriarch snorted and chuckled. "My dear boy, we have both worked very hard through many lives to be where we are now. A heavy soul is earned, not given. We are *entitled* to our place at the top. Let's not get ahead of ourselves though, speculating about hypotheticals. It is time for you to learn the symbols. Right where you are is fine, thank you."

Noah had begun to stand, but she gestured him back down upon the carpet. The open book in his lap, he stared down at the illustrations and tried to connect them with the rapid mumbling which rose to greet him. The Matriarch didn't understand Noah any better than Noah understood these books, but at least Noah could learn.

QARI OLANDESCA ILLUSTRATIONS

THE CONTRACT ENDS

Every other night in the hours before morning, Noah returned to The Matriarch's office to study. At first she would hover over his shoulder with anticipation, constantly needling him with questions he had no answer to. She swiftly grew bored with his rate of progress however and returned to her own readings, which suited Noah just fine.

There was another book or two waiting for him on the carpet every day he returned, each mumbling or hissing or chittering in its own way. Some contained dense paragraphs of symbols, while others were nothing but pictures and geometric patterns that wouldn't have looked out of place in the netherworld. Some of the pictures moved on their own, the color bleeding through the page and running down only to reform into another shape.

Noah considered asking to take the books into the netherworld to see if he could make more sense of them there, but the image of all those demons closing in on him still burned fresh in his mind, often sneaking their way into his dreams at day. Besides, he'd seen many of these patterns in the nether and they hadn't made any more sense to him there, so it stood to reason that he would not find it any harder to learn the symbols here.

Visoloth never left The Matriarch's side now. The demon dog made no attempt to speak to Noah, and its tentacled face was perfectly inscrutable as to how it viewed its change of master. Perhaps he could have helped Noah read the symbols, but again he would have to travel to the netherworld to understand it and Noah had no inclination or opportunity for that.

Noah had grown accustomed to being singled out for being a Chainer, but now that he was The Matriarch's apprentice the effect had only grown more pronounced. To make matters worse, a side-effect of Noah spending so much time studying demonic was that he'd occasionally slip those horrible, guttural words into his regular conversation without notice. This combined with the growing negative opinion of demons to prompt looks of disdain or even revulsion from his peers.

Jamie and Walter didn't seem to mind, but Brandon in particular would loudly call the slips to everyone's attention. The rumor had begun to spread that Noah's mother had been a demon, and the malicious glee which Brandon repeated it made Noah sure it had originated with him. Noah did his best not to engage or retaliate though, hoping that it would just blow over as these things typically did. Walter wanted Noah to try and get the imps to gang up on Brandon, but Noah figured that would only draw even more attention. If everyone really did find out that he had a demonic affinity, then he'd probably never hear the end of it.

The end result of these interactions was for Noah to enjoy his time alone studying the demonic books more than ever.

He began going to The Matriarch's office early, and when he found that she invited him in, he began going on his off nights as well until he spent nearly every twilight there. He still didn't understand much, but just like the complex patterns in the nether, he felt that he was perpetually on the edge of some keen insight that would magically click if he could only view it from the proper angle. Even when he couldn't comprehend the words, listening to the book's murmurings made him feel connected to something more profound and important than himself.

On one such session sitting cross legged on The Matriarch's rug, Noah encountered what he'd forgotten he'd even been seeking in the first place. The quarter sun with the door in it: not on a contract, but part of an intricate clock displayed on a double-paged illustration. The clock was rotating before his eyes, and as it did, the forest in the background was cycling through the seasons. Magnificent summer greens gave way to bright, bloody leaves, which in turn withered to skeletal trees which bloomed to life again, all in the span of about fifteen seconds. Entranced by the image, his mouth formed words with minimal input from his conscious mind.

"The contracts won't last ten years," he mumbled.

"Why do you say that?" The Matriarch asked, her voice low and musical, almost hypnotic.

"Because they're already over. They ended at the beginning of spring. Every one of them."

"You must not be reading it right," The Matriarch said curtly. "That's been weeks now, and the demons still do exactly as they're told. The contracts were written to be ten years each."

"Did Salice tell you that?" Noah asked.

A deep, warning growl rose in Visoloth's throat.

The Matriarch narrowed her eyes. "You're an obedient little slave, aren't you, Visoloth?"

The growl faded. Its yellow eyes blinked, and a single tentacle flicked the air. Visoloth rose slowly to its feet as though unsure of his own weight.

"Sit down, Visoloth," The Matriarch commanded. "I am still your master."

Visoloth flinched back toward the ground before reversing direction. It stretched its legs luxuriously, rising to its full height.

"The demons didn't know either," Noah said carefully. "They were afraid of being punished."

"I can still punish them," The Matriarch replied with a harsh edge. "Heel!"

The demon dog flinched again, but it was less discernible than the previous time and it recovered more quickly.

"It is no loss being rid of you," The Matriarch said, rising warily to her own feet. "You can join the traitor in the stone for all I care. Sit. DOWN!"

Visoloth lowered itself once more, but it wasn't cringing this time. Its body was tensed, preparing to spring. The full bloom of tentacles flared from its mouth in defiance.

"Visoloth, don't!" Noah shouted. "You need to tell the other demons in the school!"

The Matriarch rounded ferociously on Noah, brilliant diamonds now in place of where her eyes had been. "What did you tell him?"

Noah hadn't even realized that he'd spoken in demonic. He picked through his limited vocabulary to say something to the effect of: "Tell them all they're free! Then down to the village, and tell all the ones there too."

Visoloth replied something in demonic, but it was too fast

and complicated for Noah to follow. The dog's tension was apparent from his frozen stance and stiff tone however.

"Stop using those filthy words," The Matriarch demanded, turning rapidly between the two. "What are you saying?"

"I'm not giving you an order," Noah added to Visoloth in plain speech. "It's advice from a friend."

"Enough!" The Matriarch bellowed. "Traitors, both of you! To think I welcomed you to my school. You didn't deserve the lives you had, and now you've lived your last."

Visoloth began to lunge toward the old woman, tentacles springing in a wide sweep through the air. She defensively crossed her forearms, prompting twin beams of light to spring into the air which rotated to form a searing shield. Visoloth never followed through with his attack however, and instead turned away at the last second to bound toward the door.

The Matriarch dropped her shield the moment she realized the deception. She pointed an index finger, trembling with rage. If Noah was going to resist her, it was now or never. He flung the demonic tome at the woman which opened in the air and began to shriek. The Matriarch reacted at once, blasting it from the air with a torrent of wind which dismantled the book into an explosion of loose pages. The room was momentarily obscured in a blizzard of flying sheets, each screaming and cursing in a maddening chorus of rage.

The Matriarch was shouting something, but Noah couldn't hear her over the cacophony. A booming crash resonated an instant later, but this too was instantly swallowed by the screaming paper. Another gusty nova spread from The Matriarch to flatten the pages against the walls where they slid to the ground in rumbled heaps.

When visibility returned, the door stood thrown wide and the demon dog was gone. The Matriarch lifted the ends of her long dress and dashed after it with a supernatural blur of speed which made mockery of her apparent age.

"Harpies!" she shouted as she ran. "Catch that dog! Bring him to me!" Then pausing for a moment at the doorway, The Matriarch turned to glare through Noah with her diamond eyes. He was trapped with nowhere to run. All it would take was a blink, and his soul would be sealed within one of the stones.

"Don't leave this room," she snarled, "or it won't just be your soul that pays the price."

The door slammed behind her, but that was hardly the end of the chaos. The door then flipped around in its frame, so that the outside face was now pointed inward and the lock was on the other side. Hundreds of moaning pages from the ground flooded the room with a wave of despair, and outside the screech of harpies mingled with the confused shouting of students.

"Out of my way, imp!" The Matriarch's muffled voice howled. "I'll skin the lot of you, don't touch me!"

Noah didn't need a beating heart to feel terror, and his heaving lungs didn't need to move the air to feel flustered. He moved instinctively toward the door, grasping the handle only for a seething jade arc of lightning to leap across his hand. He jolted backward and clutched his injury, cursing, only realizing after he did so that he'd done so in demonic once more.

"The top drawer of her desk. Quickly, child."

Noah jumped in surprise. It took him a moment to realize that a page from the shattered book was speaking to him.

"It isn't locked. She was in too much of a hurry," another

page chimed in. Then a dozen voices in susurration around him: "Open it—open the drawer—look inside!"

Noah cast a nervous glance at the gargoyle in the corner of the room which had remained as still as stone. He then did as the pages instructed, bracing himself for another shock that never came. A small stack of parchments, a jewelry case, a bag of gemstones, quills, sets of keys, satin gloves, Brandon's confiscated mermaid skull, and other personal effects—as well as a blood red diamond. Noah had no doubt that Professor Salice's soul was still bound inside.

He looked questioningly at the pages around him, but their incessant voices were growing weaker. He thought he could distinguish the demonic words for "your friend", but it was almost too faint to hear. Then a whispered shout said "look inside," and this too was gone, replaced by the softest of tremulous moans.

Noah carefully lifted the red diamond to the light of a will-o-wisp and tracked it across the air. The stone glittered as the light pierced it, and Noah could faintly see something moving inside. He glanced around at the scattered pages again, but they were too faint to hear now. Back to the diamond, he lifted it to his eye and peered inside the stone.

Noah had the sensation of looking into a telescope revealing something very far away. A hexagonal room built entirely from the blood-red diamond mirrored the external facets. Professor Salice was sitting cross-legged on the ground with his back against one of the walls, his hands folded in his lap. His eyes were open and he immediately met Noah's gaze, apparently aware of his presence.

"Are you angry?" Salice asked. The voice sprang up in Noah's mind, only distinguishable from his own thoughts by the barest intonation. "It's alright if you are. I'd be angry if I were you."

"She's not very nice, is she?" Noah asked.

Salice chuckled dryly. "You don't know the half of it. I heard some of what is going on though, so I know her mask must be starting to slip. Is Visoloth alright?"

"You really care about a lowly demon?" Noah asked.

The light of the blood diamond caught in the Professor's eyes. "I care about all souls, but him more than most. I know he was the one to betray my plans, but I know he was only following his own conscience. I have no one but myself to blame for not being open with him about the full extent of my charge."

"You lied to me too," Noah was quick to add. "I was your apprentice, and you used me. And if you think I'm going to help you now just because I don't like The Matriarch either—well you can rot in there for all I care."

The Professor's head hung limply and he sighed. "I don't expect to be rescued. For any of us to be rescued—because I am far from the only one she has sealed broken from the cycle of life and death." He lifted himself wearily to his feet, then straightened himself rigidly with his old look of haughty arrogance returning. "I do, however, expect you to be taking up the fight in my place."

The horrible cackling screech of the harpies interrupted them. It was answered by a squeal, agonized and terrified. Noah imagined an imp being hoisted into the air by those long, curved talons and perhaps hurled down the pit as well.

"We don't have time to waste," Salice said. "We cannot let their suffering be in vain. Take the keys in the desk and my diamond and be prepared to run. I will show you why The Matriarch must be destroyed."

"I can't open the door. It shocks me when I touch it—"

"Only from the inside. Someone is approaching to open it soon. Be ready."

Noah took the set of keys, barely turning toward the door before it had already begun to open. His relief was immediately cut short as the face he least wanted to see in the world peered through.

"Brandon?" Noah hissed in shock.

Brandon's beady eyes quickly scanned the room. He opened the door the minimal amount to slip his pudgy body inside, and Teresa slid in behind him.

"Don't close the door!" Noah warned. "You won't be able to open it again."

"Teacher's pet hiding from the demons?" Brandon leered.

"What are you doing here?" Noah demanded. "Doesn't matter, get out of my way."

Noah darted toward the door but Brandon shoved him roughly back. "Not so fast. Where's my skull?"

"Your what?"

"My mermaid skull!" he demanded. "The Matriarch had it confiscated. It's your fault, and I want it back. Now while everyone's busy."

"Give it to him," Salice said, "we have no time for this foolishness."

"I won't," Noah protested. "Let me through!"

"Professor Salice?" Teresa asked uncertainly, looking everywhere around the room. "I thought you already came back to life. Where are you?"

Brandon looked suddenly fearful as well. His greedy eyes fell upon the skull in the open desk drawer though, and he lunged to seize it. This time it was Noah blocking his way, the two boys pushed and wrested to keep the other from moving around.

"Stop it, both of you!" Professor Salice shouted. "Noah, let him have the skull. Brandon, let him pass!"

Noah reluctantly broke away and stepped aside. Brandon gleefully snatched his skull, although the instant he picked it up he already seemed to be losing interest in it. "Where are you going that's more important?" Brandon asked suspiciously. His eyes fell upon the keys clutched in Noah's other hand. "You're going to steal something too, aren't you? Something better."

"I am not," Noah said. He didn't waste his chance and was already almost out the door. He didn't know where he was actually being led though, and the lack of conviction in his voice seemed to fuel Brandon's suspicions further.

"You're not taking anything without sharing it with my boy," Teresa said.

As soon as Noah made it outside the office, he tried to shut the door to lock the pair of them inside. Teresa had gotten in the way however, so instead Noah turned and sprinted toward the stairs as Professor Salice was instructing.

"You'll understand when you get there," the professor promised. "These keys will open the final door leading to the road from death."

The Mortuary was in chaos. Noah had never realized how many demons operated the school until this moment when they were all running wild. Imps were swarming along the ground, biting and scratching at the legs of panicked students. A Lava Salamander had climbed onto the central tree and was spitting sticky molten gobs at the harpies, and those that missed were starting fires all over the place. The harpies in turn were trying their best to lift demons and hurl them outside the school. The entranceway was dominated by the roaring Manticore whose barbed tail was being pinned down by a pair of Gobblers, their fleshy bodies melting into puddles like glue to hold the enraged beast down.

Noah was vaguely aware of Brandon and Teresa closely pursuing him, but there was so much going on that they were the least of his worries. He made it a few steps down the first helical stairway, but swiftly had to retreat and choose the other one as a patrol of zombies came marching up from the lower floors with Professor Wilst at the lead. This reversal allowed Brandon to close the distance on Noah even more tightly, so that he was only barely out of arms reach as Noah raced down the second flight of stairs.

Undead moans echoed through the stairway, and it quickly became apparent that Brandon had used his skull to peel off a pair of the zombies from the troop to join in his pursuit. His ability had advanced considerably throughout the semester, and the corpses were bounding down the stairs with a ravenous impetus that put the class' initial shambling to shame. Professor Salice was urging Noah on with every step though, and Noah had no time to question anything about this mad dash.

Past the second floor and its marching zombies, past the screeching owl and the frightened animals on the third, through the demonic fourth floor echoing with Visoloth's word of freedom. Onward to the fifth floor and its whispering room, all the way to the iron doors crossed with chains. At Salice's instruction, Noah plunged the largest key, ornate and gilded with gold, into the ponderous padlock and heaved to turn it. The chains slithered sinuously back like snakes, and just as Brandon and his zombies came thundering down the last stairs, the iron door swung open which led to the road from death.

The zombies staggered to a halt, throwing up their arms to shield their eyes against the searing light. A dozen or more bright beams crossed the path horizontally, with another dozen vertical beams criss-crossing in a regular pattern. Noah squinted to peer through them and could just barely make out the descending stairway vanish into the darkness beyond.

"Is it another door?" Noah asked. "I don't understand."

Before Salice could answer, more footsteps sounded pounding down the stairs above them. A moment later and Walter and Jamie had appeared, stopping short a little higher up the tree. Brandon raised his skull prompting the zombies to shuffle into position to defend him as the corpses braced for impact.

"Aha!" Jamie shouted. "I knew something was up when I saw you chasing Noah. Why can't you leave him alone?"

"Where's the treasure?" Brandon demanded. "Is it on the other side of the light?"

"Life is the only treasure!" Professor Salice cut through the tense standoff. "And there's no life to be had, so everyone needs to calm down. Not for you, not for the graduating students, not for the other schools or the furthest monasteries and temples in the highest mountains of the spirit world. The Matriarch has lied to you. Everyone has lied to you. There is no going back."

"Professor?" Jamie asked, mystified.

"Every way has been blocked," Salice continued. "The Matriarch doesn't serve her students, she serves the Trans Dimensional Department. Together they have created the Soul Net you see before you now."

"I don't understand," Noah said. "Why would she bother teaching people how to come back to life if it's impossible?"

"She's a peddler of false hope," Professor Salice said. "Six years of education, all to give students a sense of false confidence that they are ready for the journey home. The moment a soul passes into the net however, they belong to her. Trapped forever between life and death. In this way does the department seek to control both worlds, allowing only those they choose to return to life while filtering out all who would resist them. That's why I made it my mission to summon the Rasmacht and destroy The Matriarch, so that I could be rid of her net and free the souls she has been keeping from their fate."

"But what makes you so sure?" Teresa pressed. "How did you know about all this?"

"Because this is not the first time I've tried to be rid of her," Professor Salice said. "The Purges all those years ago were not a response to the evil of demons, as the T.D.D. would have you believe. They were a demonstration of the good that resides within all souls. The demons rose up to destroy the first soul net, giving up their freedom in mass to accomplish their task. I myself was killed during that violent time, and it has taken me a lifetime to relearn everything that I once knew. The net is back though, and there aren't enough free demons left in the world to destroy it again.

"I'm sorry, Noah," Salice continued, his voice heavy with weariness. "I thought that I could use you and your family to be rid of her, but in doing so I resorted to the same lies and secrecy that have plagued her tormented reign. I should have trusted you and been honest from the beginning, but I feared that my plan would be discovered before it was ready and I would lose my chance to be rid of the witch. I have no power in here, so you must be the one to summon the Rasmacht and destroy The Matriarch now."

Echos of the conflict above filtered through the stairway in the silence after his words. Noah could never remember feeling so small and helpless, even when he was surrounded by demons in the heart of the nether.

"I can't possibly," Noah said. "I don't even know how to start."

"You've already started," Professor Salice said, "and you won't be alone. Your friends here all carry the same secret, and now it is their charge to bear as well."

"I'm not his friend," Brandon said, sneering.

"You have a soul, don't you?" Professor Salice snapped. "In the face of such evil, all souls must be united. I fear that the demons alone will not be able to tear this school down, but at the very least they will be able to disrupt the resurrection ceremony that was planned for the end of the year. You will have time to prepare yourselves for what must be done, but know that the longer you wait, the more helpless souls will be ensnared as they cross the path nature intended.

"Now I must swear you all to secrecy, for the moment The Matriarch discovers what you have learned she will doubtlessly trap you as she has done with me. Noah, it would be best if you locked yourself back into her office and return me to her drawer before she realizes you escaped. She will not dispose of you as long as she thinks she can benefit from your Chainer soul. Brandon, you must return the skull as well. It is not worth risking her suspicion until you are ready to be rid of her completely."

"Do you think I'm an idiot?" Brandon asked. "It sounds like she's won and you've lost, and I'm not going to be on the side of a loser. And I'm definitely not giving up my skull."

"You will do as you're told," Teresa scolded him, much to Noah's satisfaction. He'd never heard her use such a tone with him, and Brandon seemed as shocked as he was.

"But mother—" he protested, his voice taking on a particularly obnoxious, nasal whine.

"No excuses. This is far more important than anything you can do with your toys. I'll make sure Nepon Vasolich gets you a new skull, or something even better. We're all going to work together to stop The Matriarch though, and I'm not going to hear another word about it."

At least as shocking as anything else Noah had seen today was Brandon's slump capitulation. "Yes, mother," he consented, shuffling his feet.

"Go now, before she returns," Professor Salice said. "A darkness will befall this school after the demons are driven out, and you will all be told many lies about them. You must remember that a soul burns in the heart of all beings, great and small, but no matter how clouded the mind or the spirit may become, no falsehood can ever tarnish the divine in you. The Matriarch is not the first to try and poison the well of life, nor will she be the last, but though individual leaves may wither and die, the eternal vine will always remain. Not always in the same shape, not always as we wish it to be, but this too shall be endured."

There was no victory or cherished treasure in the heavy hearts which ascended the stairs once more. The upper levels were as wild as ever and the tree itself burned in many places, but Brandon's zombies helped to push through all the way back to The Matriarch's office. Through the stained glass they saw the mighty bulk of the Daymare rearing into the air with its hundreds of flailing legs, battling against a seething host of undead specters. The Matriarch was nowhere to be seen, and it was likely she was part of this battle. This gave Noah ample chance to slip back inside her office without being seen.

Brandon seemed more upset to give up his skull than at any revelation, and he fled the moment he relinquished his prize. Jamie hugged Teresa and thanked her for helping. Teresa seemed so taken aback by this that she was at a complete loss for words, but after a few seconds she relaxed and loosely held Jamie back. Teresa quickly excused herself to dart after her son with a thousand apologies and promises on her lips.

"I'm closing you in now," Jamie said to Noah after she'd gone. "Just play along with what The Matriarch wants and please don't do anything stupid to make us worry."

"Yeah, leave that for us," Walter added, grinning. "I'm more worried about Brandon than you though. I don't trust him for a second."

"I'll be okay. It's getting quieter out there. You need to go."

Noah waited until after the office door was closed before he said to Salice, "I know what you said, but I want to take the blood diamond with me. The Matriarch might think it was only lost in the confusion."

"It is not a sacrifice for me to remain," Professor Salice said. "Stopping The Matriarch is more important to me than my freedom, and I will not jeopardize you again."

"I'm frightened." Noah hadn't wanted to say it in front of his friends, but now that he was alone it came rushing out unbidden. "I don't understand any of it, not really. I don't understand anything more about death than when I was alive. Every time I think I'm starting to, it all gets mixed up again. I can't summon the Rasmacht without your help."

"When you say 'I', who are you referring to?" the Professor asked.

"I'm me. I'm Noah," he replied, confused.

"Noah. The name of the seventy-five year old man who died last year. That Noah? Or what about the one who lived before that? Or the hundred other lives before? Are they not also you? And how many times do you think they all were afraid? How many times do you think they could not possibly go further than they were?

"It is a common mistake to think our current perspective is who we are. We think ourselves limited by the tiniest sliver of what our recent memory has done. You are not this thin slice of life, this forced perspective of reality that you are familiar with. You are not your mind, or the habits it has acquired, or the things it's done. I believe that you will access those other lives just as you learned to speak demonic, and I believe you will find a way for everyone to live again. You are life itself, Noah, and through you all things are possible."

The next half hour waiting for The Matriarch to return was agony for Noah. He was forced to listen to the roiling chaos and battle outside his door while being helpless to aid the wounded or block the aggressor. Even more difficult were the words he forced himself to say when the door finally opened and The Matriarch reappeared at last.

"I'm so sorry," Noah blurted out at once. "I never should have gotten in the way of you chasing Visoloth. It was those demon books telling me what to do, and I was listening to them for so long and I got so confused—"

"Hush, child, all is forgiven" The Matriarch replied, the sweetness in her voice turned poison. Her star-lit robes were immaculate despite the battle she'd returned from, and every curl on her head was exactly in its place. Noah stiffened as she crossed the room toward him, but he did nothing to resist as she put her arms around him and drew him close.

"The demons are all gone now, and there's nothing left to be afraid of. Of course, it would have been better to dispose of them before they learned of their freedom, but perhaps this way is for the best. The people of Teraville would have given me quite a fuss if I'd tried to force away their precious servants, but at least now everyone realized that those nasty things cannot be trusted."

Noah cursed himself silently, realizing for the first time the full extent of the damage he'd done. The Matriarch drew away from him but left her hands on his shoulders, her smile fixed upon her face. "If you truly repent for what you've done, then I will not send you away from The Mortuary. This is your home, and you are my apprentice. Someday you will have learned everything I have to teach, and perhaps you will be the one to run this school. Would you like that? To help all those lost souls find their way back to life?"

"Yes ma'am," Noah said, doing everything within his power to keep the anger from his face and voice. "There's nothing I'd like more."

The Matriarch stared deeply into Noah's eyes. For a moment he thought he saw the diamonds in her eyes flash once more, their gaze penetrating the deepest parts of him. Her eyes darted to her desk, then back at Noah, her smile cracking at the edges. Casually, she released him and strolled to her desk, looking inside the top drawer. She stared down for a long moment before withdrawing her satin gloves and putting them on, one meticulous finger at a time.

"The school is a mess, and we don't have any more demons to clean it up," she sighed. "Let's hope a good war brings in enough souls to do the job for us, eh?"

Noah wasn't sure whether he was supposed to agree with her, or whether she was joking. She held her fixed smile a few moments longer before chuckling to herself, and Noah forced a similar sound to come from somewhere inside him.

"Ah well, at least we have the whole summer to clean it up," The Matriarch added. She mimed filling an invisible glass and raised it as if toasting. "To a demon free school, and a new semester."

Noah mimed his own glass and clinked with her in the air. "To eternal life," he replied.

BOOK 2

Keep reading with book 2 of the "School of Rebirth and Reincarnation" series.

READ MORE HORROR

Read more from Tobias Wade

TobiasWade.Com

Join the Haunted House book club and get free advanced copies every time a new book is published.

PUBLISHER'S NOTE

Please remember to
honestly rate the book on Amazon or Goodreads!

It's the best way to support me as an author and help new readers discover my work.

ABOUT THE AUTHOR

Former neuroscience researcher, born again novelist. During my studies it struck me as odd that I could learn so much about behavior without understanding the intricacies of human nature. I realized that I learned more about what it means to be human from reading stories than I ever had from my text books, and I was inspired to write.

I spent several years selling scripts in Los Angeles, but was ultimately frustrated with my lack of control over my projects. A general stubbornness and unwillingness to compromise my creative pursuits led me to starting my own publishing house to do things my own way.

I now work full time as a novelist and publisher with Haunted House Publishing.

Made in the USA
Middletown, DE
05 July 2019